PARANORMAL UNIVERSITY: FIRST SEMESTER

PARANORMAL UNIVERSITY: FIRST SEMESTER

PARANORMAL UNIVERSITY™ BOOK ONE

JACE MITCHELL

MICHAEL ANDERLE

DISRUPTIVE IMAGINATION

Copyright © 2019 Jace Mitchell & Michael T. Anderle
Cover by Fantasy Book Design
Cover copyright © LMBPN Publishing
This book is a Michael Anderle Production

LMBPN Publishing
PMB 196, 2540 South Maryland Pkwy
Las Vegas, NV 89109

First US edition, October 2019
eBook ISBN: 978-1-64202-537-8
Print ISBN: 978-1-64202-538-5

PARANORMAL UNIVERSITY: FIRST SEMESTER TEAM

Thanks to our Beta Readers:
Mary Morris, Larry Omans, Kelly O'Donnell, Nicole Emens, Erika Everest

Thanks to the JIT Readers

Misty Roa
Jackey Hankard-Brodie
Dorothy Lloyd
Deb Mader
Dave Hicks
Jeff Eaton
Jeff Goode

If I've missed anyone, please let me know!

Editor
SkyHunter Editing Team

For Tucker. No one could ask for a better friend.

— Jace

To Family, Friends and
Those Who Love
to Read.
May We All Enjoy Grace
to Live the Life We Are
Called.

— Michael

CHAPTER ONE

"*No way!*" Claire's head whipped to the right, desperately searching for whoever had just stripped the purse from her shoulder.

The man's head barely came up to the waists of those around him.

Claire saw him barreling through the crowded amusement park, and a thought raced through her mind.

Is he a midget?

Claire gritted her teeth as she watched him flee. *Doesn't matter how tall he is! I've got $16.53 to my name, and every bit of it is in that purse.* She couldn't even afford to be in this amusement park, except her friend Rachel had offered the ticket.

Claire took off after the thieving bastard.

"What are ya—" Rachel called, but Claire lost the words as she rushed forward.

She'd find Rachel when this was all over. Right now, she had to get her freakin' purse and the twerp who took it.

Claire reached the crowd the little man had thrust

himself into, which immediately slowed her down. She pushed on, moving people out of the way with the confidence of someone much older than her eighteen years.

"Hey! Watch it!" someone shouted from her right.

Claire paid them no mind.

She'd always had sharp eyes, and right now, they searched for any kind of quick movement—someone trying to bolt. The man was actually short enough to hide inside the crowd.

Is he a man? Or a kid?

There!

Except, what Claire thought was movement was actually a brief flash of light. She thought she might have heard someone else yell about it too.

What the hell? she wondered, slowing for a second. Doesn't matter. *I've gotta get my purse!*

She pivoted and rushed forward, slicing through gaps in the crowd as they appeared before her.

The freakin' joker was getting away! He'd made it out of the crowd and was heading deeper into the park.

How is he that fast?

Claire glanced ahead of him and saw the bend in the road. If he got there, he could slip into the wooded area lining the street and simply hide until she gave up.

"Not happening," she vowed under her breath. She lowered her body some and surged forward, breaking free from the crowd.

Now they were in a flat-out foot race. Claire didn't know this man, but she knew he didn't want to be in a race with her.

The wind blew through her hair as her feet pounded

the pavement. She was gaining on the jackass, although he was fast, faster than most people Claire had ever come in contact with.

She was fifty feet away when he turned around to check on her.

What the heck? Her feet kept moving though her mind froze in disbelief.

His face looked green! Not like he'd just vomited or something, but actually *green*.

Doesn't matter, she thought. He could be Neapolitan ice cream-colored, he wasn't getting away with her purse.

Claire was ten feet away when they hit the bend in the road. The man kept his head down, hurtling forward as if his life depended on it, and mayhap it did because Claire was beyond mad now.

He banked a right and headed toward the woods, obviously hoping he could lose Claire since he couldn't beat her in speed.

"No, you don't!" She leapt forward.

Claire grabbed the little man by his shoulders and roughly threw him to the ground.

He rolled onto the grass, flipping head over foot. Claire's purse flew to the right, but she didn't even glance in its direction. The money honestly didn't matter right now. She wanted some freakin' *justice*. This man tried to *rob* her.

He turned one last somersault and landed on his back, staring at the sky.

Claire trotted over to him.

And there she froze.

Claire Hinterland was staring at a *green* man.

No. Her mind spun in defiance. *He's not a man. He's a freakin' leprechaun!*

It turned out the thief's name was Frank, and also... He most definitely was a leprechaun.

Over the next six weeks, Claire learned a lot about Frank, but the two most important things were this: he liked beer, and he liked bowling.

In that order.

Turns out, Frank wasn't such a bad guy. A thief, yes, but he was also pretty nice once you got to know him. Just...Well, if he ran out of beer, he might try robbing someone.

"It's not exactly easy to get a job," he'd told her. "Trust me, I've tried."

Claire had rolled her eyes, knowing *that* was a lie. "You're an alcoholic, Frank."

"That's not possible," he'd responded with a wink and a sly grin. "I'm a leprechaun. We can't be alcoholics; it's a rule."

Claire had raised an eyebrow. "Aren't leprechauns supposed to have my skin tone? You know, be *white*?"

Frank glared at her. "Some are white. Some are green. I'm green, damn it, and I won't put up with any racism about it, you understand?"

Claire had shrugged and laughed, putting up her hands in protest. "Hey, that's fine with me. Just learning about you and your ilk."

The two of them were now inside Frank's favorite

haunt, a rundown bowling alley called Midtown Pins.

A plate of fries sat on the table in front of Claire, a glass of beer opposite for Frank. She dipped her hand down to the plate and grabbed a fry, hearing the now-familiar crash of Frank hitting a strike as she tossed it into her mouth.

"Badda-*boom!*" he shouted, shoving his hand into the air and twirling to look at her. "I tell ye, if all ye humans weren't trying to murder me, I'd be the number one bowler in the country. Probably the entire world."

"Frank, no one is trying to murder you," Claire told him with a sigh. "You've been going on about this for a week, but look around." She lifted her next fry, taking in the entire bowling alley with a wave. "No one is here. Just you, me, and Charlie over there making my fries and your beer. It's like this every time we come."

Frank walked back to the table and picked up his beer. He took a long pull. When he pulled it away from his mouth, he belched, then turned to her. "That's your problem, lass. Smart as you are, you don't listen to your elders. I'm over six hundred years old, and you think you can tell me my business of staying alive? I'm being *followed.*"

Claire grinned as she took another fry. She popped it in her mouth and chewed in silence as she studied the mythological creature.

It'd been a shock to see Frank lying in the grass six weeks ago, his big green nose pointing at her like an oddly shaped pickle.

She understood now what was happening, as did the rest of the world. The news had been covering it *constantly* since it broke about a week after Claire met Frank.

The "Mythological Invasion."

Claire thought that last part, the invasion piece, was just the media creating hype. Frank wasn't invading anything besides a brewery.

There were all kinds of theories about what was happening; Claire didn't know what to believe. She understood a few things, but that was because of her relationship with Frank.

It looked to her like not everyone could see the mythological beings, at least not at first. For example, Charlie, at the front of the bowling alley, viewed Frank as just a short, odd-looking man. He didn't see the green skin or the large nose.

To Charlie, Frank was just *weird*.

Claire had heard of a few more sightings. Some kind of rainbow-colored snake in Australia. A Chupacabra that got loose in a zoo and hurt a bunch of animals.

That one had really made Claire sad.

"So who is it, Frank?" she teased. "What do these people following you look like?" Claire liked needling him about this.

Frank picked up a bowling ball and turned around to look at her. "Men in black cars without kind faces, little lady. Zeus help me, she thinks she knows better than Frank!" He shook his head, turned around, and rolled the ball down the lane without hardly looking at the pins.

Another strike.

He twisted back toward Claire and spread his arms out to the side in a "What can you say?" gesture as he walked back to the table. "I might be the best bowler ever."

"Isn't Zeus from like...a different mythological era or something?" Claire asked with real curiosity.

"Sure. But I've met him." Frank swigged his beer as if that was the most normal statement in the world.

That he'd met *Zeus*, a Greek god.

"Frank, you ever consider yourself an exaggerator?" Claire tossed another fry into her mouth, grinning at his reaction as she chewed.

"This wee little lass! Zeus!" He took a deep pull on his beer, nearly finishing it. He sat it down and leaned against the table, meeting her eyes. "Is he a mythological creature? Zeus?"

Claire said nothing, only kept the grin going.

"I'll take your silence as knowing you were bested. *Yes*, he is a mythological creature, as you humans call us, and *yes*, I've met him. Every once in a while, he comes down from Mt. Olympus and takes a break from his shagging proclivities. He's a nice enough guy." Frank leaned back and burped again. "Deep voice, though."

Claire laughed. Sometimes it was still hard to believe all this stuff, even though she was staring at a drunk leprechaun.

Frank turned to look at the pins being set back up. He wasn't swaying yet, but Claire thought he might begin to soon. He'd still hit his strikes though, probably even if he was falling over.

The doors to the bowling alley opened.

Light poured into the dimly-lit building, casting the two entering figures in darkness.

Charlie looked up from the little bar he stood behind. "How are ya? Here for bowling or food?"

"We're meeting friends," the man on the right told him tersely.

"Heeeeey, Frank," Claire whispered as she slowly stood up. She didn't like the look of this, especially not after what Frank had just told her. "I don't ever like saying you were right, so let's just say that you might want to dip out the back. I'll go distract whoever these jokers are."

Frank drunkenly turned to see the men walking toward them.

The doors had closed, so they weren't shrouded in shadow anymore. Black suits. White button-down shirts. Black ties. Both took off their sunglasses at the exact same time as if they were synchronized robots.

Claire moved around the front of the table. "Go, Frank. I'll hold them as long as I can." Frank may have robbed her once, but he might as well be her best friend at this point.

She wasn't going to let any government types just show up and snatch him.

"I owe ye one, little lady. Next round's on me." He burped a little at the end of his sentence, but still wasn't moving.

"I don't drink, Frank," Claire reminded him. *"Now get out of here."*

Frank tipped a wink at her. "Aye, think I will!"

He rushed off toward the back door, while Claire kept her focus on the two approaching men. She didn't know exactly what she was going to say or do. She just hoped she could give Frank some space to run.

"Sorry, gents, but you're early. Bingo isn't until later." Claire went with sarcasm when they finally reached her lane. "The senior crowd usually gets here a little after nine."

She stepped up to them, trying to keep their eyes on her

and not looking behind her, where Frank was making his getaway.

The men looked very similar. Both had brown hair, parted to the right. The one on Claire's left was a little older, a bit more overweight.

"You're Claire Hinterland, right?" the older one asked with no emotion.

"Depends on who's asking." Claire was young, but she hadn't grown up in what might be called a "privileged" environment. She'd been in bad positions before, and each time her spine turned to steel.

Just like it was now.

"You mind if we sit down?" the same man asked, nodding to the table Claire had just been at.

Claire raised an eyebrow. "You want to talk to *me*?" Meaning, this *wasn't* about Frank?

"Yes, ma'am. We know about your friend, but that's not who we're concerned with." The man gestured with his hand to the table. "May we?"

Claire wasn't sure what was going on, but it didn't look like they were going to run Frank down, nor arrest her.

Plus, I could outrun these two if needed. She moved to the table and sat down in front of her fries again.

"Don't ask. You can't have any." She grabbed a fry and bit off half of it. "Now, if you're not here for Frank, but you know what he is...Well, start with, how do you know what he is? You'd be the first people besides me that can see his true nature."

The two men glanced at each other briefly, then the older man spoke again. "We can explain that later. We don't see him as clearly as you do, but we probably don't see him like the guy behind the bar does either. I promise, though, that all of this will make sense in the days to come. Frank isn't important right now."

Claire raised an eyebrow. "Right *now*. Then what is important? If you're not here for him, then why *are* you here?"

"For you, Ms. Hinterland." The older man reached into his jacket pocket and pulled out a sheet of paper. He placed it on the table and pushed it over to her side.

Claire glanced from the paper to the man.

"Open it," he told her with a nod.

Claire grabbed the paper, unfolded it, and started reading.

Attn: Claire Hinterland

Congratulations! We at the University of Paranormal Studies are pleased to inform you that your application has been accepted.

Our state-of-the-art campus offers a wide range of courses, cutting edge resources and equipment, and respected industry specialists as your tutors.

You may not be aware that graduates of UoPS have the benefit of guaranteed employment options with the US government, who will reimburse your course fees after three years of service.

Alternatively, the option to move into the private sector with globally recognized qualifications is also available.

We understand you may have questions about this unique opportunity. Please make use of your handler, who will address any of your queries or concerns.

Regards,
Dr. Kristin Pritcham,
Dean, University of Paranormal Studies.

Claire placed the sheet of paper back down on the table. "Not sure if either of you is aware, but I didn't apply to any school. Let alone a University of Paranormal Studies, whatever the hell that is. My finances don't really stretch to education. Now, how about we cover a few basics. Who are you?"

"I'm Special Agent Remington," the older man told her. He nodded toward the man next to him. "This is Special Agent Lance."

"Special Agents? For what?" Claire's eyes narrowed, and she leaned back in her chair.

"We're with the FBI." Remington glanced at the mostly empty beer sitting on the table, Frank's dregs. He moved it out of the way.

"And you're here to offer me a place in a college?" Claire crossed her arms over her chest. "Forgive me if none of this is making much sense, but I think that's part of your job description, isn't it? To confuse people."

"We understand your disbelief." Remington looked at Lance for a second.

The younger man nodded but made no other movement.

Remington turned back to Claire, his face set in a frown. "The world is changing, and it's happening faster than our government can keep up with. It's all hands on deck at this point."

Claire's eyes were still narrowed at the agents. She didn't like what she was hearing, mainly because these two weren't telling her much of anything. "Why don't we cut through the nonsense, and you tell me what this is about?"

"You're aware of the mythological invasion, obviously, from your drinking buddy's constant presence." Remington gave a slight nod toward the back of the building where Frank had disappeared. "Not everything that's happening is on the news, however, and not everything coming through the Veil is as nice as your friend."

"The 'Veil?'" Claire leaned forward, unable to help herself. This was new. The television never said anything about a "Veil."

Remington nodded. "It's how these creatures are coming across to our world. We were woefully underprepared, but our scientists are quickly learning. These creatures are from another dimension, and we're calling the separation between them and us the Veil. The scientists believe that it's tearing, though, and the tears are growing in size with each incident." He was quiet for a moment. "Creatures are coming through faster than we can react."

Remington looked at the basket of fries.

"Don't even think about it," Claire snapped.

She thought she saw the smallest indication of a smirk on his lips as he dipped his head in acquiescence, although she was probably wrong.

Humor didn't appear to be a part of a FBI agent's job description, either.

Remington looked up and continued. "There are a lot of theories about what's happening, and different agencies are operating on different mandates. The FBI is focused on the *invasion*. We cannot be naïve enough to believe that this is benign, that we are not at war. We're looking for people to help us fight it."

Frank's face suddenly appeared in Claire's mind. "I'm not going to kill Frank. No matter what."

"Told you," Lance cut in, still looking directly at Claire.

Remington gestured in the air with his hand, as if swatting lazily at a fly. "Right now, your little green buddy is the least of our worries."

Claire's eyes flashed to Lance. "What's that supposed to mean? 'Told you?'"

It wasn't Lance who spoke, but Remington. Lance simply held Claire's gaze as if she were no more than a statue. "We know a lot about you, Ms. Hinterland. We know you come from a poor family, and we know that your physical aptitude is pretty much off the charts for both males and females of your age group. Chasing down that leprechaun was more impressive than you probably realize. You know how many people could catch one of them? Maybe one in ten thousand."

Claire knew she was fast. She knew her reaction time was better than the guys back in high school, despite the fact that she'd never played sports. None of that really mattered right now. She turned her gaze from Lance to Remington.

"That's all well and good, but it doesn't answer my question. What did he mean by "Told you" when referring to Frank?"

Remington smirked and glanced at Lance. "Now *I* told *you*." He looked at Claire. "There are two other things we know about you. You're smart, which was what I meant.

You immediately saw we weren't answering your question. Can I be honest with you?"

Claire tapped hard on the paper. "If you want me to even consider this, you'd better be."

"There's a bit of a disagreement between my partner and me regarding what skills will be the most important in the upcoming battle. I believe it's a person's physicality and intelligence. Lance is convinced that it's another part. Their empathy."

Claire raised an eyebrow. "Go on."

"Two things put us onto you. For me, it was you chasing down a leprechaun through a crowd. We heard about it and immediately started looking into you. The second thing was how you didn't hurt the creature. You, in fact, befriended him. Now you're hanging out with him daily. You probably understand that mythological being as well as he understands himself. Lance believes it's going to help us fight them."

"Why?" Now both of Claire's eyebrows were raised. She didn't know what answer she'd expected, but not *this*.

"Because you'll understand the enemy as well as they understand themselves." Remington leaned forward on the table and touched the corner of the paper. "This offer is good for forty-eight hours. We know your monetary situation. Everything is paid for. Travel, books, equipment—"

"Equipment?" Claire interrupted.

"You're not going to be fighting these creatures with your bare hands," he told her. "You're going to have access to the best weapons available."

Claire chuckled disbelievingly. "I'm eighteen, and I've

never touched a gun in my life. The government's just going to *give* me one?"

Without moving anything but his mouth, Lance muttered. "Told you again."

Claire's eyes flashed to him, her face stern. "Lance, I'm starting not to like you very much."

Remington finally smirked. "Well, Lance likes *you*. He just thinks you're extremely stubborn, which you are. It's okay. We think it *helps* your profile, not hurts it. We give eighteen-year-olds guns all the time during war and ship them to other countries. We're not talking about guns here, though. We'll be fighting this invasion...*differently*." He looked at the paper again and tapped it gently. "Everything is paid for. You're old enough to sign up without your parents' permission, but we know you still live with them due to financial reasons. We know you'll want to discuss it with them—"

"You seem to know everything, Special Agent Remington." She looked at Lance with narrowed eyes. "You both do."

"We're trying to save the world here. We're trying to get you to help us. In forty-eight hours, that offer is off the table."

Claire reached down and took the piece of paper. She folded it again and put it on her lap. "You two practice such dramatic flair?"

"It comes with the job." Both men stood up and stepped back. "Your country needs you. The world needs you. We hope you come along with us."

CHAPTER TWO

.

After the *Men in Black* guys left the bowling alley, Claire sat there for a few minutes by herself, just staring at the empty lanes.

It took her a little while to stand up and catch the bus home. She was in a daze, unable to quite process what was happening to her.

Claire didn't love the life she'd inherited, but it was her life, and so she'd accepted it. She'd known that she would grow up, graduate high school, then get a job at one of the fast-food restaurants and probably end up being a manager there.

It wasn't like the lives of the famous people she saw on television, but it was still a life. She never thought she was too good for it.

She stared out the bus window watching as the town passed by.

It was her town.

And now she was being told that it didn't have to be. Those men with their letter had told her she could leave it, and everything would be paid for, and the life she'd always thought would be hers would no longer be.

The bus finally pulled up to her stop, and she got off. She walked the block south to her small two-bedroom house and into the front door.

"Mom! Dad! We gotta talk!" she called as she closed the door behind her.

"We're in the kitchen!" came the reply.

Claire crossed the living room, tossing her bag onto the couch on her way through to the kitchen area.

Her mom and dad were moving around the stove and sink, both of them cooking. They had the day off today, and whenever that happened, they liked to cook together.

Claire was poor. She had grown up on the poor side of town and seen how a lot of parents in her neighborhood behaved. Fights, both physical and verbal, were the norm. In front of their kids, too.

Not so in Claire's house.

Her parents loved each other, and Claire watched now as they moved around the kitchen.

Sometimes it grossed her out, how affectionate they were. Light touches on the back. A stolen kiss on the cheek here and there.

Today, though, she thought she was going to miss it.

"I've got, well, I don't know if it's good news or bad news, but I got news." She walked over to the table and pulled the letter out from her back pocket before sitting down.

Both of her parents stopped what they were doing and turned around.

"If you're pregnant, you're out of the house." Her father

deadpanned the statement, but couldn't hold it for long. Especially not when her mom elbowed him in the ribs. He broke out in a grin.

"What is it, honey?" her mother asked.

Claire unfolded the letter and pushed it across the table toward them. "That. It's an invitation to college. Or a college *of sorts*."

Claire shook her head as she stared at the letter, not exactly sure how to explain it. "You know about the Mythological Invasion?"

Her father nodded and moved to the table. He picked the letter up as her mother stepped to his side, and both started reading it.

Claire continued talking. "Apparently, it's not a hoax, and apparently, the government wants me to help stop it."

Her dad slowly handed the letter to her mother, having finished it. "This is for real? That letter, it's real?"

"Yeah." Claire sighed. "It's real."

"This thing doesn't really say much, Claire." Her mother was holding the letter with both hands, scrutinizing it intensely. "What are you going to do at this college? If you're fighting an invasion, what are you learning? I mean, is any of this going to be applicable after you get out of the college?"

Her father walked closer to Claire. "Who cares?! This is great, honey!" He reached down and wrapped her in a giant hug.

He held on for a few seconds before pulling away. "Your mother and I never had a chance to go to college. It's wonderful that you will."

"Just hold on a second, Bill," her mother chided. "I'm

not agreeing to send my only child to some school that might get her *killed*." She let the paper fall to her side. "I need to talk to the college president or dean or whatever they call those people."

Bill turned to look at her. "You're kidding, right?"

Her mother didn't even give him a glance. Her eyes remained on Claire. "Can you get hurt? You're fighting an *invasion*."

"I don't know, Mom." Claire didn't look up. She knew the argument her parents were about to have, but she also knew it didn't really matter what they thought. Not when it got down to bare bones.

"Mary, she's working at Kickin' Chickin down the street," her father interjected. His eyes were large, unbelieving. "This is a godsend. She's got a chance to go to *college*, and if that paper is right, the government is the one recruiting her."

"No. She's not going if she can get hurt. I'd rather her safe at Kickin' Chickin than dead at college."

Claire was coming out of the daze she'd been in since hanging out with Frank. Her parents still didn't know she'd been palling around with a leprechaun, and this was the reason why.

Her mom would have put an end to it immediately.

Her mother had always been the protector, and her father the one trying to push her. Claire hid the hard stuff from both because it would only worry them.

She couldn't hide this, though. She was moving out of the house.

Her mom gave her large eyes. "Claire, honey, I just want what's best for you."

Claire shook her head, still not gazing up from the table. Her mother had always wanted what was best for her, or at least she *said* that. Maybe she just really wanted Claire close by her side, even at the expense of her future.

"I don't want to stay here forever," Claire whispered, a steely determination growing inside her. "I don't think I realized that until I was given an option."

"What do you mean?" her mother's voice became shrill, as if such an idea had never occurred to her.

Claire raised her eyes. "I don't want to work at a place flipping chicken my whole life. I love you. I love Dad, but I don't want to stay in this town where nothing happens. This is my chance to get out. It's a chance to do *something*."

Her dad nodded, still standing next to her.

Tears filled her mother's eyes. "You could get hurt, Claire-bear."

Claire nodded. "Yeah, and I could get robbed at Kickin' Chickin one night, too. But this is a chance to get out of here. To *try*." She tapped her finger hard on the table with the last word.

"Okay, okay." Her mother raised her hands, palms out in surrender. "Let's think about it some, hey? Let's sleep on it and think about it."

Claire shook her head. The steel was taking hold of her spine now, giving her a strength that wasn't going to break.

Not for her mother. Not for *anyone*.

"I'm going, Mom. I'm going to call the agents today, and then I'm going." Claire stood up from the table as tears welled in her mother's eyes. "I love you, Mom. I love Dad, too, but I can't stay here my whole life. I *can't*. I can't do what you guys do. I wish I could, but I want more. I'm going to go to this college, and I'm going to try to do something worthwhile with my life."

Her mother looked like she was about to break right there in the kitchen, just crack and fall apart.

Claire couldn't take it. She didn't want to make her mother cry, but her mind was made up. This might be scary, and it might end badly, but what was the alternative? Putting flour on chicken legs and sticking them in a fryer forever?

No.

Not if she didn't have to.

Claire left the kitchen and ran down the hall to her room. She closed the door quietly and let her tears go.

"When are you going to call?" Frank asked. He was sitting on the end of Claire's bed, his back to her.

It was dark outside, and Frank had just teleported into her room a few minutes prior.

Leprechauns, Claire now understood, had the ability to do that.

He appeared in the same flash of light Claire had seen in the crowd when she was chasing him. Frank had actually teleported further down the path.

She'd asked him why he didn't just teleport further away.

"The longer we teleport, the less control we have over where we land," he'd replied offhand.

She'd asked why Frank didn't just teleport a second time, why he had tried to outrun her.

"A couple of things." Frank had informed her, raising a finger. "The first is that the more times we jump in rapid succession, the less distance we can go, and the less control we have. So, I wouldn't have gotten as much distance if I'd jumped again, and after a few times, I might not even have gone in the direction I wanted."

He'd raised a second finger and grinned. "I also didn't think ye had a chance in Hades of catching me."

Claire had smirked. "Well, you were wrong."

"Won't happen again, lass. Bet on that," Frank had promised.

Now, Claire sat against her headboard with the covers pulled up to her neck. She hadn't minded when Frank appeared. She wasn't sleeping but only thinking. "I told my parents tonight, but I'm going to wait until the morning to call the agents."

"Where's this school at?" Frank stood up from the bed and walked over to the dresser. He picked up one of the ornaments on it and eyed it in the window's moonlight.

Claire pointed at her light-fingered friend. "Don't even think about it, Frank. You're not taking that."

"Wouldn't consider it, me dear," Frank's voice was far away as he turned the curio around in front of his face like a diamond.

Claire glared for a second, but Frank wasn't facing her to see it. "The university is in Boston."

"*That* is what I was hoping for." Frank placed the ornament back down and picked up another. "Boston is a place that appreciates creatures of my kind. Aye, the Irish are the best people to ever grace this pathetic excuse for a universe. I'll fit in fine up there."

Claire's eyes widened. "You?"

"Aye, lass. Me. Ye think I'd see ye go up there alone?" Now he did turn around, a wide grin on his face. "I know a good bit about Boston. Truth be told, I'm something of a scholar."

Claire's own small smirk grew on her face. "Frank, the only thing you know a lot about is beer, and from what I can tell, not the good kind. All you drink is garbage down there at the bowling alley."

"That's because we live in a town where there is nothing but swill for the swine. Boston?" His eyes glinted in the moonlight. *"That's* a town where they'll have fine beer on every street corner."

Claire chuckled. "I knew you weren't going for me."

"Not true, lass. Ye are going to need me, ye just don't know it yet."

"How do you figure?" Claire asked. She was feeling a bit better now, better than she had all day, in fact.

Frank was a jackass, but he was *her* jackass.

"Well, for one, the Veil is weaker up there. It's letting through more creatures like ye fine friend Frank here, but not all of them have such good intentions. While in yer corrupt human world, I cannot find a job, but among those from beyond the Veil, I will be esteemed. What *ye* refuse to give me." Frank flicked his hand, dismissing Claire's interruption. His grin returned. "I can keep my ear to the streets, as the kids say. Either way, I'm going. Ye don't have any choice, lass."

Claire almost had to laugh. He sounded just like she had with her parents. "I'll be working with the people who are trying to capture you."

"Yes, and that's something ye will have to deal with when you meet yer maker. But for now, I'm going to try to keep ye from meeting him—or her, since yer fine friend Frank is not a sexist." Frank's left hand snuck behind him to the dresser to palm one of the ornaments.

"Not on your life." Claire shook her head. "Drop it."

Frank's face grew wide in mock surprise. He held the ornament in front of his face, staring at it in bewilderment. "I don't know what yer talking about, nor how such an object got in me hand. If I didn't know better, I'd say it's ye that has magic and might have placed this trinket here to trick an innocent leprechaun."

Claire hopped up from the bed, and the blanket fell away, revealing the old, oversized t-shirt she slept in instead of wasting her hard-earned money on fancy pajamas like Rachel's.

She snatched the small glass angel from Frank's fingers. "All right, go home, Frank. I'll call them tomorrow. How are you getting to Boston? I know the FBI isn't going to give you a ride."

"Aye, lass. I wouldn't take one from those prejudiced ne'er-do-wells, anyway. Leprechauns are self-sufficient, I'll get there just fine. Ye need not worry about me." Frank stepped over to the window. "I'll see ye in Boston."

A thin silver light flashed in the middle of Frank's chest and the leprechaun was gone, leaving Claire alone in her room.

She'd made up her mind that she was going to this new college, regardless of what her parents thought.

Staring at where Frank was a moment before she thought, *I'm glad he's coming too.*

CHAPTER THREE

C laire made it to the university, although the entire trip left her feeling like she'd been thrown into a whirlwind.

From the first call to Remington until she boarded the plane, it took only a few hours. The FBI had kept one of their own planes overnight for her, ensuring if she said yes, there wouldn't be much delay.

Claire had never seen a city as large as Boston before. As the car rolled through the streets, she stared up at buildings that appeared to stretch into the heavens. Claire couldn't even think of missing her parents or home, she was too enamored with the world around her.

I've only seen things like this in pictures, she marveled.

As for the university building itself, Claire's lips parted in awe when she saw it.

The car turned onto the entrance of a horseshoe driveway. If that wasn't fantastical enough, the sprawling construction at the end of the driveway blew Claire's mind.

She leaned against the door and stared at the building,

still open-mouthed. "You must have the wrong address," she told the driver.

"No, ma'am. This is the place."

Claire didn't reach for the door handle. She didn't roll the window down. She didn't move.

Truthfully, she felt like she had when first meeting Frank, a creature from another plane of existence. Because of the luxury in front of her now? It had to be from another universe, certainly not meant for her.

To call it a house would be like calling a dragon a bird.

The mansion sprawled forever, or as near to forever as Claire could see. Two massive double doors sat beneath Greek-style columns, with windows lining the entire front of the building. Claire had caught a glimpse of the lawn as they pulled in, and impossibly, the property was larger than the actual house.

A mansion, she thought. That's what I'm looking at. Not a school, but a mansion for the rich and famous.

"This isn't a college." Now Claire turned to the driver. "Someone must live here. A movie star or something."

The driver's eyes flicked to the rearview mirror. "The federal government purchased the property a couple of years ago, during the first tear in the Veil."

"You're with the FBI?" Claire raised an eyebrow.

The driver nodded and turned his face back to the windshield. "Everyone you meet within this operation is with the FBI. Even your professors are contracted to work for the Bureau."

Claire swallowed, suddenly feeling a weight on her shoulders. "Well, let's hope I don't flunk out and end up in one of your black sites somewhere." She offered a weak smile.

The driver didn't take to the joke, just continued to stare out of the window. "Have a good day at school, Ms. Hinterland."

The trunk popped, and Claire knew that was her cue to grab her bags.

Remington had told her to bring only two, and that everything else would be provided. Claire had crammed as much as she could into those two bags, and despite her strength, they were *heavy*.

Her gaze was fixed on the three stories in front of her as she left the vehicle and walked around to grab her bags from the trunk. *I hope I'm on the ground floor.*

Claire headed to the front doors. Once there, she placed her bags down and stared at them for a few moments, listening to the vehicle pull off behind her.

It hit Claire all at once. She was alone now. No way to turn back. She didn't even have a cell phone since her parents couldn't afford the expense, and *she* certainly wasn't wasting her hard-earned money on one when they had a perfectly good landline at home.

The steel in her spine returned. "Don't start thinking like Mom now," she whispered to herself. "Alone doesn't mean anything but an opportunity to meet new people. If you don't want to be alone, you can always go home and hang out with Wilma and Myra at the Kickin' Chickin."

That thought made her raise her hand to knock on the door.

She paused, thinking, *what is the etiquette when entering a mansion? They don't teach that in high school. Knock? Ring the doorbell? Don't do anything and demand a butler come get the bags?*

She was just about to knock when the door swung slowly open and revealed a kindly-looking old lady. She came up to Claire's shoulders and had straight white hair that cupped her face. She was plump, but that only added to the friendliness Claire felt coming from her.

"May I help you?" The matronly lady smiled and Claire returned it, unable to help herself.

The lady looked Claire over. "Claire Hinterland, I presume? You may address me as Miss Reilly."

Her accent was decidedly English, and the entire scene grew more surreal.

Never met an English person before, Claire thought as she nodded. "Yes, ma'am."

"You're late. The first class has already started." Without dropping her smile, Miss Reilly waved at Claire's luggage. "Come along. I'm not in the business of carrying luggage or else I'd be working at an airport, wouldn't I? Pick your bags up and follow me." She clapped her hands to snap Claire from her daze. "Chop-chop, dear. Professor Byron doesn't take kindly to people walking in after he's started talking."

Miss Reilly's smile broadened just a bit more, glee crinkling the corners of her eyes. She held Claire's gaze for a second, then turned and walked into the house, obviously expecting Claire to follow.

"Well, that's a good start," Claire whispered sarcastically. She reached down and grabbed her bags, then followed her into the mansion.

CHAPTER FOUR

Claire arrived at her class, sweating, out of breath, and quite honestly pissed off after hustling her ass to follow Miss Reilly up three flights of stairs to her room, lugging her own bags the entire way.

She'd dropped everything on her bed, grabbed a notebook and pen, then practically flown to the mansion's other wing to make it to class before she missed too much.

This wing of the mansion had obviously been remodeled. Claire opened the door and found herself in what looked to be an actual lecture hall instead of a bedroom.

The floor slanted downward so that each successive level of the tiered seats had a view of the white-haired professor standing at the bottom.

"Excuse me?"

Sonofabitch! Claire exclaimed silently as she closed the classroom door behind her. She'd hoped to just walk in, sit down, and start learning.

No such luck.

"*Excuse me?*" the professor repeated, his pitch rising

with indignation.

Claire looked up, taking in the room quickly as she did.

It was a large room, though only eleven people filled the seats, each one of them sitting in the third row.

"Are you *lost?*" the professor asked. He was a tall, skinny man with a severe face. He looked as if he hadn't had a happy thought in perhaps a century or two, and thus the muscles had forgotten how to form a smile.

Based on how old he looks, I'm guessing he served in the Revolutionary War. Probably was a turncoat. Fought for the British. Claire offered him a polite smile. "This is Veil and Invasion Theory, right?"

The professor shook a finger at Claire. "That's correct, but you did not answer my question. Are you lost?"

You prick, Claire thought. You know I'm not lost. No one just stumbles onto a FBI site, gets inside, and finds your class.

She decided discretion was the better of valor and did her best to keep from letting her anger show. "I'm Claire Hinterland. Apparently, the recruiters got to me late. I'm sorry, Professor Byron. It won't happen again."

"Ms. Hinterland," the professor mused, stringing out her last name like a song lyric. He raised a hand in the air and waved toward himself. "Please, don't sit in the back. Come down to the front, and let's all be friends."

Now we're friends? Claire said nothing, but walked down the steps and sat at the first open seat on the third row.

A girl with long blonde hair sat next to her. Claire only caught a glance, but that told her everything she needed to know.

I'm late, and now sitting next to the prettiest girl in the whole school. Could the day get any worse?

Professor Byron smiled thinly. "Thank you for joining us, Ms. Hinterland. I presume that you met Ms. Reilly on your arrival?"

Claire nodded, wishing this whole episode would end. Her face wasn't red from embarrassment yet, but if this guy didn't give her a break, it would be, and then she'd probably be unable to hold her tongue.

The professor nodded as though Claire had just revealed some deep philosophical truth to him. "Did Ms. Reilly let you know that I *loathe* it when people are late to my class?"

Claire nodded again.

The professor took a step toward the front row. "Did Ms. Reilly happen to tell you *why* I loathe it?"

No, Claire thought. *She also didn't give me your date of birth, social security number, or sexual proclivities.*

"No, sir," she replied, her voice gravelly. She felt the steel firming up in her spine again and was starting to think she may be expelled before she wrote her first word down on paper.

"Well, let this be your first lesson, Ms. Hinterland. It's one I hope serves you well. I know it has me. Being late is a passive-aggressive way of telling the people around you that their time doesn't matter. That only *your* time matters. So, today, you have told us all that our time is not important."

The professor smiled sadly. "I do hope that in the future, you'll come to respect us more, and think that our time and lives matter as much as yours."

"I apologize." Claire's hands gripped the bottom of her

seat so tightly that her knuckles were white. She could feel the bones in her hands straining. "It won't happen again."

"I'm sure it won't." He held her gaze for a second, then stood a step back. He clapped once, the sound cracking through the classroom. "Now, let us return to the subject at hand, shall we? The Veil."

The professor turned around to a table behind him and grabbed a binder, then walked to the front row. He handed it to Claire, who took it without a word.

Claire placed the binder on the small table attached to her seat and opened the cover. A single sheet of paper was titled *The Veil & Invasion Theory*.

"Ms. Hinterland, I'm not going to explain this binder to you, since that would be wasting everyone else's time. If you can't figure it out, please ask one of your classmates later."

Claire looked up from the binder to nod, but the professor was no longer watching her. Instead, he'd backed up and was facing the class again.

"Now, where were we? Can someone please remind me? My train of thought has been thrown from its rails and is careening to a fiery crash in which everyone aboard will most likely burn alive. It is a terrible thing. Can someone save us?"

A young woman on the far end of the row lifted her hand.

The professor dropped his head in mock exasperation. "Oh, Ms. Drins, this is not elementary school. There is no need to raise your hand and wait for me to call on you. I have asked a question. When you are talking to others and they ask a question, do you raise your hand? No, I think not. Please, just tell me the answer. What were we talking about?"

Claire looked down the row at Ms. Drins. Her face was bright red, and Claire immediately felt pity for her.*Might be best if you don't remind him, Ms. Drins, and let him die in that fiery crash,* she thought.

"You were explaining what the Veil is," Drins answered.

The professor nodded without looking up from the floor. "Ah, that's right. What the Veil *is*. Very good. First things first, no one actually *knows* what the Veil is. That may sound like a cop-out, but regardless of what the FBI is paying me I did not come here to lie to you. We have ideas, but we don't know. Now, at orientation you were told to read the first chapter in your binders. In said chapter, you will have been introduced to the most likely of the hypotheses that have been put forward by the scientific community. Please, for the love of all that is holy, can someone tell me what it said?"

He didn't move, didn't raise his head, but simply waited for the answer.

Ms. Drins continued as if they were the only two in the class.

Claire had seen people like this before in school. The overachievers.

"It's a border between Earth's reality and another reality. We have a few guesses as to what it might be, but our best guess is a new type of matter called Titan Matter—"

"Yes, Titan Matter!" The professor interrupted her reply, light in his eyes for the first time. Real excitement now, not just piss and vinegar toward the class. "Why do we call it that, Ms. Drins?"

"It's named after the Greek Titans," she responded.

She sounded just as interested as the professor, though Claire didn't know if it was the subject matter or simply being right.

The professor nodded then began to pace slowly across the room, his hands behind his back. "Titan Matter. I myself named it. There are other types of matter, namely, baryonic matter, which is the type we are traditionally able to interact with, and what scientists called Dark Matter. Dark Matter is somewhat trickier to pin down since our only way to observe it is by tracking its effect on the objects *around* it."

A new voice interrupted. "It's invisible? Sounds like bullshit to me."

Claire looked along the row. Sitting slumped deep into his seat three chairs over from her was a guy with short brown hair. His binder wasn't opened, and he had neither pen nor paper in front of him.

The professor stopped his pacing and turned to look at the guy. "I wouldn't term it that way, Mr. Teams. Since I'm an educated person, I would say it's the place of science to disprove the theories that came before as we advance in knowledge and ability."

The guy smirked but didn't sit up. "So Titan Matter is bullshit, too?"

The professor sighed. "If you are the best we have, then we are indeed doomed. Regardless, I must go on with my endeavors as any good soldier would. Please, Mr. Teams, keep your vulgar opinions inside your vulgar head and let the rest of us continue on in our less animalistic ways."

Claire watched the professor resume his pacing lecture, unconcerned by Teams and his careless attitude.

The class had started out awfully, and she didn't rate the other students highly so far. The girl at the end seemed to be trying to make an A, as if that mattered. Teams was an asshole, plain as the jackass grin on his face.

However, Claire was fascinated by Professor Byron's lecture.

This was cutting edge stuff.

This explained *Frank*.

"Titan Matter is easier to observe than Dark Matter. The proof, you ask? All the mythological creatures now running amok in our society. We've seen the Veil, or, rather, it becomes visible to the human eye when it breaks. Otherwise, it's as invisible to us as Dark Matter. There are two instances of a rip being recorded, although we can easily hypothesize that the actual rate of occurrence is much higher due to the volume of mythological creatures crossing over."

The professor paused in his flow to give the students time to absorb the mass of information he was providing before continuing.

"My hypothesis states that the Veil is made up of Titan Matter, a completely new state of energy. Right now, governments are spending a tremendous amount of money to understand it, but that is not relevant to our current purposes. More, based on the quality of intelligence I sense in this room, you will likely not understand it, so I will not waste our time."

The professor stopped pacing and faced the class with his hands clasped behind his back. "Which one of the geniuses before me can recite what your binder says is happening to the Veil?"

"It's tearing apart," the pretty girl to Claire's right said. She was staring at her binder as if she didn't want to be noticed, and her voice sounded like speaking might be the hardest thing she'd ever have to do.

"I was beginning to think you were mute, Ms. Hallor. Perhaps blind as well, the way you keep staring at that binder."

He's going to be lucky if I don't blind him. Claire had experienced a lot of different teachers in her life, but none who walked around thinking they were above everyone else, like this pompous jackass.

"It's tearing apart? Or these are random failures that we think will stop?" the professor pressed. He took a few steps forward to stand in front of Hallor. "Speak up, please. Perhaps in the town you're from, everyone has super-hearing? Unfortunately, in this class, we all hear at a normal decibel level."

"Hey," Claire interrupted, unable to take it anymore. "Give her a freakin' break. She's here to learn, not let you walk all over her."

Claire narrowed her eyes and gripping the desk tightly. The last comment from the professor had pushed her over the edge. All thoughts of failing or being expelled and getting sent to a FBI black site left her mind.

She wasn't going to stand here while this pretty-but-almost-unbelievably-shy girl was belittled. It had probably taken everything in her to speak up at all.

The professor slowly looked at Claire as if the effort was hardly worth it.

"I have offended the delicate Ms. Hinterland." He stared at her as if she were a bug, one he didn't care enough to squash. "My apologies."

Which *really* meant, "Why are you still here?"

The professor turned back to Ms. Hallor. "I will do my best to not offend our flower at the end of the row. Ms. Hallor, is the Veil tearing apart, or are these temporary blips?"

The girl's face was maroon, blood filling her cheeks. "It's tearing apart," she mumbled.

"That's right." The professor backed up and resumed his pacing.

Claire was relieved. Not for herself, but for Ms. Hallor, and perhaps the professor. If he'd continued to mock her then Claire and he might have had to go toe to toe.

The professor was oblivious, lost once more in his own narrative. "It's ripping apart. As of now, we don't know why, and we don't know how to reverse it." He smiled as he walked, either finding himself humorous or completely unfazed by his part in the interaction that had just occurred. "So perhaps we are doomed, and not just because of the lack of intelligence in this room. Yet, onward. Am I right?"

He stopped walking and glanced at his watch. "It seems my time with you today is up. I must say, I'm beyond grateful. However, we did not cover what we needed to in this session."

He looked around the students, his face serious. "That will *not* happen again. Every day that you're here, we will cover the planned material from this moment forth. I will see you all tomorrow at eight sharp. You're dismissed."

"Thank God," Claire whispered as she closed her binder. She was beginning to think coming here had been the worst decision of her entire life.

She stood up without looking at anyone and started up the steps toward the front door.

"Ms. Hinterland," the professor called after her. "Would you mind staying for a few moments? I promise not to waste too much of your time."

Claire repressed a sigh. *Can this day get any worse?* she wondered.She turned around and walked back down the steps as the rest of her classmates flooded the opposite way. She didn't sit down but stood holding the binder in front of her.

The professor had walked over to the table and was gathering papers, acting as though she wasn't there.

Claire waited impatiently but said nothing. She'd already spoken enough, she imagined, and would very shortly be asked to leave the university.

She didn't much care at this point.

If being at this university meant she had to stand by and watch people be bullied, she'd rather be at home putting chicken in deep fryers eight hours each day.

The door closed behind her as the last student left, echoing through the now silent room.

The professor gathered all of his papers together and lightly tapped them on the desk to straighten them.

He stood, but kept his back to Claire. "You didn't like the way I talked to your classmate, did you?" he asked.

Claire swallowed and made a very quick decision. She didn't come here to lose her nerve or start breaking for other people, even if they held more power than her. "I didn't like the way you talked to any of us."

The professor chuckled lightly. "I know that you were late getting here, but did Ms. Reilly tell you my name?"

"Dr. Byron."

He turned around, and the sternness that he'd carried the entire class had dissipated. His face looked softer, wiser, and his eyes held that glee she'd seen when he first started discussing the Veil.

Claire's own eyes narrowed, unsure exactly who she was looking at.

"Yes, that's right. I'm Dr. Byron." He half-sat, half-leaned on the table, holding the papers in his hand. "It's good that you stuck up for your classmate. You're going to need to continue doing that in the days to come, and they're going to need to stick up for you. Not necessarily from me, but from the things you'll face."

Claire didn't know exactly what to say. That was the last thing she expected to hear.

"Ms. Hinterland, I'm serious about not being late again. I do not know much about you. Nothing at all, really. But I do know what we are facing. Or, I have an idea, and it's not pretty. I've been in a war before, the Vietnam War, and there's nothing beautiful about it."

He stood up and took a step forward, the hand holding the papers dropping to his side." You're here for a reason, and it's not my job to know what that reason is. At the age of nearly eighty, I find myself in a war again, only this time it's my job to train the soldiers. You're one of those soldiers. It took guts to walk in here late and still stand up to me, and I respect that." He paused for a moment, his dark green eyes staring intensely at hers. "Do you know why I said we're going to cover everything we're supposed to?"

Claire lowered her binder from her chest, feeling slightly more comfortable with the man for the moment. "When you said it, I thought it was because you were a control freak."

What she meant was, "I thought you were a prick."

"A control freak, huh?" Professor Byron smiled, and it wasn't nearly as gruesome as Claire imagined. "Perhaps, but that's not how I see it. I insist we progress forward because there isn't time to waste, Ms. Hinterland. I came out of retirement for this war, and I mean to help us win it. If I allow us to miss our schedule, I might be setting us up to lose."

The professor turned around and walked back to the table. "While I am tough, there are reasons for it. Please remember that going forward. You're dismissed."

Claire didn't move for a few seconds but only looked at Professor Byron. She'd never been in a situation like this, and certainly never met anyone like him. Claire felt pretty sure they didn't make people like Professor Byron where she was from, and that she might have misjudged him.

"I said you're dismissed, Ms. Hinterland."

Claire wanted to say something but wasn't sure what. Perhaps she'd said enough to him already. She turned and headed out of the classroom.

She'd only been at the university for a few hours, and it was already unlike anything she'd expected.

Claire could only imagine what the rest of the day would hold.

CHAPTER FIVE

Claire's return to her dorm room was yet another dip in her already sinking expectations.

The smart-aleck from class sat with his feet up on Claire's desk, blowing cigarette smoke out the open window. "I'm Jack Teams," he offered by way of introduction. "I am sure the pleasure is all yours."

Claire's eyes widened in disbelief at what she was seeing. "You're not my roommate. You can't be."

"Of course not." He didn't look at her, but simply put the cigarette in his mouth, took a long drag, and blew the smoke out the window.

"Don't be an ass, Jack."

Claire turned toward the new voice. She hadn't seen anyone else. She'd been so shocked to find a guy in the room that she'd completely missed everything else, which was highly irregular for her.

"I'm your roommate." The pretty girl who had been next to Claire in class —Ms. Hallor, as Professor Byron said—was sitting on the other bed, her back against the wall. "I'm Marissa."

"My name's Claire." She let the door swing closed behind her and walked over to drop her book bag and binder on the bed before turning her attention back to Jack. "One, I'm pretty sure you're not allowed to smoke inside the building, and two, I'm *definitely* sure you're not allowed to smoke in my room. So put it out, and then get the hell out."

She'd had a rough enough day already and didn't want anything to do with this guy. She'd encountered too many narcissistic a-holes like him in high school, and she had no time for them.

Jack still didn't even glance in her direction. Rather, he flicked the cigarette ash out the open window.

Okay then, Claire thought. She walked across the room and knocked the cigarette out of his hand before he could try to move it. It flipped out the window and fell from sight. "There. Now the cigarette is gone, and the next thing I need is for you to be gone."

Jack smirked without taking his feet off the desk. "That was pretty fast."

"He's part of our unit," Marissa told Claire, her lip curling as she spoke. "I'm not exactly thrilled about it, either."

Claire wasn't sure she liked the sound of that. "A 'unit?' With *you?*"

"Yes, ma'am." Jack snickered. "You, me, and Ms. Hallor are a unit. That's why I'm here in your room, and it's also why you should treat me a bit nicer."

Claire had no idea what was going on, but that was par

for the course at this point. Everything about this day had been a disaster, so why *wouldn't* this jerk be part of her life or the foreseeable future?

"Unit or no unit, get your feet off my desk." She grabbed his ankles and pulled them away from the desk.

The chair whipped around as Jack's weight shifted, causing him to sit up awkwardly.

"There. That's a start." Claire took a few steps back and sat on the edge of her bed, ignoring Jack in favor of Marissa. "Listen, it wasn't my fault I was late as hell to this place. I did everything the FBI guys told me to, but still, I've been griped at by the house mom. You saw what happened in class, and *now* I'm being told about a unit that includes *him*." She jerked a thumb toward Jack, who smirked in return. "Can you explain what this unit is for? What did I miss?"

"It's okay." Marissa offered a soft smile and unfolded her arms. "They told us someone was coming late."

"They *knew* I'd be late?" Claire leaned forward. "They knew, and they still acted that way?"

Marissa shrugged but kept her smile. "I think that's the way this place operates. The orientation person, I don't remember her name, mentioned someone had been found at the last minute and would join us shortly. I guess that's you."

Claire's eyebrows drew together. "Dr. Byron mentioned orientation, too. What are you talking about?"

Marissa shrugged apologetically. "Yeah, it was last week. Most of us have been here for six or seven days already. Got our books and binders and everything else."

Claire groaned and looked down at her feet.

"Welcome!" Jack chuckled. "The three of us are going to save the world."

"It hasn't been easy, but I'm starting to get used to him. Either that or you become immune to him after a while." Marissa scooted away from the wall and toward the edge of the bed. "Where was I? Oh, yes, the units. We're the first class. There are twelve of us, with three people to each unit. You, me, and him are one unit."

"What do units do?" Claire asked.

"Well, for one," Jack interjected, "we don't throw people's cigarettes out the window. It could be a fire hazard." He stood up and stuck his head out the window, looking down at the cigarette. "You're lucky this time, Hinterland. It landed on cement." He pulled his head back in. "Otherwise, this whole place could have gone up in flames."

Claire rolled her eyes. "Maybe you should think about the hazard you're causing with your filthy habit?" she shot back.

"Basically, a lot of our work is going to be done in groups or units," Marissa continued, ignoring the spat. "There are rumors about a private academy on the West Coast, but nobody knows much about it. The rumors are it's owned by a billionaire, and it's not a FBI site. To be honest, I'm not sure *anyone* knows very much about *anything.*"

"We're their guinea pigs." Jack took a step closer to the bed, shoving his hands into his pockets. He sounded as if he didn't have a care in the world. "It's not all bad since you two get the pleasure of working with me. I'm really happy for you both."

That angered Claire, although she couldn't say exactly why. She groaned and fell back onto her bed to stare at the ceiling. "Great. Just *great.*"

Jack just laughed.

CHAPTER SIX

The days came and went quickly, passing in a blur for Claire. She got up early, spent all day in class, and studied at night. Most of her classes were theory focused. However, she was also taking combat classes, and the physical demands on her body increased her exhaustion even as they strengthened her.

Still, she wasn't going to quit. Claire was beginning to understand how big an opportunity this was for her. The sheer amount of money being put into this place told her that the government was taking the Mythological Invasion very seriously.

Claire *never* had to cook for herself, which was something of a miracle in itself. She sometimes supplemented her diet back home when she had the cash to go to a fast-food joint, but here they had three meals a day, all provided without a dime expected from them in return.

Claire sat bookending Marissa, with Jack on the other side. Neither of her teammates seemed to notice how ridiculous of a notion free food and board was to Claire.

Claire had finally gotten more than six hours of sleep last night, meaning she felt more rested than usual when Dr. Byron took his place in the center of the classroom.

"It does seem like time is flying by," Dr. Byron began, folding his hands in front of him. "We've been here, what, a month already?"

A few nods went around the students at the professor's question.

Has it really been that long? Claire wondered. *It doesn't feel like it.*

She'd spoken to her parents a few times, but still, it didn't feel like that much time had gone by.

"A month is gone, and I look out upon my students and wonder if we will ever have enough time to educate you properly." He shook his head in mock exasperation. His cheerful nihilism was beginning to grow on Claire. "Today, however, we will journey forward in hopes that I can impart some very important information to you."

He turned around and moved to the whiteboard behind him. He picked up a dry-erase marker and wrote a question.

Who can see the Mythers, and how?

Dr. Byron put the marker down and turned around. "If you have seen a Myther—in person, so to speak, not on a video—raise your hand."

Claire glanced around the room before she raised her hand. The rest of the class had their hands raised too, so she wasn't the odd one out.

Dr. Byron's own hand was down. "That's right. I'm the only one here who can't see Mythers. Yet you all can. Who knows why?"

"You're too old," Jack blurted.

The professor gave a wry smile. "You're not far off. You're not close, either. Does age have anything to do with it?"

Claire nodded, thinking of Charlie at the bowling alley. "Yes. Typically, older people can't see them."

"That is true," Dr. Byron agreed. "But what about very young people? Can they see them? Say, ten-year-olds?"

"No," Marissa whispered from Claire's side.

"Ah, the genius mute!" Dr. Byron cheered. He glanced at Claire. "Kidding. Let us not get into another tussle, Ms. Hinterland."

He turned back to Marissa. "You're right. Younger children typically cannot see Mythers, and the same goes for older adults. While there are always exceptions to the rule, there is a certain age range we have found to have the innate ability to connect with creatures from beyond the Veil."

Dr. Byron turned and wrote on the whiteboard again.

18 - 23.

He faced the class. "The five years between eighteen and twenty-three are the prime window for seeing Mythers. It's a short window, which is why we have so little time."

"How sure of that are you?" Jack asked.

Claire sighed. *That guy! Always wanting to cause problems.*

"As sure as we are about anything else regarding the Invasion," Dr. Byron answered, unperturbed. "We're constantly making new discoveries, but right now, that's what it looks like. Before that age, very few people can see them, and after twenty-three, the same. My turn to ask you a question. Why do you think that is, Mr. Teams?"

Jack grinned but was quiet.

"He doesn't know," Claire scoffed. "You know he doesn't know, so can we keep going?"

Dr. Byron grinned. "You're catching on, Ms. Hinterland. I like that. We must advance forward, or our enemies will overrun us."

He stepped away from the board. "As a child, you are given restrictions. Children by design have great imaginations, but their lives are run for them by their parents in order to assure they reach adulthood in one piece. Eat this, not that. Go to sleep at this time, wake up at that."

"What's that got to do with anything?" Jack cut in again.

Dr. Byron stopped in his tracks and pointed at him. "Mister Teams, unless you can provide me with a note stating you have some neurological condition that prevents you from allowing your intellectual betters to impart wisdom to you, I will politely suggest you do not interrupt this lecture again."

Byron raised a bushy eyebrow at Jack and continued in the next breath. "We believe that around the age when people are leaving the construct of their parents' rule, their ability to accept the unexpected peaks. This means their minds are flexible enough that they are able to see these creatures. So, people going to college or entering the workforce. People leaving home for the first time." He held up a finger to emphasize his point. "The common factor in all of these situations is that the person is placed in a situation where they are given power over their own lives. But, as I'm sure some of you are aware, power comes with responsibility. In this case, the responsibility of finding self and discovering the world without the innocence of childhood to filter out the truth of things. All of these factors create the perfect environment for the brain to be receptive to the true nature of the Mythers. Why else do you see so much 'radical' thought on college campuses? It's the first time people are exposed to complete freedom."

"And what happens at twenty-three?" Claire asked.

Dr. Byron nodded at Marissa. "You're smiling. Happen to know the answer?"

"We get jobs," Marissa replied, still smiling.

"That's right. You go out and get jobs, and the weight of the world crushes your spirit. Either way, the brief freedom you had is gone."

"That doesn't make sense," Claire called out. She leaned forward on her desk. "Some adults can see them, right?"

"Sure." Dr. Byron nodded. "Some adults can swim the English Channel at seventy years old. That doesn't mean ninety-nine percent of people at that age wouldn't drown if they tried."

"Why can some see and others can't, then?" she asked.

"You and Mr. Teams just love trying to poke holes, don't you?" He glanced at Jack. "At least your interruptions have some logical thought driving them." Turning to the rest of the class, he continued. "It's not a bad question. Much as with everything else in this jumbled mess, we only have theories. Neuroscientists understand that our brain is malleable. It is designed to change, to adapt to challenges and overcome conflicts. Lucky for us, since we wouldn't be able to learn much otherwise. Some adults can see

Mythers. I want to be clear here: this isn't *only* a matter of belief. Belief is neither necessary nor sufficient by itself."

The professor held a hand to his chest. "I believe the Mythers exist, or else I wouldn't be here. However, I cannot see them. My brain won't let me. It's too *old*, as Mr. Teams put it. Probably it's too set in its ways, at least for now. Some adults, a very small fraction, don't have that problem."

He paused while Marissa whispered, "I read that when the Europeans arrived at the New World on their giant ships, the natives didn't see them. They looked right at them, but couldn't see the ships sailing toward them, not until the ships reached the shore. Their brains simply couldn't compute what they were seeing because it was so far beyond anything they knew to be true."

"I've heard that story too," Dr. Byron answered, his voice low. He shook his head. "You're tricking me into sounding like you, Ms. Hallor. Some adults can see them, but the vast majority can't. Unless *what*?"

An alarm started going off before anyone got a chance to answer. Dr. Byron's phone suddenly began vibrating on the table.

"Ah!" He chuckled as he made his way over to retrieve it. "Trying this new technology to see if it helps. Did you all know your phones have alarms on them?"

He looked up with a grin on his face.

"Did you like that, Mr. Teams? An *old person* joke for you." He put his phone into his pocket. "Okay, we're going to pick up there at our next class. Go forth and do your best to be somebody or something."

CHAPTER SEVEN

C laire opened her eyes when the hand covered her mouth. A scream bubbled up in her throat; she was certain she was only seconds from dying—

"*Shhh*, lass. It's only yer good buddy Frank. See?"

Frank's green face filled Claire's vision. "You don't want to wake your roommate." He glanced at Marissa, still sleeping soundly in her bed.

"Frank!" Claire whispered harshly. "What the fuck are you doing here?"

"Checking out the new digs, lass." Frank straightened and slowly turned around, eyeing the room. "I must say, this isn't much better than where you were before, Claire." He completed his circle and looked down at her bed, grinning wildly. "I thought you were coming up, not falling down?"

"Frank, you've got to get out of here!" Claire sat up in bed, pulling the covers around her. "You know where you are? This place is the training ground for *killing* creatures like you!"

Frank looked into the air in mock exasperation. "Oh, Zeus, here we go again. This wee lass telling *me* about the business of staying alive." He turned back to the bed. "Come on, let's get out of here. I found a twenty-four-hour bowling spot we can hit."

Claire shook her head. "*No.* I've got class tomorrow. I'm not about to ruin all this by sneaking out with you."

"Class, schmlass," Frank said with a wave of his hand. He grabbed the edge of the blanket and yanked it off.

Claire glared at him. "You're lucky I've got clothes on, or you'd be flying out the window right now. You can't just teleport in here whenever you feel like it!" Claire moved her head to check on Marissa when she let out a tiny snore. She was still asleep.

"The mouth on this one!" Frank danced in indignation, bouncing from one foot to the other. "Do ye think I'm likely to take orders from ye? No, lass, Frank is a free leprechaun. I do no one's bidding but me own. Now, enough with the jibber-jabber. We've got some bowling to do, me lady."

Frank wasn't lying. The scoundrel had scouted out a twenty-four-hour bowling alley in downtown Boston. There'd been some more arguing before they'd left, mainly consisting of how Claire was going to get out of the university.

Frank had a solution. "I could teleport us outta here?"

"If I end up in some kind of alternate universe, or

behind the Veil, for that matter, I'm going to strangle you," Claire told him.

Frank winked. "Sure, and how'll ye get back again if you do?"

Well, it was hard to argue with that.

Claire had seen Frank teleport before, but she'd never *experienced* it. Her body felt very light for a second, as if she weighed no more than a feather, and then everything got very, very fuzzy.

The next thing she knew, she was staring at a Porsche on the side of the road.

"Ye got new digs, Frank got a new car." He still had hold of her wrist. He looked up at her and winked.

Claire stared at the vehicle, her eyes wide. She was unsure if she was more shocked that she just teleported out of the university or was looking at a car Frank couldn't afford if his life depended on it. "You robbed me for beer money, and now you're telling me you've got a Porsche?"

Frank reached into his pocket and pulled out a single key. "Yes, lass. Ye may be falling down, but Frank is on the come up. I told you, Boston is the place for an ambitious leprechaun. Now, enough prattle, let's take it for a spin."

Frank drove like a madman, and the entire time Claire was too worried about vomiting to even consider what was going to happen if someone found out she wasn't in bed.

He spun the car into the bowling alley's parking lot, wheels screeching and smoke rising from the concrete. The vehicle jerked to a stop, and Frank looked at her. "I haven't gotten my driver's license yet, but I don't think that'll be a problem."

Claire gripped the door handle, her eyes wide. "I'm going to kill you."

"You just aren't cut out for city life, lass. Me, though? I know what I'm doing. Come on, let's get to bowlin'." Frank opened the door and hopped out.

It was amazing that he'd been able to see over the steering wheel and touch the pedals with his feet. He was barely tall enough to see out of the driver's window.

Claire looked at the pedals. She wasn't sure *how* he'd managed to do it.

I nearly died, she thought, stepping out of the car and slamming the door. "Frank, that's the last time I go anywhere with you behind the wheel. Next time, *I'm* driving."

"Hah!" Frank tossed the key into the air with his right hand then grabbed it with his left before pocketing it. "I've heard about you women drivers. You're not very good from the sound of things."

"Also," Claire shook her fist and ran to catch up to the leprechaun marching across the parking lot. "If you make another sexist remark, I'll cut your balls off."

Frank laughed. "Always with the threats!" He hustled through the front door.

It took a few minutes for Frank to get his bowling shoes and beer.

Claire was more than grateful the kitchen was still open this late.

Thank goodness for the stipend they're giving us, she thought as she ordered fries.

Frank started bowling. He hit strike after strike, making wisecracks when he came over to sip on his beer.

Claire thought he was drinking slower than usual, although she didn't say it. It was good to see Frank. It felt like it'd been longer since they last spoke, probably because of how dramatically different Claire's life was now.

Seeing Frank reminded her of home and of the life she'd left behind.

Frank hit another strike, and the falling pins echoed through the empty bowling alley. He looked over his shoulder, his green lips spread in a smile, then moon-walked back to the table without saying a word.

She'd seen that move before and acted like she wasn't impressed, although he did it remarkably well. "Frank, you haven't been in Boston two months. How did you get a Porsche? Are you wanted for grand theft auto, now?"

"I've changed me ways, lass." Frank grabbed the tall glass of beer and took another sip. "I no longer commit such horrendous crimes. I'm a stand-up guy and a model citizen."

Claire rolled her eyes. "A leprechaun saying they're a model citizen is like a polar bear claiming to be a vegetari-an." She nodded toward the beer. "Did you also join a sobriety movement? I've never seen you drink so little in all the time I've known you."

Frank placed the beer on the table and stared at it for a second. His ball rolled into the holding area, but he didn't look at it.

Claire raised an eyebrow. "Everything okay?"

Frank was quiet for another second, and Claire felt her stomach drop. *He's never been like this,* she thought. *Not once. Not even after you beat him up for robbing you.*

Claire pointed at Frank. "Frank? I'm gonna need you to

start talking. You didn't just come get me out of my room to bowl, did you?" She then pointed toward the half-full beer. "Because *that's* not like you."

The leprechaun looked away from the table toward the bowling pins as if he didn't want to look her in the eyes while he spoke. "I'm worried, lass."

"I told you not to come to Boston," Claire scolded.

"No, I'm not worried about me." He finally met her eyes. "I'm worried about you."

"Me?" Claire shook her head. She grabbed a fry and chewed it while she considered his confession. "There's nothing to be worried about with me. I'm surrounded by the FBI. You know who they are, right? Federal Bureau of Investigations. I mean, they pretty much run the USA, for God's sake."

"Sheesh, the wee one is too stubborn to even listen." Frank sat down and picked his beer up. He eyed it for a second, then set it back down. "For leprechauns, word travels fast in Boston. I've heard things, and they're not good things, lass."

Claire frowned, her concern growing deeper with every second Frank refused to spill. "All this gloom and doom and secrecy. Frank, your mouth is twice the size of your whole body, and today you won't say a word. Just tell me what you called me out here to tell me."

Frank stared at his glass as if answers to unvoiced questions might be found in it. "I never knew why I was here. Why I crossed over, you see? I didn't ask, either, Well, it's not in my nature. But there are rumors here in Boston about why the Veil was opened. Why us mythical creatures are here. Why we were brought here from our side of the

Veil. The media is saying that it's happening naturally, or when you have a lot of worshippers in certain places. But those are not the only reasons." He was quiet for a moment, his green face as pensive as Claire had ever seen it. "Someone *called* us over."

Claire raised an eyebrow, her hand pausing in midair before she grabbed another fry. "You want to say that again, Frank?"

He nodded without looking away from the beer, smiling forlornly. "They didn't tell you that in class?"

Claire shot him a sour look. "No, and you're still not saying much. Tell me what exactly you're talking about." Her hand still hovered over the basket of fries, her food completely forgotten.

Frank placed his hand on the glass but didn't lift it. "Someone is calling us over. I don't know why, but we're not all accidents. The rumors say the summoner is human." He looked up and met Claire's gaze. "One of you."

CHAPTER EIGHT

D r. Byron stood in his usual place after all the students had taken their spots. "Mr. Teams, have you had time to think about the question from last class?"

Claire was exhausted, much more so than usual. She'd half expected to get back to her room last night and find security or someone waiting to escort her right back out. No one had been there, though. Frank had simply teleported her in, then left.

It had been late, but she hadn't been able to sleep. Who could, when someone told you something like that?

She hadn't mentioned what Frank had told her to Marissa or Jack, and she didn't think she was going to either. She didn't know what to expect if word got around that a leprechaun was feeding her information, and more, she didn't know what to do with the information anyway.

It wasn't Claire's job to know that stuff. It was her job to learn.

Let's hope that's the right decision, she thought. *Lives could depend on it.*

"What question was that, Dr. Byron?" Jack asked, shifting in his chair.

Claire leaned forward and looked at him. He couldn't be serious.

Jack didn't pay her any mind.

"Your memory is comparable to that of a goldfish, Mr. Teams." Dr. Byron sighed. "The question was, under what circumstances can adults see Mythers? When do their brains adapt?"

"Ohhh," Jack said. He stretched his legs forward and leaned back in his chair. "I thought you were asking a hard question. Adults can see them when they're about to die."

Dr. Byron smiled. "Perhaps your work ethic is not as horribly lacking as I had originally thought. Or perhaps you opened a book for once." He turned to address the whole class. "Mr. Teams is right. Adults who cannot see have been reported as being able to see when being attacked. Why?"

Claire raised the hand holding her pen.

Byron flourished a hand. "Ms. Hinterland. Do enlighten us."

Claire tapped her pen absently on her notepad as she spoke. "The brain resists a lot of things, but if someone is nearing death, it reacts. The instinct to survive, to keep the body alive, forces the brain to adapt."

"Good answer." Dr. Byron nodded and walked to the left side of the class. "Let's say that I am being attacked, and at the moment where I'm in real danger, I gain the ability to see the creature. Let us also say Mr. Teams somehow awakens from his lifetime of apathy and clownsmanship and is able to save me. What happens to my brain then? Do I continue to see Mythers? Ms. Drins?"

"I don't know," 'Ms. Drins answered.

Dr. Byron looked around the room. "Anyone else have a clue?"

Jack pointed his thumb to the left. "I bet Marissa does."

Dr. Byron glanced at Claire. "Does he not get the same treatment as me for his behavior toward Ms. Hallor?"

Claire shrugged. "Eh, he's part of my unit. I give him more leeway."

"Fair enough." Dr. Byron continued his line of questioning. "Ms. Hallor, is he right? Do you have a clue?"

Marissa went bright red as she spoke. "I think it depends on the person. On their individual mind, and on their age."

Claire could tell she wanted to punch Jack in the face for bringing her to attention.

The professor pressed his fingertips together and smiled. "Tell us more."

Marissa continued. "Some people can see them immediately if their minds are more fluid or...adaptable. Others?"

She shrugged. "Well, it's not likely they would see the Myther in the first place. Except...there *are* stories of moms who have lifted cars to save their children. Maybe it's not all about neurology. To answer the question about continuing to see Mythers, I think they couldn't do it just anytime. But for that split second, that moment of life and death, they stop kidding themselves and *see*."

Byron nodded with a slight smile. "That's right, Ms. Hallor. If the person's mind is set, it's likely they will not ever see another creature again. Some may be in between those extremes, seeing something every once in a while. We believe those to be in between the 'seeing' and non-seeing' state."

"What about people who already see? Like us?" Claire asked, crossing one leg over the other. "Can we ever go back to not seeing?"

"Hmmm..." Byron raised his hand to his chin and started rubbing. "There's never been a case of that happening." He peered out over the class, trying to come up with an answer. "I do not believe any of you will ever return to not seeing. Not when this is all said and done. Once you can see the Mythers all the time, your brain cannot be reverted back. Someone who has only seen one or two Mythers and has not had time to accept them?" He shrugged, dropping his hand down. "I think there's a good chance their minds would go back to being under society's chains. The answer is, we don't have the answer yet. However, the Mythers are here, and those who haven't seen one for themselves won't be able to deny them forever when their recorded images can be seen by all."

Dean Kristin Pritcham wasn't sure if she'd made a brilliant career move or a massive mistake. This deep into the decision, though, there wasn't much she could do about it.

A year ago, the FBI had plucked her from complete obscurity. She'd been a professor at Oviedo College in Florida, with a focus on teaching Greek and Roman mythology. Now she was the dean of her own university.

If you can call it that, she thought. *Twelve students, four professors, and a former Russian secret ops agent as a weapons and combat expert, a house mom, and a mansion. Maybe you're just running a daycare center.*

Only, the FBI didn't show up at daycares, and they were supposed to be entering Kristin's office any moment now. She glanced at the clock on the wall in front of her, which said two minutes until five in the morning.

They'd requested the meeting late last night. That was something else Kristin was quickly coming to understand —the FBI didn't keep normal business hours.

Kristin's stomach grew cold. It happened every time she had to meet with these guys. She'd taken the job because she knew there wasn't a whole lot of room to rise where she'd been before. People weren't exactly banging her door down with job offers for professors of Greek and Roman mythology.

She hadn't believed the offer when she'd gotten it. "You've got to be shitting me."

"No, ma'am," Lance had said, looking decidedly awkward. "No one's shitting you."

"Why me?" she'd asked. "I'm nobody. Even in my own field, I'm nobody."

Lance had kept staring right at her and simply said, "Told you," to his partner.

Remington had taken over the conversation. "Quite simply put, Dr. Pritcham. You can see them."

"Who?" Kristin had asked, although she'd known exactly what they were talking about. Kristin hadn't told anyone what she'd seen, but that apparently didn't matter.

Because she'd done something even dumber. She'd anonymously uploaded the video online.

"The Mythers," Remington had said with an even look. "We know it was you who uploaded the video. We want a mind like yours to run the east coast school. One that isn't set in its ways. If you can see Mythers, then your mind is flexible. It's agile. It's going to be able to handle what we throw at it."

The knock on the door was firm, pulling Kristin from thoughts of the past.

"Come in," she called loudly.

The door opened, and Remington and Lance entered.

Kristin figured they had first names, but she didn't know what they were, even after a year.

Lance nodded to Kristin as he closed the door behind him. "Hello, Dean Pritcham."

"Hi, gentleman." Kristin stood up and walked around her desk to offer her hand to each agent in turn. "To what do I owe this pleasure?"

Remington gestured toward the chairs. "It's okay if we sit down?"

"Of course," Kristin said with a welcoming smile. She sat down in her own chair. "How are you today?"

"It's been a busy morning," Remington said. "We got off the plane about an hour ago, and we're already working on recruiting the next class. It'll be at least twice as big as what you currently have."

Kristin smiled. "That's good. Twelve students don't constitute what I'd call a university in any real sense of the word."

Remington nodded. "We understand your concerns, but

right now, we can't really focus on them. I'm assuming you've seen the news this morning?"

Of course, she had. The video had gone viral. A group of people on safari in Africa had been recording video of a herd of zebras as they drove across the plains. A unicorn had trotted out from the middle of the herd. White as a dove, with a horn in the middle of its forehead.

"Yeah, I saw it," Kristin said. "How did the adults see it, though? How did they know what they were looking at?"

Lance spoke now. "Best we can ascertain, they had a teenager with them who saw it. The parents didn't see anything until the teenager uploaded it."

Kristin understood the rules of these creatures. At least, she thought she understood them as well anyone could. The "rules" were still being invented, however, and everyone was constantly learning.

It was much less common for adults to see the creatures, but once a Myther had been recorded, everyone could see it on the image without a problem. Thus, the video's virality.

"So, Dean Pritcham, we understand your concerns about class size," Remington continued. "But please trust us. You're not running an elementary school here. The problem is growing more and more severe by the day. That's actually why we came."

Kristin leaned back in her chair as she did any time she was about to start thinking hard. "I'm listening."

"What's the curriculum for this semester?" Remington asked.

Kristin raised an eyebrow and smirked. "You don't have a copy in that briefcase by your chair?"

Remington smiled back. "Sure, I do. Just want to hear you explain it to me."

Kristin narrowed her eyes at the agent. *He's making sure you're at least as on your game as he is. Fine.*

She rattled off the courses on her fingers. "The first semester is based on *what* is happening, as well as beginning physical training. They cover the Veil and invasion theory, mythology and structure, mythology in the present day, hand-to-hand combat, and basic weapons levels one and two. That's five classes. Two of them are physically focused, but all will require a tremendous amount of practice. It's a full load."

"We're going to need to alter it," Lance told her quietly.

Kristin's mouth opened slightly. She didn't say anything for a moment, just folded her hands over her chest and letting the words sink in.

When she had herself under control, she fixed the agents with a hard look. "You know the amount of work it took for us to get this up and running, right? The number of approvals that had to be sought? You expect me to just *change* it?"

"Well, Dean Pritcham, that's what we're hoping," Remington responded. He leaned forward, placing his elbows on his knees. "We're constantly receiving more information about what's happening here. The FBI hasn't placed *all* its hope on this university. We have assets in other areas, and we're using them to better understand the nature of what we're facing. Right now, we're getting an idea of what's coming next, and it's not going to be a unicorn or a rainbow snake. Those things are just accidents, more or less. Our assets are telling us that something much more dangerous is on the way, and that it's coming soon. We need to get these kids prepared to face whatever it is."

Kristin brought her index fingers to her temples and started to rub her head. She closed her eyes. "You two are going to be the death of me, I think. What's coming? How much time do we have?"

Remington leaned back in his chair and smiled. "You know something, Dean Pritcham? Lance and I find ourselves to be pretty serious about life. I like talking to you, though. You may take it even more seriously than we do, and that makes me feel good. Makes me smile. Thank you for that."

Kristin didn't open her eyes. "I'm very glad I can be of service. Now, how much time do we have?"

"That's the good news," Lance said. "We're not exactly sure."

Kristin groaned at the smile in his voice.

CHAPTER NINE

C laire was the first person in class. She'd been coming in early for the past few weeks, wanting to ensure she didn't fall behind. Claire knew already that she wasn't the smartest person in the class. She wasn't even the smartest person in her unit. Marissa held that spot.

Her binder was out in front of her, but she was looking at Dr. Byron.

He sat at his table, looking down at a large book and reading intensely.

That wasn't there yesterday. Claire had seen papers, but no ancient-looking book.

Claire wasn't going to interrupt him and ask him about it. She didn't want to chance pissing him off again. Instead, she turned her attention to her own binder and kept studying.

After a few minutes of concentration, the sound of students entering the room broke her focus.

Claire turned around and watched her classmates make their way down the steps. She'd come to know them better as the semester progressed, though the Units were sort of sticking together.

Marissa came down the left side of the room and sat next to Claire. "Seen Jack?" she asked as she put her bag down and pulled the binder from it.

"Nope. Don't care to either," Claire answered.

"You'd miss me." The voice was right by Claire's face, a soft whisper. She jerked around, ready to slap whoever had gotten that close to her, but Jack was already backing up and grinning wildly. "Oh, Ms. Hinterland, you have to be quicker than that."

He moved down the row and squeezed past Claire and Marissa. "Excuse me, ladies. Excuse me. Just tryin' to get to my seat here."

He was grinning the entire time, and Claire did her absolute best to hide her own smile. He was an asshole, definitely, but there was something kind and humorous about him, too.

Jack sat down, but he didn't pull anything out. Not so much as a pen. "You two ready to learn more? Personally, I want to know if these creatures come over fully clothed, or if it's like *The Terminator* and they arrive buck naked. If they're naked, that leads me to wonder if Aphrodite will be coming and where I might be able to get a peek."

Marissa shook her head and Claire put her hand to her mouth, hiding the grin that had burst onto her face.

"Okay, my pupils," Dr. Byron said, standing up from the desk. He didn't close the book but left it open. He walked around the desk to the main area of the floor. "You can put your Veil binders away. We won't be needing those."

Claire's eyes narrowed, but she did what the professor asked.

"There's been a pretty drastic change of curriculum, and I only received word of it a few hours ago. Unfortunately for you, I'm not the best person in the world to teach what they're asking me to, but we must deal with the situations we face, yes?"

Claire's eyes darted to the open book behind the professor. *That's what it was,* she thought. *He was studying just like us. He's a scientist, an expert on cosmology, or physics, or something. But what they want him to teach us doesn't have anything to do with that.*

Professor Byron began to pace just as he had the day before. He looked down at his feet as he walked with his hands clasped behind his back. "You see, the curriculum was laid out in a very specific manner. First, we wanted you to understand what was actually happening. Next semester, you would begin to focus on different types of mythology, giving you a broad overview of what might be faced. As the year progressed, you were to continue to broaden your understanding of specific mythologies based on your chosen specialization."

He reached the end of the room, turned, and started pacing again, never once looking up.

"However, the powers that be have decided that isn't what will happen this semester. What that looks like for your overall education, I cannot say. Most likely, based on the aptitude already shown in here, this university will be a dismal failure." He stopped and faced the class. "Yet, the decision is above my pay grade. So, for this semester, in here, you all will learn no more about the Veil."

"We got that, Byron," Jack shouted. "You gonna give us a clue as to what's goin' on, or what?"

Professor Byron smiled, a wry thing that said he knew more than Jack did, but one day, Jack might discover it all.

Perhaps Byron even hoped he would.

Byron met the eyes of the class with concern. "By the time this class is over, you all are going to be experts on Eastern European Mythology. Specifically, vampires."

Jack raised an eyebrow. "Tell me they don't sparkle."

CHAPTER TEN

Agent Remington liked almost everything about Boston. He liked the historical buildings, the Catholic cathedrals, the small streets. Hell, he even liked the sound of the traffic.

He only had one issue with the city—its frigid air. The cold was so bitter he could barely stand to breathe it.

Remington had a large overcoat wrapped around him and gloves on. He hadn't bothered putting on a hat or earmuffs.

Perhaps he should have because at three in the morning, there was no warmth to be had on Boston's streets.

Lance stood next to him, silent.

Both men knew why they'd been called out this late at night, although neither wanted to admit it to the other. The car ride down here had been silent.

More than anyone else involved in this, Remington and Lance knew what the world was facing. There were people with more authority, of course. A lot more authority,

Remington knew. But they weren't in the thick of it day in and day out.

Remington and Lance were in charge of recruitment and managing the assets who brought them information about the invasion, as well as assessing the destruction being caused.

Right now, they were in a Boston back alley looking at some of that destruction.

Each end of the alley had been taped off since the local police had been notified about the body a few hours earlier.

Every police officer in Boston was under a strict directive to alert their superiors to anything that didn't make sense to them. Those superiors? Well, they sent it up the chain until it got to Remington and Lance's attention.

"We reported it soon as we heard." The Boston cop's New England accent was heavy on the night air as the three moved down the alley toward a large dumpster. "Hold on to your cookies, agents. Wicked bad scene."

He flashed them a pale smile. "Me and my partner, we came out here, got one look at this thing, and knew we had to turn it in. Boss told us, we see something like this, don't turn it in, and that's our badge. I got fifteen years in, and I ain't losing my pension over not reporting something, ya know?"

The cop was talking up a storm, and Remington didn't want to hear it.

Lance didn't even look at the man but kept his eyes on the dumpster ahead.

"You sure he didn't freeze to death?" Remington asked as they reached the large green trash bin.

The cop's eyes widened. "Am I sure? Sure, I'm sure. I've been working this city for fifteen years. You know how many bums I done seen freeze to death? Too many to count, that's how many." He knocked on the dumpster with his fist. It echoed in the close alley quarters. "The body's inside there. You need me for anything else? If not, I'm gonna go sit in the car with my partner."

Partner sounded like "pahtnah."

"No, we don't," Lance said.

Both agents stood about three feet from the dumpster, not yet looking in.

"Okay, then, gents. Let me know if ya need anything." The cop turned and left the agents by themselves.

Remington turned to Lance. "If I ever get that annoying, I want you to shoot me, okay?"

"If you ever get that annoying, I expect you to shoot yourself," Lance responded.

Remington chuckled. "Let's get a look." He pulled out a flashlight from the inside of his overcoat and pressed the button.

A stream of white light spilled out from the head, illuminating the otherwise dark alley. Both agents walked forward and peered over the lip of the dumpster as Remington shone the light inside it.

Remington peered at the dead body lying on top of the garbage bags. "What's with the pale skin? We got a corpsicle on our hands, you reckon?"

"He didn't freeze to death," Lance concluded with a glance. "Eyes are wide open. Would have closed if he'd frozen to death. You don't think..."

Rigor mortis hadn't set in yet. Remington put on a pair of gloves and used his pen to lift the victim's chin.

"There." Lance pointed at the left side of the victim's neck.

Remington saw them too.

Two tiny incisions.

"The asset wasn't wrong." Lance took a step back from the dumpster and looked back down the alley. "They're calling over vampires."

Remington stared for another few seconds then pulled himself away, too. "You know anything about vampires?"

"Seems to run the gamut." Lance was looking toward the police lights at the end of the alley. He pulled his jacket tighter around him. "You've got Dracula. Those like vegetarian vampires from *Twilight*, or whatever. They didn't eat people, right?"

Remington chuckled as he walked up next to his partner. "Beats me. Didn't read it."

Lance smirked. "I always knew I was the more educated of us."

Remington raised an eyebrow. "You read that shit?"

Lance shrugged. "I'm married. She wanted me to read them, so I did. I think it increased my getting laid percentage by about fifty percent over two months, so worth it."

Remington chuckled again for a moment before his amusement died away. He sighed, his breath coming out as white fog. *This is going to be a long night.* "The problem is, people have believed in vampires for a long, *long* time. That means there's got to be a lot of them behind the Veil. If they're coming here, then this is only the first of many bodies."

"The new theory," Lance asked. "What do you think about it?"

Remington raised his left hand as if tossing something in the air. "There's always a new theory with this shit. Which one?"

"That there is an infinite number of these creatures," Lance whispered, not wanting the words to travel to the cops at the end of the alley. "If Dracula was to come over and we killed him, there would be another Dracula, and another, and another. All the ways humanity has imagined that vampire just waiting to suck the blood of sleeping virgins."

Remington frowned. "If we get the Adam Sandler one, we don't have a problem. Can you imagine the cast of *Underworld* made real?"

Lance shook his head. "Endless iterations. Each one is different, but they're infinite. What do you think?"

Remington shook his head, his eyes widening. "I think that's a scary fucking thought, and I hope it's not true. But what do I know? I'm here to recruit."

"Yeah. I guess you're right." He nodded toward the dumpster. "We need to keep this out of the news. We don't need a panic."

Remington shoved his hands deeper into his pockets. Lance was right. There were people who believed this all to be a hoax, something akin to the crop circles in the nineties. The more things that came up like this, the fewer hoaxers would exist.

Hoaxers were the people who refused to believe any of

this was real. They didn't believe creatures were crossing from another dimension, nor did they believe in a Veil. In short, they thought it all was some grand conspiracy.

"We need the hoaxers," Lance said, clearly thinking down the same path he was. "They'll help keep this manageable."

"For now," Remington agreed. "Sooner or later, the world's going to believe. Those kids have to be ready to fight this."

"They will be. We picked the right ones. Let's go see if we can keep this out of the media." Lance started walking down the alley, and Remington followed.

The television was small and in the corner of the room. Jack sat in Claire's chair, while the two girls sat on her bed.

"No freaking way." Jack shook his head, grinning like a madman as he stared at the television. "I don't believe it. No way."

Claire looked over to Marissa, who was sitting next to her in their dorm room. They'd gone to Jack's dorm yesterday, and Claire had quickly decided she wouldn't be going back there. The place had been a disaster. Claire didn't understand how anyone could live like that.

The messiness of Jack's room didn't matter right now, though.

Marissa met Claire's eyes. She looked scared. "You think?"

The question trailed off, but Claire didn't need to hear the rest.

The writing on the television screen proclaimed *Vampires in Boston*, while the commentators were railing on and on about the invasion.

"This is why they changed classes around," Jack commented. He had a bowl of popcorn in his lap, and he tossed a few pieces into his mouth. He didn't stop chewing as he spoke. "They knew vampires were coming, so they're trying to get us ready to fight them. Unbelievable."

He shook his head as he dug his hand into the popcorn again.

"What's unbelievable about it?" Claire asked. "That's why we're here, isn't it?"

Jack took another bite of popcorn kernels. "Well, yeah. Eventually. But look at the body right there. That thing has freakin' *bite marks* on its neck. We're not ready to fight that yet. I think that's what they're about to have us do. Just throw us to the wolves."

"No." Marissa shook her head. "They're going to teach us about them, but they're not going to have us fight them. Not yet. They can't."

Claire looked back toward the television. "You think it's true?"

Jack pulled his impression of Professor Byron's most pompous tone. "This isn't the National Enquirer, Ms. Hinterland." He picked up a few pieces of popcorn and tossed them lazily at her.

Claire swatted them off her lap, still staring at the television. "This is freakin' CBS. Yes, it's true. Sure, the skeptics will say it's a lie or a government plot to take away our guns or something else, but it's real, sweets. We've got vampires walking among us."

"I...I didn't sign up to fight vampires." Marissa sounded scared, more scared than Claire had ever heard her before.

Claire placed her hand on Marissa's knee. "Hey, it's okay. We don't know what's going to happen. This is just the news, and they always fluff stuff up to make it sound worse than it is."

Jack looked at the two of them with an eyebrow raised.

Claire met his gaze quickly, knowing he was about to say something insensitive at best, and straight mean at worst. She shook her head hard.

Jack grinned but looked away. He was an asshole, but he walked the line carefully. Claire was starting to appreciate it. He wasn't a *cruel* asshole.

"Come on, you two," he said, standing up from the chair and spilling popcorn from his pants to the floor. "We've got to get to class. Dr. Byron might feed us to the vampires otherwise."

Well, everyone knows about it, Claire thought as she looked down the aisle at the rest of her classmates. Their faces were pale and drawn as if perhaps each one of them had just received news that a person they cared about had died. *Do I look like that?*

Marissa certainly did.

So did everyone else but Jack, who was actually smiling.

That kid, she thought as she pulled out a pen and paper, setting it on her desk. *Does anything get to him?*

Dr. Byron turned around from his table and looked at the class. His face was severe, as always when they began, but he didn't look scared. "Anything fun going on outside of here?"

Jack burst out laughing and all eyes fell on him. He doubled over in his chair and clutched his stomach. "Jesus, Dr. Byron! That's a good one!"

The rest of the classmates started eyeing each other, unsure of exactly how to react. Claire shook her head, smiling at the outburst, but also glad he'd broken the gloomy atmosphere. This place was tense enough. They didn't need to make it worse by dwelling on possibilities before they became real.

"All right, Mr. Teams. All right." Dr. Byron waved his hands to quiet the class. "Calm yourself before you have an aneurysm. I will most certainly lose my job, and that would be the worst part of the whole incident." He clapped his hands, bringing the entire class's attention to him. "You've all seen the news. So have I. It has cleared up a few things, I believe. I am a lot like you. Oh, not in intelligence, education, charm, or other things that matter, but when it comes to knowledge about the future. I was surprised we were starting vampires, although I am less so now."

Dr. Byron moved in front of the table, revealing more binders behind him.

"My role here is to prepare you for what might come, and that's what I intend to do. Here are your new binders for the class. Obviously there aren't any textbooks on vampires, so I've done my best over the past two nights to cobble together all the information we currently have on them. Please come get the binders and return to your seats."

Claire got up with Marissa right behind her. The other

students followed suit, all walking down to the bottom level to get a new binder. Claire felt the weight of hers, noticing immediately it wasn't as heavy as the last one.

Jack raised his hand as he took his seat. "I've got a question, Professor."

"Of course you do, Mr. Teams," Dr. Byron shot back. He moved to the front of the class. "Please ask it now so that I can continue your education."

"We talked about the Veil, and I understand that, but what are these things made from? I mean, how do they *exist*? It doesn't seem possible for two realities to meet this way, regardless of what the news is saying."

"That's the first smart thing you've asked, Jack," Claire said as she turned her head back to the professor. "Maybe there's some reason they brought you in here besides your ability to make the class laugh when everyone is freaked out."

"We were actually going to spend quite a bit of time on that exact question before the powers that be decided we must change course." Dr. Byron looked at Rebecca's seat. "I'm sure you've read ahead, Ms. Drins. Can you tell the clueless Mr. Teams about how this might all exist?"

She doesn't look like she wants to answer one bit, Claire thought. The entire class was frightened. The news of vampires had shaken them to their core.

Had they *all* thought they would come here and just get an education but not have to put themselves in danger? Claire wondered. Maybe.

Right now, it seemed like only she and Jack were holding it together.

Rebecca opened her mouth to talk, swallowed, and then

opened her mouth once more. "They... They think the universe behind the Veil is filled with the physical representations of our beliefs."

"Yes, that's partially true." Dr. Byron looked at the rest of the class. "Has anyone else read ahead? Ms. Hinterland?"

"Actually, yes," Claire answered.

"How shocking," Dr. Byron replied with a smirk.

Claire didn't resent him for it. She'd met the man behind the barbs, and he wasn't half as bad as he pretended. "Maybe you can teach Mr. Teams, given that you two are in the same unit. Enlighten us."

Claire hadn't had much time since she got here, from sneaking out with Frank to the changing curriculum. Everything had been a whirlwind. Still, she didn't come here to flunk out, so she'd buckled down and done her reading at night after everyone else was asleep.

"The Veil separates our two universes," she started. "We can't see into the other universe, so we can't find out how it exists or what happens inside of it. Rebecca is mostly right, though. Somehow, the things humans have believed in throughout history were born over there. Best we can tell, it's the ideas that aren't real that show up on the other side."

Dr. Byron nodded. "Is 'belief' the right word, though? The one Ms. Drins used. Does, let's say, a belief like the sun revolves around the Earth show up over there?"

Claire remembered all this easily. "No. Not those kinds of beliefs. Beliefs in *things*—creatures, gods, monsters. That's what is on the other side. Beliefs in systems and structures, as far as we can tell, don't exist over there. Some say when things are worshipped, they pop into existence. Worship can mean any number of things, like fan art, or comic cons."

"And," Dr. Byron asked, "how confident are we in that?"

She shook her head. "Not very. We're not very confident about anything regarding the Veil or the other side, because we can't cross over. So far, it seems to be a one-way street. Things come this way."

Dr. Byron nodded. "Late to class, but perhaps not last, Ms. Hinterland." He turned to Jack. "Does that answer your question, Mr. Teams?"

"About the same as everything else," Jack said, looking nonplussed. "'We think it's because of this, although it may not be. Just a load of bull—"

Dr. Byron's eyebrows went up, and his face *dared* Jack to finish the sentence. A sly smile crossed Jack's lips but he only said, "Bullish. Just a load of bullish."

Dr. Byron sighed, his eyebrows dropping. "I suppose that's the best we can hope for from you, Mr. Teams. Now, let's move onto the subject at hand, the thing that has all of you looking white as sheets. Vampires. What do you know about them?"

"They drink blood," a guy from the middle of the row said. Claire didn't know his name yet.

"They're the undead," Rebecca commented.

"They're immortal," Jack threw in, "so not sure how we're supposed to kill them."

Dr. Byron raised his hand palm out, requesting the answers to stop. "Yes, that's all true, except for the last bit that Mr. Teams threw in."

"As usual," Claire whispered so that only Marissa could hear. Marissa *finally* cracked the tiniest smile.

Good, Claire thought. *That's something.*

Dr. Byron walked backward until his legs touched the tabletop. He leaned against it. "Today I want you to learn the basics of these creatures. We all need to be on the same page about what they are and what they can do. The news says that they're crossing the Veil now, and truth be told, I hadn't actually considered that. When we think of mythology behind the Veil, horror movies don't really come up, do they? No one thinks Michael Meyers or Freddy Krueger is going to come waltzing down Fifth avenue."

"Can they?" Claire asked.

Dr. Byron shrugged. "Who knows at this point? Perhaps. Perhaps not. If I had to guess, I'd say yes, because people 'worship' them, at least in a sense. They might be fictional characters, but every year, we dress up like them by the millions. Now vampires, or witches and werewolves for that matter? You'll see in your binders that belief in these creatures goes back hundreds of years. So, probably sometime in the seventeen hundreds, vampires began appearing behind the Veil, because that was when we first started believing in them here."

He turned around and walked to the whiteboard, picking up a marker. He quickly sketched out a rough outline of Europe and then circled a few places around the Balkans.

"Most likely, a belief in vampires came about due to racism," he continued as he turned around. "One group of Europeans hating another group, which doesn't really matter for our purposes. Now, we have to assume vampires are real, and we have to assume their powers are real too. What can they do?"

Marissa raised her hand, and Claire nearly groaned. *Please don't chastise her, Dr. Byron. Give her a pass for raising her hand.*

"Ms. Hallor, I *would* ask why you're raising your hand like a child, but I know that your friend, Ms. Hinterland, would rake me over the coals." His eyes briefly flashed to Claire, gave her a quick wink, and went back to Marissa. "Please, tell us."

Marissa didn't look up from her binder as she spoke. Her voice was little more than a whisper. "It depends on what version of a vampire you're thinking about. The oldest legends say they have super strength, enhanced senses, and shapeshifting abilities. Some were rumored to fly, others had psychic powers. They were all very fast and healed much quicker than humans."

Claire's eyes widened. *What is she, some kind of expert?*

"There have been many, many versions," Marissa continued. "Every new movie or book putting a spin on it—"

"Sparkles," Jack interrupted with a disgusted shake of his head.

Marissa didn't notice. "Older vampires are represented as more powerful, with younger ones not capable of doing as much. Some myths say they can reproduce like humans." Red flowers bloomed in Marissa's cheeks at that. "But, the most popular myths all say that they reproduce through sharing their blood. That means they can either kill you or make you one of them." She looked up, her face full of the question that had just dawned on her. "Can they make new vampires here, Dr. Byron?"

Claire couldn't stop staring at Marissa long enough to even glance at the professor. Her usually meek friend had hit the nail on the head. She was definitely an expert about fictional vampires.

As if she wrote Dracula, Claire thought.

Dr. Byron started clapping slowly and loudly. "Well done, Ms. Hallor. Well done. I'm not sure I could have asked it any better, and I know your classmates couldn't have either." He stepped away from the table and walked over to the front row. "As to your question, I don't know. The person on the news this morning didn't have any real answers, and the agents haven't been very forthcoming with the Dean, either."

Dr. Byron looked at the rest of the class, his eyes sweeping across them. "By tomorrow, I suggest you all be as well versed on these mythological creatures as Ms. Hallor here."

Claire leaned over to Marissa as the others began to leave. "What the hell? How do you know all of that off the top of your head?"

Marissa grinned, staring down at her binder. "I've *always* thought vampires were sexy."

CHAPTER ELEVEN

Hannah Townsend watched the creature enter the room, studying him carefully. The room they sat in was windowless, as were all the rooms down here. Hannah's "partners" sat next to her. How she hated that term. Partners.

The vampire looked *polished*. His suit was tailored, his tie perfectly knotted in a full Windsor. His shirt was crisp, and his shoes shone. His hair was dark and parted to the right. His skin was pale like porcelain, as if it had never seen sunlight.

Bradley Baker sat to her left. He was a fat man with a bald head. He wasn't so big that he fell out of the chair, but it was clear anyone sitting next to him on a plane would be a bit uncomfortable. Matthew Lowndes sat to her right. He looked like he might start crying at any moment. He appeared to be in a state of mourning.

They shouldn't have been allowed in the same room with her, let alone in the same organization, but the decision hadn't been hers to make.

For Hannah's part, she knew what she looked like to this creature. She was thin almost to the point of frailty, and her eyes were cruel little beads that darted around the room. Hannah was fine with that. She hadn't invited this creature here to speak kindly to him.

That wasn't the plan, because if any of these Mythers thought that they were beneath them...

We'd have no chance at all, she thought.

"I was hoping I would never have to return to these catacombs," the creature said as he closed the door behind him. "When I escaped the underground, I wanted that to be forever."

Hannah reached into her pack of cigarettes and withdrew one. She took her lighter from the table and lit it, taking a drag before looking up. "What's your name?"

The creature raised an eyebrow. "I've been called a lot of names, but I suppose David will suffice for now."

Hannah nodded. "David is fine." They had called quite a few vampires over, but this was the first one they'd summoned to their location. Rather than trying to engage at first, they'd simply been honing their techniques to call over the *right* ones.

There were a lot of mistakes before we got to your kind, she thought, eyeing the aristocratic creature.

"How are you liking Earth?" Hannah asked before taking another drag of her smoke.

The creature smirked. "That's the name of this place, 'Earth?'"

Hannah nodded but said nothing.

"Yes, I do like this place." David moved farther into the

room, looking around. "Though this type of confined space reminds me of our long sleeps. I'm not fond of it."

Bradley spoke for the first time. "Well, you won't have to be here much longer if you cooperate."

The vampire looked at the fat man and then turned his head to Matthew. "You look like you might have an accident in your pants. Are you okay?"

Matthew's left leg was bouncing. He dropped his gaze from the creature. "Um, yeah."

How in the hell did I end up stuck with someone so weak? Hannah wondered. "Never mind that. We called you here for a reason."

The creature walked to the table but didn't sit down at the chair placed there for him. "I would hope so. I don't really like being summoned."

"We're sure you don't," Hannah agreed. She flicked her cigarette ash onto the floor. "But that's not really our concern. We have things we need you to do."

The vampire smiled and let out a harsh laugh. "You summoned me here to give me commands? I'm curious, who do you think you are?"

Bradley placed his fat hands onto the tables, his knuckles looking like tire irons. "We're the ones who called you over, and we're the ones who are going to call over your master."

The creature's smile dropped away.

That's right, Hannah thought. *Now you'll understand.*

"You're calling him?" David asked, his whole demeanor changing. "The original Dracula? Can you even do that?"

"Soon," Hannah answered. She took another long drag on her cigarette, holding the creature's gaze as she did.

"We're getting closer. Each one of you we find brings us closer to locating him."

David's eyes narrowed. "How is that possible? How is any of this possible?"

Hannah let her ash fall to the floor. "That's not your concern right now. Your concern is doing what we ask before we locate him and bring him over."

"You're talking about Dracula, yes? Just so we're all on the same... What's the phrase I'm looking for? On the same page?"

Hannah nodded. "That's the one."

Again, he took on a smirk. "Even if you could bring him over, why would I do your bidding? You are not Dracula. You are a human. Your kind don't command mine."

Hannah knew that the other two could speak just as easily as she, but also that only Bradley was even capable of talking right now. Matthew was far too scared to do anything more than not bolt from the room. "You've been feeding, right?"

The vampire nodded, still smirking.

"How do you like all that human blood out there?" Hannah asked. "Does it taste good?"

David said nothing, only stared.

Hannah smiled back. She put her cigarette out on the table and withdrew another one. "I'm sure it tastes wonderful." She lit the cigarette, pulled on it, and blew the smoke into the air. "You'd like to continue feeding, yes?"

The vampire nodded slowly.

"Well, we want you to keep feeding." She looked at Bradley. "Don't we?"

He nodded, smiling too.

Matthew only stared at the table, barely able to handle what was happening here.

The powers that be have to get rid of him, Hannah thought. *He's not cut out for this, regardless of whether he can see them.*

She turned her attention back to the vampire. "If you want to keep drinking human blood, you will do as we tell you. Otherwise, we'll send you back where you came from." She shrugged as if it were no matter to her, even though having a sizable number of vampires on this side of the Veil before bringing Dracula over was crucial to their plans.

David placed his hands behind his back, straightening and taking on the appearance of it not mattering. "What do you want me to do?"

Perhaps it doesn't, Hannah thought. *It's not like you're going to die out there. A lot of people don't even believe you exist, let alone can see you.*

"We've brought over quite a few like you," she replied. "I'm sure you've sensed them?"

The vampire nodded. "What do they have to do with me?"

"It's simple, really. We want you to organize them and just feed." She smiled, putting one hand in the air with her palm up. "That simple. Nothing else."

David raised an eyebrow. "Organize them?"

"Nothing substantial. Just let them know that they're to cause some mayhem, raise a ruckus, feed as much as they'd like." Hannah pulled on the cigarette once more. The smoke slowly rose to the ceiling. "When we finally locate him, we'll have more for you to do."

The vampire sighed and looked down at his feet,

smiling again. "We don't typically organize well, not unless *he* calls on us. But I may be able to meet your request." He looked up. "Unless, of course, you're bluffing about being able to send me back. Then maybe I can't."

Here it is, Hannah thought. *The place where we decide who is in charge. Him or us. And Matthew had better keep his damned mouth shut.*

"Is that something you want to test out?" She raised an eyebrow. "Because we can put you right back behind the Veil. It's no trouble. You're not the only vampire we have summoned here. There are plenty of others who can do what we want. If you don't want the opportunity to be the one who paved the way for your master's arrival."

The vampire nodded, still smiling. "Do you think you'll control him? Dracula?"

"None of your concern," Hannah answered.

The vampire looked over the three of them before letting his eyes fall back on Hannah. "He won't be controlled. He's not like me. Not like any of us that came over. He's the original. We're just lesser beings compared to him. He's older than us. Stronger."

Hannah waved her hand at his talking points. Smoke wafted into the air as she did. "You let us worry about that. You just go up to the surface and do as we've asked. We'll let you know when we need you again."

The vampire was silent for a second, his smile saying that they were fooling with things they didn't understand. Finally, he shrugged. "Okay. I'll go cause some mayhem for you. Anything else?"

"That'll do," Hannah responded. "You can go now."

The vampire dipped his head slightly, then turned and walked out of the room as quietly as he'd entered.

Matthew let out a large sigh. "Holy shit."

Hannah turned to him, disgust written all over her face. "You really helped us out a lot there, you know that?"

"This is too much. We shouldn't have gotten involved. We should have picked something *else* to call over." Matthew shook his head, his left leg still bouncing.

"Hush your mouth," Hannah chastised. "Everything is happening exactly as we want it, and the higher-ups are happy with our progress. All we have to do is get Dracula over here, and we're on easy street."

Finally, Matthew met her eyes. "We don't even know if we *can* call him over. This isn't a science, Hannah."

Hannah smiled and turned to the door that was now closed. "Ah, but we're getting closer all the time, aren't we?"

Dean Kristin Pritcham watched the two men walking across the courtyard without a hint of joy. The sun was falling behind them, and Kristin still had more work to do when she went back inside. She lived on the university's premises, wanting to give this her all. No husband, no kids. Her life had been her work, and so it was still.

Only now she wasn't teaching a class, but rather, trying to figure out how to train teenagers to save the world.

Remington smiled courteously as he and Lance reached the small garden. "Good evening, Dean Pritcham."

Kristin didn't get up from her seat but nodded at the two gentlemen. She raised her glass of wine and tilted it toward them. "I'd offer you some, but it's all the way inside."

Remington's smile faded slightly. "I've got to say, Dean, you don't seem very happy to see us."

"Aren't you hot in that suit, Agent Lance?" He hardly ever spoke, and it was almost becoming a game to get more out of him.

"Him?" Remington looked at his partner. "He skis in that thing. Can't get it off him." He looked back to Kristin, all levity disappearing. "You've seen what's happened the past week?"

Kristin sighed and looked away from the two men. She didn't bring her glass to her lips, but rather just gazed at the vast lawns stretching as far as she could see. This was where they would train the kids. Where their physical skills would reach peak performance.

"Yes, I've seen," she answered solemnly.

Lance's eyes didn't follow hers to the lawn but were cold and hard. "How's the curriculum going?"

"We're adapting it as you requested." Kristin took a sip of wine. "They're going to be experts on vampire slaying."

"That's good. Experts are good. They'll be able to teach next year's class, then?" he asked sarcastically.

Kristin turned her head. "I'm doing what you told me."

"This week, we had seven people turn up with bite marks on their necks." Lance stuck his hands in his pocket and leaned forward slightly. "We need them ready for the field."

Kristin shook her head in exasperation. "I've spoken to their professors. The students aren't ready. Not mentally, not physically. We're a few months into the semester, for goodness sake."

"We gave you peak specimens," Remington reached for Kristin's glass. "Give me a sip."

Kristin raised her eyebrows and smiled quizzically. "They let you drink while on duty?"

Remington made a "gimme" gesture. "They just put a new memo out. Anyone who has to deal with you is mandated to drink."

Kristin shrugged and handed him the glass.

Remington took her glass and drained the wine without bothering to sniff it. He glanced at Lance. "Sorry, there's not enough."

Lance's eyes fell on Kristin. "I'm beginning to think there's not enough in the world."

"Yeah, yeah," Kristin thrust her hand at Remington. "Give me the glass back."

He handed it to her. "We need these kids in the field. These creatures—either they're converting humans, or more are coming over. We have to start killing them before there's an epidemic."

Kristin's ire rose. "You're going to get *these kids* killed. They simply aren't ready. When I took over, you said I would have a year to get them up to snuff."

Remington shook his head regretfully. "We're not the ones setting the pace, and you know it. The people calling these creatures over are dictating that, and they're speeding it up. Each day you have them in a classroom is a day more innocent people are dying."

Kristin wanted to snap at these two men, but when it

came down to brass tacks, she knew they were all on the same side. She stood up and let the empty glass drop to her side. "Why can't you fight for the time being? I know the FBI has trained agents who can try to stop what's coming across."

"You also know why we can't," Lance whispered.

"We can't see them," Remington reminded her. "That's why we're recruiting teenagers. You know that. Anyone over twenty-three is unlikely to see anything that crosses the Veil. At least until it's too late, and one of those bastards has their teeth sunk in their neck. Can you guess how many adequately trained agents there are? You're rare when it comes to adults who *can* see these things. That's why they have to be in the field and not us. I wish it wasn't the case."

Kristin breathed in deeply and then sighed. "I know you're right." She turned to look at the mansion. "I just don't want to get them hurt."

"Do you have any standouts yet?" Remington said as he moved behind her, his shadow casting out over hers.

"The professors are telling me each stands out in a different way." Kristin's eyes narrowed as she thought about each of the students. She'd only met them at orientation, but she was keeping close tabs on their progress. "Probably Claire Hinterland. She's a leader, even if she doesn't know it yet. Byron has seen a lot of leaders in his time, and he says she's going to be something special—*if* we give her the time to grow into it."

Remington ignored the last part. "How quickly can we get her hunting vampires?"

"Well, if you two have some wooden stakes in your car, we could get them handed out to everyone now and send them into the wild once the sun goes down?" Kristin put a hand to her chest. "Heaven forbid we waste another precious moment ensuring the children have the training to survive."

Lance cracked a rare smile. "Actually, we just finished whittling some wood before we got here."

Kristen sighed before speaking again. "Give me the rest of the night. I'll think of something. I'll need to get the laboratory focused on this. I wish you had given me more warning. I'll get back to you in the morning."

Professor Byron's face was calm as he stared down into the amber drink he held in his hand. "Kristin, you've got to be kidding me." He swirled the ice gently inside, causing it to clink softly in the quiet office.

Kristin had her own glass; this one contained more wine than the last one. "I wish I *was* kidding, Patrick." She sat behind her desk, staring out the window to her left. "The agents just left an hour ago. I've been sitting here wracking my brain trying to figure out what to do."

Byron was a Scotch man, and luckily for him, Kristin had both types of alcohol in her office. "We haven't been in school a semester yet." He looked up at Kristin as the ice slowed its swirl in his glass. "You're really going to send them out there vampire-hunting tomorrow night?"

"Maybe not tomorrow night, but the night after?" Kristin raised her eyebrows. "The agents made good points. It's hard to argue."

Byron frowned. "The FBI agents?"

Kristin nodded. The sun was almost below the horizon outside, the view from the window quickly turning dark.

"What points are those?" Patrick raised the glass to his lips and took a sip. "We can get more kids their age, so giving them to vampires as food isn't the worst thing in the world?"

Kristin wasn't able to help the laugh that escaped. "Ever the cynic, Patrick."

"Yes, that happens when you serve in a war." Byron walked over to the desk and placed his glass on it. "You're serious, though? You want to put them in the field this early?"

Kristin shrugged, then shook her head. "I don't want to, but the agents are right. These threats are real, and we have to try to combat them. That's our whole purpose for creating this university. We've got people showing up dead with marks on their necks, and we're the ones who are supposed to stop them. We can't very well say no to that."

Patrick's hand remained on the glass, the skin beneath his nails turning white from how hard he held it. "Even if the kids aren't ready? Because they aren't, Kristin. You know that."

"That's what I want to talk to you about." She turned from the window and looked at Patrick. "We don't have to risk everyone. I've been thinking about it, and I think sending the best we have is the way to do it. We've got four Units. Let's send the unit with the highest chance of making it through."

Patrick relaxed his hand and forced himself to take a sip of his drink. The top shelf liquid hardly burnt as it flowed down his throat. He stared into the glass as he spoke. "So, we send the best and brightest off to die?"

"Do you think the worst and dumbest will have a better shot?" Kristin snapped back. "What unit do you think is the best?"

Patrick was quiet for a moment. He began to swirl the liquid again as he thought. "Claire Hinterland's," he responded eventually.

"Why? You've told me about her before."

Patrick looked up and found Kristin's eyes. "What do you know about the three inside the group?"

"It's Hinterland, Hallor, and Teams, right?"

Patrick nodded. "Yes, that's the three. Have you looked at their profiles?"

Kristin shook her head. "If I can be honest, Patrick, I'm doing my best to stay above water. Recruiting the professors, assessing the quality of the curriculum, all of it. I've trusted the FBI profilers to get us the right students to build strong Units from."

Patrick raised one hand with his palm out. "No need to defend yourself, Kristin. I'm going through it right alongside you. I know how hectic it is. Hell, I had to change an entire curriculum over the course of two nights." He put his hands down. "Hinterland's unit. I looked at their portfolios, the writeups the FBI sent over with each student. In a class of remarkable students, those three stand out."

"How?" Kristin leaned back in her chair.

"Teams is an asshole." He looked down at his drink and grinned. "No other way to put that. However, the FBI did a deep dive on him, on all of them. He's extremely smart, and his physical skills are above satisfactory, but what really sets him apart from the rest is his loyalty."

Kristin raised an eyebrow quizzically. "I know Teams. I think he commented on my heels the first time I met him. He's loyal?"

"That's what the psychological profiling says. He was sentenced to juvenile lockup for six months because he refused to give up a classmate."

"You're telling me the FBI brought in someone with a criminal record?" Kristin asked.

A small smile crossed Patrick's lips. "Not exactly." He met Kristin's eyes. "It was expunged on his enrolment here, but there are other examples in the file. Those two girls he's with might not like him much right now, but if the excreta hits the fan, I imagine he'd die for them."

Kristin's eyes were narrow, and she grew quiet for a second. Still leaning back in her chair, she finally asked, "What about Hallor?"

"She's the smartest in the entire cohort. Not just her unit—"

"Smarter than Hinterland?" Kirstin interrupted.

Patrick nodded. "Oh, yeah. I mean, it's not that Hinterland can't keep up. It's just that Hallor reaches conclusions before the rest of the group. Before you and me, even. Right now, we're dealing with pretty easy stuff, the history of these creatures, so her gift isn't completely visible. When we get into headier things, she'll shine."

Kristin brought her hands together and interlaced her fingers. "So. We have a loyal person and a smart person. What about Hinterland?"

Patrick stepped away from the desk, carrying his drink

with him. He went to the window, where the outside world was now dark. He chuckled. "Based on her test results so far, she can kick both our asses at once, and maybe the entire class's at the same time. Physically, she's a beast, plain and simple. But more than that, she's a leader. A natural one. The FBI profiler noted her high empathy; maybe that's what makes her suited to leadership. She showed that in class her first day. I was going off on Hallor for pretty much no reason. Hinterland had never met the girl, but she spoke up and put a stop to it. She *felt* for Hallor and the embarrassment I was putting her through."

He turned around, his back to the window now. "She's smart. She's beyond capable physically, but what separates her from everyone else is that people follow her. They're going to die for her, if necessary."

Kristin leaned forward, putting both hands on the desk. "You're sure of that."

Patrick was quiet as he brought his drink to his mouth. He took a long sip. When he put the glass down, he nodded. "Without any doubt. She's a leader already, and she has only just begun to discover her capability."

"So why wouldn't we send those three out?" Kristin raised her eyebrows. "If they're the best, why not see how they do in the field?"

"Oh, I don't know..." Patrick said whimsically. "Maybe because we're sending them to fight vampires?"

"Loyalty, brains, brawn, and leadership," Kristin countered. "Sounds like all we need are a few weapons and a night on the town for those three. They'll bring us vampire heads, don't you think?"

Patrick raised both eyebrows. "You convincing yourself or me?"

Kristin smiled. "Maybe both?"

Patrick shrugged. "You're the boss. I just hope you're right."

Kristin stood and grabbed her glass. She walked across the room to the open bottle of wine and removed the cork before pouring another. She took a sip, then sighed. "Me too."

CHAPTER TWELVE

J ack stood in front of the full-length mirror in Claire's room. "This is the easiest assignment I've ever heard of."

Claire was using the smaller mirror on her desk. She'd thought about kicking Jack from the larger one, but didn't want the headache associated with it.

Jack turned a circle to get a good look at the jacket he'd just put on. "All I have to do is show up at the bar, and these vampires are going to come find me. They won't be able to help themselves. I mean, do you see how good I look?"

Claire rolled her eyes.

Marissa didn't say a word. She was sitting on the bed, her legs folded beneath her, on the verge of tears.

They'd gotten word a few hours ago what was expected of them, and to say that it was shocking would be an understatement. *More like putting the three of us in an electric chair and turning it on for a good thirty minutes,* Claire thought.

Marissa still wasn't over the initial shock.

"We need you to go out and hunt vampires," Dr. Byron had told them like he was asking them to pick up a head of lettuce at the grocery store.

"How do we do that?" Jack had asked.

"She knows," Dr. Byron responded, nodding toward Marissa.

Marissa had known.

Didn't want to tell us, though, Claire mused as she applied blush to her face. She hardly ever wore makeup. Didn't even have any; she was borrowing Marissa's right now.

"Seriously, you two are going to have to watch out for me." Now Jack was messing with his hair, getting it to take on the messy look he always wore. "These vampires won't be able to keep their hands off me, and they'll probably try to take me home."

"I hope they won't be able to keep their *teeth* off you," Claire shot back. She glanced at Marissa in the mirror. "Hey, you gonna get ready? We've got to be out of here in two hours, and we still need weapons."

Claire had seen Marissa scared before, but perhaps not like this.

Of course not, you dope, she chastised herself. *When was the last time Marissa was told she was going out to try to find, then kill, vampires? Probably sometime around the Never of Neveruary.*

Marissa only nodded in response to Claire's question. She stared down at the bed without moving to get dressed.

Claire stood up from the desk and walked over to Marissa. She sat down on the edge of the bed and faced her. "You're pretty scared?"

Marissa looked up, her eyes narrow.

Claire took on a small smile. "Dumb question, I know."

"What I don't understand is how you two aren't scared as hell." Marissa's voice was louder than usual, almost as if she was angry at the two of them.

Or jealous, Claire thought. *Jealous that Jack and I aren't showing how scared we are. Of course, she's going to be mad if she's the only one scared out of her wits. Jack certainly isn't going to show it, no matter what.*

"Hey," Claire whispered, dropping the smile. "I'm scared. Like *really* scared. I don't know if numbnuts is over there or not, but I am. I don't know half of what you do about vampires, but they're telling me to go out there and fight them. Our training is at a bare minimum. So yeah, I'm pretty damn scared."

Marissa's eyes narrowed as if she didn't trust what Claire was saying. "You're over there putting on makeup. He's walking around like his dick is so big it might as well touch the floor."

"It does!" Jack shouted good-naturedly. "Thank you for noticing."

Claire didn't even glance at him. "One thing I know for sure is that everyone deals with fear in different ways. Me? I remind myself that I can do whatever I put my mind to. I focus on that, and my focus grows into real belief. Right now, instead of focusing on how scary this is —and believe me, it's really scary—I'm thinking about what I've learned from Dr. Byron and you in class. I'm thinking about how I *know* I can identify these blood-suckers if I see them. I'm thinking about how I'm strong and fast, I can get out of tight places if I need to. I'm focusing on what I *can* do. But none of that means I'm not terrified."

"I'm not scared a bit." Jack turned around and faced the bed. "Only that I may be raped by ten female vamps because of how good I look."

The problem was, Claire couldn't really say much about his looks, because he was extremely attractive, especially when he dressed up, like now.

He's also a jackass, she thought and looked at Marissa. "He's scared, and I don't care what he says. He's covering it up right now; maybe that's how he deals with it. But I can tell you this, no one goes out to hunt vampires their first time and *isn't* scared. Hell, these things aren't supposed to exist, Marissa. People get scared just going to the movies to watch them. There's nothing wrong with being scared. The only issue is, if we let that fear stop us, we're not moving forward. We're at a standstill."

Marissa looked down at the blanket. Tears still resided in her eyes, but they were welling less, and Claire thought she might actually be doing some good.

"You're right." Marissa unfolded her legs and scooting closer to the bed's edge. "They didn't bring me here to get scared and cry into my pillow. They brought me here to fight."

"You're damn right they did." She jerked a thumb over her shoulder at Jack. "From the looks of Jack-ass back there, we're going to need all the help we can get. He's going to be too scared of moving a strand of hair to actually help."

"You probably think you're clever," he commented, turning back to look at himself in the mirror. "Using my great name in such a lowly fashion. *Jack*-ass. I will not even respond to such poor wordplay. However, my hair does look good, and if things get bad tonight, I'd appreciate it if you both did the heavy lifting. I don't want to mess up what I got going for me."

Claire shook her head as Marissa stood up from the bed.

"Jack, any time you think you look nice, I want you to just look at me," Marissa moved to the small mirror at the desk. "No matter how good you look, I promise, I'll always look better."

"Damn." Claire was stunned. Marissa hadn't spoken like that before, but the girl was telling the truth. Marissa was stunningly beautiful, so much so that Claire had thought she'd be a snob when first sitting down next to her. Yet, Marissa had never once acknowledged her looks. Until now. To shut Jack up.

Claire laughed. "She's got ya there, Jack-ass."

Claire had never been in a bar before, and she didn't like it. Sure, she'd been to bowling alleys and the like that served beer, but she'd never once gone to the lowly holes in the wall back in her home town. She knew that most college kids loved the first chance they had to get into a bar and drink. The illegality of it probably made it even more fun. Claire didn't feel like that one bit.

The damned FBI gave us the fake IDs, she reminded herself as she handed the card to the doorman. He looked at it, looked at Claire, and flipped it around to the back.

After another second, he handed it back, and she walked through. *Thank God.*

That would have been the most embarrassing thing in the world to get caught with a government-issued ID on a mission to kill vampires. That would be an interesting one to explain to a judge.

Jack came in next, and Marissa followed.

Jack walked past Claire and headed deeper into the bar. "This place is insane."

"Bar" might have been the wrong word. Actually, it was *definitely* the wrong word. This place was in the heart of Boston, and three stories high. They were inside, meaning they'd gotten past security, but the real action was farther into the building.

"You feel that?" Marissa asked as she reached Claire.

Claire nodded. She didn't need to ask what Marissa was talking about. The bass. It was vibrating in her chest, and she wondered what in the hell they were in store for once they got to the dance floor.

"We better catch up." Marissa pointed at Jack, who was rounding a corner. "He's legit going to lose us."

"Maybe a vampire will grab him." Claire started walking, following Jack's lead. "Which head do you think he's using right now?" she yelled to be heard over the bass, which only got louder the farther they went inside the club.

"Hopefully, the one on his shoulders," Marissa shouted back. "But who knows?"

They rounded the corner into a dark hall. Neon lights outlined the ceiling and the floor, allowing Claire to actually see where she was going. *How nice,* she thought. She had no idea why people would subject themselves to music this loud, or quarters this dark and close.

They reached the end of the hallway and emptied out onto a huge dance floor. Claire had to move quickly because more people were coming out of the hall, but none of them stopped to look at what was in front of them.

The bar appeared to wrap around the outside of the dance floor, though Claire wasn't completely sure. It certainly didn't look like anywhere she and Frank had ever been. Neon lights ran through everything—the floor, the ceiling, the bar area. The place looked like some kind of throwback to the club that Sarah Connor went to in the first *Terminator* movie. Claire had seen it a few years ago with her dad. He said that all new cinema sucked and she needed to learn the classics.

The music here was different, too.

In the middle of the dance floor was a stage with a DJ on it. Scantily-clad women danced around him, though they paid him no mind and he ignored them as well. People filled the entirety of the dance floor, with someone constantly either entering or exiting to the bar.

"Once we find these vampires, I'm going to enjoy myself."

Claire's head whipped to the right and saw Jack standing next to her. *At least he didn't run off and try to hump the first thing he saw*, she thought.

"What do we do?" Marissa asked from Claire's left. She appeared to be just as mesmerized by this insane scene.

"This thing's got three stories. Let's go up to the second floor and talk for a second," Claire responded.

"You think it'll be quieter?" Jack shouted.

"I don't think it can get louder!" Claire went to her right, knowing instinctively that the other two would follow. She found the staircase and started up, the world growing darker again, as well as quieter. Her ears were ringing, but she'd still be able to hear her partners.

They reached the second floor. This place appeared to be more like a lounge, and the bass was less severe.

We should have discussed this stuff outside, Claire thought as she led them to a group of chairs by the wall. She made a note to not make this mistake again. If they were going into a place, they'd all be on the same page before they got there.

Another thought quickly appeared: *Why didn't one of the professors tell us this before they let us out?*

She pushed the thought away. They didn't have time right now, but she'd ask later. Seemed like something they should have tried preparing their students for.

The three sat down, but Claire didn't look around this time. It was a quieter floor, with maybe fifty percent fewer people, but still pretty busy. The three of them needed to get a plan together.

"Okay." Claire leaned on the table in front of them. "We're not going to be able to talk down there, and from the sound of it, upstairs either."

"Good." Jack smirked. "You both talk way too much anyway."

"Quiet," Claire snapped. She thought she might get some pushback, but Jack said nothing. "We don't have time to mess around right now. We also can't keep leaving the dance floors. This is my fault. I should have thought of it before, but it's too late now." She looked at

Marissa. "Our goal is to, at the very least, locate a vampire. Get his or her description and report back. Best result possible? We kill one. What do we need to do to find one?"

"We know what they look like," Marissa answered. She leaned forward as well, her voice just above a whisper. "They're thin, and they're pale. They aren't pack animals like werewolves, they're seducers. They will be alone, and they will most likely prey on people who are alone. For the most part, they're asexual—"

"That's until they meet me," Jack quipped. "Then they won't have much choice but to turn *very* sexual."

Claire rolled her eyes but didn't chastise him. Sometimes the Jack-ass couldn't help it, she supposed.

"*So*," Marissa continued, "you might see a man hitting on a man or a woman, or vice-versa."

"Okay," Jack said, his smile fading. "Then what do we do? Ask them if they're a vampire? Or maybe we just stake them through the heart?"

Claire felt the wooden stake strapped to her leg. It wasn't big, not like they portrayed in the movies. This was more of a wooden dagger. Each of the three had one, and the club's security hadn't checked them.

Marissa looked at Claire questioningly. "Identifying is easy. If you want to kill one, that's going to be a lot more trouble."

"Let's just find the damned things first," Claire said. "We might not even be able to do that."

Jack lowered his hand to his calf and absently stroked the dagger strapped to it. "If we find one, we should kill it." His voice was soft, and the normal humor was gone.

"Boy Danger over there," Claire joked, "if you find one, alert the rest of us, and then we'll decide what to do, okay?"

Both Jack and Marissa nodded.

"Okay." Claire stood. "Let's cover the bottom floor first. If we don't see anything, then we'll take the third floor. Let's get started."

Holy hell, Marissa wasn't lying.

Claire was standing against the bar, watching the dance floor. Her eyes were sharp, even in the darkened area. She couldn't see Jack or Marissa from this vantage point, but that was okay. She felt safe, as long as she was inside a public place.

Or, at least she did until she saw one.

Marissa knew her vampires, that was for sure. Claire had been watching for maybe twenty minutes before her eyes fell on the creature. He was just like Marissa said— pale, his skin closer to porcelain than anything human. He was exquisitely good-looking, but in a regal sense, as if he were a prince from hundreds of years ago. He was well dressed and exuded this...

Confidence, Claire thought. *He moves and talks as if he's never heard of self-doubt.*

She didn't see any fangs on the creature, but Marissa had said there were different ways they showed. Some myths had the teeth always present, some only when the vampire bit his victim.

Am I sure it's a vampire? Would be a pretty big mistake if I'm wrong. Claire's eyes narrowed as she watched the creature interact with the woman next to him. It was as Marissa said it would be. He was alone. She was alone.

No, Claire felt no doubt about what she was watching. Just as she'd believed Frank was a leprechaun, she believed this, too.

What do other people see when they look at this vampire? she wondered. Probably just a pale but extremely attractive man. The word "vampire" would never cross their mind, not until it was too late. Despite all the news reports and media attention, the rest of the world couldn't see these creatures. Not truly. Only a few were capable of it, and Claire now realized the importance of her mission.

Claire quit leaning against the bar and straightened up. *If you don't do something about this thing, he's going to bite and kill that woman.*

They'd been told to spot one, identify it with a photograph, and give up the information when they returned. If possible, kill it, but that had been a secondary notion.

Not anymore, Claire thought. *I can see this thing, and I know how to kill it. That means it's my job, or people are going to die.*

This changed things. Now Claire had to figure out a way to get this creature of the night away from the woman he wanted.

She moved away from the bar and down onto the dance floor. People jerked and swayed, some even approaching her to try to dance. She pushed past them, her eyes on the creature posing as a man. She'd forgotten about Jack and Marissa for the moment. She would find them later.

Claire reached the edge of the dance floor and stopped. The creature was staring at her and smiling. He flashed two long incisors on his top row of teeth. *Your name is Claire? Is that right?*

The voice penetrated Claire's mind, and she had no doubt about what was happening. He'd first read her mind and was now talking to her. She didn't know if there was any way to talk back, but she'd give it a shot.

I'd worry less about my name and more about what I'm going to do to you, she thought, hoping the creature would hear it.

"That's one of them."

It was Jack's voice, and it was right in her ear. He'd managed to sneak up behind her.

The creature turned around casually and took his drink from the bar.

Claire watched him take a sip. "He's reading my mind," she told Jack. "Be careful what you think."

"No worries," Jack commented. "I usually just think about sex and my own greatness. He'll probably get bored with it."

Claire shook her head but grinned. It was good to know he wouldn't change, regardless of what stood in front of them. The vampire leaned over to the woman next to him and kept talking, acting as if Claire didn't even exist.

Which sort of pissed her off more. Like she was no threat, and he needn't worry about her.

"Did that just happen?" Jack asked. "He knows you're here, and he's ignoring you? Like you're an ex-girlfriend or something?"

"Yeah, not for long. We've got to get him away from that woman, then we've got to kill him." Claire didn't take her eyes from the vampire as she spoke. "Where's Marissa?"

"I'm here," she whispered from Claire's right.

Claire's head whipped to her. "Goodness, between the two of you, I'm going to have a heart attack. Can you, like, let me know you're here or something?"

"Usually you pay pretty close attention to things," Marissa said with a shrug. "We've got our first one, I see."

People continued to dance all around the three, none of them paying any attention. Claire was jostled every few seconds, but nothing too harsh. "Okay, listen," she told the other two. "Jack, you go outside to the back alley. Wait for us there. I imagine we'll be running fast, and I imagine he'll be chasing us just as fast. You're going to need to be ready to attack, okay?"

"What are you about to do?" Jack turned to look at her. "We found him. We've identified him. Snap the picture right now. We can report back to the university what he looks like, and let the FBI or whoever find him."

Claire shook her head. "Nope, pretty boy. If we do that, the lady standing next to him will be dead by morning. It's up to us to make sure that doesn't happen."

Jack eyed the woman for the first time. After a few moments, he let out a sigh. "Well, if I'm going to die for someone, at least she's pretty. I'll be outside. Just make sure you give me some warning because that stake is going into *someone's* chest, and I'd rather it be the vampire's than yours."

Jack said nothing else, only turned and headed to the back door.

However he acts in class, he's someone I want by my side, she thought. "Okay, Marissa, you ready?"

"Hell, no, but we're going to do it all the same," Marissa responded.

"That's right."

The vampire still wasn't looking at Claire. He truly thought she didn't matter. That was about to change. "You got the holy water on you?"

Marissa tapped the small black vial attached to her belt loop.

"Give it here." Claire put her hand out, palm up. Marissa detached the vial and handed it over. "Good. Now go wait outside with Jack."

"Me too?" Marissa asked exasperatedly. "You can't do this alone."

"I'm not doing it alone. I'm getting the vamp out of here alone, but Jack is going to need some help once we get outside, and I'm going to be running my ass off, so I won't be able to just stop on a dime and pull the stake from off my leg. It's your job to make sure this thing dies and stays dead."

"All right," Marissa agreed, "But don't get killed before we have a chance to kill it."

Claire nodded. "Fair enough. See you in a minute." Marissa stepped away, leaving her alone on the dance floor. Sure, people were dancing around her, but none of them knew a nearly immortal entity from an alternate universe stood twenty feet away.

Claire closed her fist around the vial. She silently unscrewed the cap, letting it drop to the floor, and held it up so the water didn't fall out. Claire wasn't Catholic. She didn't think Jack or Marissa were either, but apparently the creatures still abided by the rules.

Sure hope so, Claire thought.

She walked to her right, but the vampire didn't turn to watch. Claire exited the dance floor and went back to the small platform surrounding the bar. The door Jack and Marissa had exited through was behind her, the vampire in front. Truth be told, Claire had a vague plan but not much else.

Of course, she hadn't told the other two that.

Let's hope vampires don't react well to pain, Claire thought. She walked across the dark room, strobe lights flashing from the ceiling and people passing her on the left and right. The vampire's back was to her, which was what she wanted. *Hold like that for just a few more seconds.*

When she was five feet away, the vampire spun. "You again?"

"Me again," she agreed. Her right hand flashed upward, the liquid from the vial spilling into the air.

Claire's aim was impeccable, and the holy water splashed across the creature's face.

"YOU BITCH!" he screamed. His skin sizzled and burned beneath the liquid, his hands reaching up to his face instinctively. As he swiped at the holy water, the flesh on his palms started to burn and smoke.

The woman next to him screamed.

Time to move, Claire thought, and as the words flowed through her mind, the vampire looked up.

His skin was red and badly burnt, raw flesh staring back at her. His mouth was wide, and his fangs were pure white. He hissed at Claire.

Nope, no thanks. She whirled and her feet pounded the floor. She took off, dodging drunks left and right.

"I'M GONNA KILL YOU!" the creature bellowed.

Claire didn't turn around to look. She had to hope he was as pissed as he sounded and wanted vengeance.

The door was thirty feet away, and Claire sped up. People had stopped walking now, but were instead standing and staring at her rushing past them. They were staring behind her too, hopefully at the oncoming vampire.

Ten feet.

Five.

Claire burst through the door and out into the back alley. Her right foot touched down and she bolted to the left. Jack had asked for warning, but what was she supposed to do? She saw two figures out of the corner of her eye but kept running.

The vampire wasn't as nimble, and he slammed into the opposite brick wall, unable to pivot as quickly as her. The bricks cracked beneath the force, sending red dust into the air. The vampire growled as Claire came to a stop and turned back around. Jack and Marissa were on the other side of him, trapping the creature in the alley.

Trapped. That's one way to look at it, Claire thought. *The other is, only one side is escaping this alive.*

The vampire stood up and straightened his coat while eyeing Jack and Marissa.

"You were supposed to stake the bastard!" Claire screamed.

"I wasn't getting in the way of the train wreck!" Jack called back. He did have the stake in his hand, although he was probably right. He would have been pulverized on the brick wall.

The vampire's skin was already starting to heal, his face

looking less burnt by the second. "I'll let you two live." He glanced toward Jack and Marissa before turning his attention to Claire again. "You're dead, though."

He started forward, and Claire got down on one knee. She pulled her pant leg up and unsheathed the wooden stake, then stood. Claire couldn't see if Jack and Marissa were moving. She hoped they were getting out of here.

The vampire reached her and slashed with a hand, his nails suddenly claws like a feline's.

Claire dodged to her left, barely avoiding having her neck ripped open. The other hand came just as quickly, and Claire had to duck to avoid it this time.

He's fast, her mind thought coldly. She took the stake and thrust it up, hoping to impale the creature...

But he wasn't there.

"Behind you!" Marissa screamed.

Claire didn't have time to turn around. She felt hands on her back, and nails ripping into her flesh, and then it *shoved*. Claire flew into the air, her arms flailing at her sides.

Jack dropped his stake and rushed forward, catching her just before she hit the ground face-first. "Gotcha."

They both stood quickly and whirled. The monster was coming forward again, his face healed now and his fangs bared.

Jack retrieved his stake, and the three students spread out. They didn't look at each other but moved as a team, as if they'd been training for this their whole lives and hadn't just met weeks ago.

Claire stood in the middle, her stake in her right hand, her body loose. Jack went to her left and Marissa to her right. Marissa reached into her collar and pulled a crucifix out, then ripped from her neck and brandished it.

"Silly girl," the vampire said with a grin, his gait not slowing. "It's not the cross, but the faith behind it."

Marissa didn't drop either the cross or the stake.

Jack moved forward when the vampire was ten feet from them. Claire followed his lead, hoping that two would be enough to kill him. Jack sliced forward with the stake, and the vampire's hand lashed out.

"AH!" Jack screamed as his stake clattered to the ground.

Claire didn't wait to see the injury but darted forward. She slashed with the stake, pointing it directly at the thing's heart. It's left hand moved to swat her—

WHOOSH!

The sound filled Claire's ears, and wind rushed by her cheeks.

The creature's hand remained frozen in the air, its nails ready to gash her forearm open. His mouth had turned into an awful circle, as if he wanted to scream but couldn't. His eyes were wide, and the smooth confidence once written all over his face had vanished.

"What the fuck!" Jack shouted, still holding his right arm with his left hand.

A stake protruded from the vampire's chest, and it was wedged in deep. His hand dropped to his side, and he wobbled for a second, an unbelieving look on his face.

He didn't think this was possible, Claire thought. He didn't think he could die.

The creature fell backward, hitting the ground much more softly than he had hit the brick wall.

Claire whirled in the direction the stake had come from. "What the hell was that?" she whispered, immediately thinking there was more danger lurking. The alley was dark beyond the club's exit light, and when Claire peered into it, she couldn't see anything.

"IS IT DOWN?!" The voice echoed through the narrow alley.

"Yes, it's down!" Jack shouted back, moving forward and passing Claire. She had never heard him so angry before, and there was blood dripping from his arm. "Who the hell are you?!"

Claire heard footfalls, and two men walked out of the shadows.

Agents Remington and Lance.

"You two were there the whole time?" she asked as she stepped up shoulder to shoulder with Jack. Marissa followed right behind her, and the three of them filled the alley.

"My arm is *bleeding*!" Jack shouted, spittle flying from his mouth.

"We'll get you patched up," Remington said. He was holding a crossbow in his right hand.

"You gave us wooden stakes, and you've got *that* freakin' thing?" Claire asked. Jack's anger was spreading to her now. They'd all almost *died*.

"Well, you couldn't very well carry it inside with you, could you?" Remington lifted it with both hands, turning it around. "Security might have seen it." He let it fall back to his side as he smiled. "Okay, kid. We need to get the wound looked at. You folks did really well tonight. Spectacular, even. Come on, let's get him fixed up and you all something to eat, and I'll tell you how we did it."

Claire looked at Marissa. She was holding the cross in her left hand and the stake in her right. She shrugged. "This is what we came for, right?"

Claire turned to Jack. He was glaring at the two agents but wearing his grin again. "If this scars and it keeps me from getting women, someone is going to pay."

CHAPTER THIRTEEN

"I'm glad you called again, honey."

Claire was in one of the mansion's sitting rooms, a landline handset pressed to her ear. "Yeah, I'm sorry it's taken me a bit longer this time. We've just been so busy. How's Mom?"

"She's better. She eventually got out of bed, of course. I haven't really pressed her on it. She's going to be fine, although she's not ready to talk to you just yet. She's still holding a grudge."

Claire nodded on her side of the call. She knew what her mom was like, but her dad was right—Mom would come around.

"How are things with you?" her father asked. "How are classes? We're seeing more and more about this invasion on the news. If I'm honest, I thought the whole thing was a hoax until those people came and recruited you. Now, when I go to work, and everyone tells me how fake all this is, I just smile and nod. I ain't told them you're at the college that's going to fight back against this stuff."

Her dad finally paused, and Claire smiled. He was rambling like always, although he didn't realize it. "Things are good. Classes are good."

"You learning a lot?"

The image of the vampire slashing Jack's wrist popped into her mind. She saw herself rush forward, and a wooden stake plunge into the vampire's chest.

"Yeah, Dad. I'm learning a lot."

What else do I tell him? That I fought a vampire last night and one of my classmates is going to have a scar from it? Mom would have a freakin' heart attack.

Claire knew she had to stay quiet about the things happening here for her parents' sake if no one else's.

"All right, Dad. I have to get to class, but I just wanted to call and check in. Tell Mom I love her, okay?" Claire's eyes grew moist, surprising her. She missed her parents.

"I sure will, honey. Do you know when you'll be able to come visit us?"

Claire shook her head. "No, not yet. They're still working out the schedule, but I'll let you know as soon as they tell me something." That wasn't exactly the truth; Claire didn't know if they'd worked out the schedule or not, only that no one was talking about them visiting home at the moment.

"Okay. Let us know as soon as you hear. We miss you."

"Miss you too, Dad. Talk soon. Bye."

Claire hung up and sat staring at the floor for a moment. She didn't have class, but something perhaps even more important. She had to go see the dean. All three of them did. She hadn't met the woman yet and honestly didn't know much about her. She didn't know what this meeting was about but certainly didn't need to go in there with her eyes wet from missing her parents.

Jack would give her hell.

She could hear him saying it now. *"I nearly got my arm chopped off and didn't shed a tear, but you're crying over missing Mommy and Daddy?"*

Claire smiled a bit. Jack was such an asshole, but he'd performed heroically last night. None of them had been much of a match for that creature, but even Marissa had stood her ground and tried to force it back.

She didn't know how powerful the three of them could be, especially based on how the FBI needed to save them last night, but she *did* know that they would stick together. Being afraid hadn't stopped them from battling seemingly insurmountable odds.

"Hey, you coming or what?" It was Jack calling from behind Claire's chair.

Claire blinked twice to make sure her eyes were clear, then stood up and turned around.

Jack's right arm was bandaged. Claire had seen the wounds when they got back last night.

The mansion had an infirmary built into it, with on-call doctors. They'd all been waiting, having gotten the word that a student was hurt.

Truthfully, Claire was impressed with the operation. They were taking this extremely seriously. Jack was going to have scars, but maybe they'd give his pretty boy look some character.

Claire crossed the room to meet Jack. "Have you been in yet?"

"Me?" He laughed. "Heck no. I forget what I said to the

dean at orientation, but I thought she was going to rip my eyes right out of my head like a hawk or something."

"A hawk?" Claire raised her eyebrows as they started down the hall.

Jack nodded. "Yeah. They eat the eyes of birds so that they can't see. I don't know, Claire—it doesn't matter. Point is, I'm not going in there alone. Marissa is waiting outside, too."

Claire glanced down at his arm. "How's it feeling?"

"Hurts." Jack lifted it into the air. "They're giving me some meds, but not enough to get me high. Just keeps the pain right under the threshold of me wanting to kill people."

"Based on last night, you don't seem to be very dangerous," Claire quipped.

Jack grinned. "Yeah? That why the vampire struck at me first instead of you? He knew who the real threat was."

They reached the dean's office, where Marissa sat on a wooden bench. She looked up and smiled.

"You okay?" Claire asked.

Marissa nodded, but Claire knew she was scared again. Getting called to the dean's office the day after attacking vampires wasn't exactly great news.

"All right," Claire said. "Let's see what she wants." She reached forward and knocked on the door.

"Come in," the dean called.

Claire twisted the doorknob as Marissa and Jack took their places. Claire walked in first with the other two following behind her.

Dean Pritcham sat behind a wooden desk. A window occupied the wall behind her and to the desk's left.

Remington and Lance occupied the leather couch against the wall to the right of the door.

"Thank you for coming." Pritcham stood and gestured at the three chairs in front of her desk. "Please sit down."

Claire gave a quick glance to the FBI agents and then took the middle chair. Jack went to her left and Marissa to her right.

"How's the arm feeling?" Remington asked.

Jack did a half-turn in his chair. "If you'd been a bit quicker with that crossbow, we wouldn't need to ask that question, now would we?" He turned back around and looked at Pritcham.

He might be a Jack-ass, but he's got some balls on him, Claire thought. She'd stood up to Byron, but she hadn't mouthed off to a FBI agent yet. Claire stifled the smile wanting to bloom on her face. Probably wasn't the best time.

"You three did a remarkable job last night," Pritcham said as she sat down again. "To be honest, it was better than anyone thought was possible."

Claire's face grew quizzical. "Thanks?" She didn't know how to respond to something like that.

"No, it's we who need to thank you," Pritcham offered. "The whole country, really. Last night, you allowed us to kill one of the first creatures summoned through the Veil. Before that, we hadn't been able to do it. It was truly an amazing feat."

Claire glanced at Marissa. She was only staring at her lap, probably wishing they could get the hell out of there and back to class.

"Did you just call us in here to thank us?" Jack asked.

"Because if so, I've got stuff to do. Putting some salve on this wound. Probably calling some of my girlfriends. Probably need to study for the next time you throw us in front of monsters without being prepared. Probably a lot of stuff."

The dean raised one eyebrow skeptically. She gazed at Jack for a few seconds, then turned her attention to the FBI agents.

Claire wanted to turn around and see what expressions they had on their faces, but she kept her eyes forward.

Finally, Pritcham looked at Jack again. "Mr. Teams, I appreciate your anger. I do. However, I have a question. What did you think you were getting into when you signed up here? Did you think you'd get some grades and then be let out into the world to find a job selling insurance? Did you think this was going to be like one of those other schools you were accepted into? Columbia or Yale? Remember, your letter said a guaranteed *government* job. It didn't specify what kind."

Claire's eyes grew wide, and she turned to Jack. *"Yale?"* She thought Marissa might have been accepted to a school like that, but Jack? Why would anyone risk their life here if they could have gone to an Ivy League school?

Jack ignored her question and kept his eyes on Pritcham. "No, I didn't think it would be like those schools. I also didn't think I'd show up here and get my arm nearly chopped off in the first few months."

Pritcham leaned back in her chair, putting her elbows on the arms and touching her fingertips together. She studied Jack for a few long moments. "That's fair, I suppose. We didn't think we would need to move this fast, either. We thought we had more time, and none of us wanted to put you in harm's way this quickly. However, as you saw, we made sure there was backup the entire time. They weren't simply letting you go in by yourself, despite what you originally thought." She gestured with her left hand toward the agents. "But as to your first question, no. We didn't call you here just to thank you. We called you here to discuss how the rest of this semester is going to go."

"How's that?" Claire asked.

It wasn't Dean Pritcham that spoke, but Remington from behind her. "The remainder of this semester isn't going to be about learning, but about attacking."

The room grew quiet for a few seconds.

Claire couldn't take it anymore. She turned around and looked at Remington. "You going to expand on that?"

Remington smiled, although Lance remained stoic. "I thought I might. There are a few things still up in the air, but it's time we level with you about what we do know."

"That would be nice." Claire's fingers were starting to grip the chair's arms. Maybe she *would* get a chance to go off on a FBI agent today.

Remington leaned forward. "I imagine your professors know more about the Veil and the universe beyond than the two of us. What they don't know, and what nobody knows besides the FBI yet, is why it's happening. Or at least, one possible reason that it's happening. We know why vampires are coming out right now in Boston."

Marissa turned around, too, and she was gripping the chair just like Claire, only for different reasons.

Claire relaxed her left hand and reached over, touching

Marissa's without looking at her. *It's okay*, she thought. *We're all in this together.*

"We're calling it a cult," Remington continued. He tried to conceal the quick glance he gave Claire's hand, but she saw the approval in his eyes. He liked the bond they were forming. "It's decentralized from what we can tell, meaning that there are multiple cells acting semi-independently."

"Gonna need you to expand some," Claire instructed. This was what Frank had told her about. The people pulling the Mythers over.

Marissa spoke before Remington could respond to Claire's demand, her voice a whisper. "The cells have to be using some organizational structure. If you think about terrorist cells, that's probably the best way to describe groups like these. White supremacist groups are often decentralized, meaning that there isn't one person who controls everything, yet they're all working toward the same evil purpose. It allows them to do things on their own and makes it harder for government agencies to track. There is probably some loose organization, and someone at the head of it all, but it's much harder to get to them because they aren't giving people direct orders."

The room was quiet for a moment, then Lance said in his normal stoic fashion, "Told you."

Claire shook her head, smiling. She didn't have to ask what that meant. Marissa was a fucking genius.

"That's just about the whole of it," Remington agreed. He was still leaning forward with his elbows on his knees. "There's a sect of this cult in Boston, and what they're doing is calling over vampires. Agent Lance and I are focused on two things right now, One is recruitment, and the other is the cult in our midst."

"We think," Lance confided, "That they're looking for Dracula. We think they're trying to pull him over."

Jack put his left hand over his stomach and slumped down in his chair, laughing. "No way. No fucking way. You can't expect us to believe this." He laughed some more, unable to keep talking. Finally, he pulled himself together. "Look, they're bringing vampires over, I can't deny that. I got the wounds on my arms to prove it. But if you're sitting here asking me to believe that they're going to bring over a character from an old book, I'm not going to do it."

"Why not?" Pritcham asked from her chair. "Where do you think these things came from? Books. Tales. Nothing else."

Jack stopped laughing, his eyes growing narrow. "Why do they want Dracula?"

Remington sighed. "That's where our intelligence dries up. We're not entirely sure what these different cults want yet. We're working on finding out how they came into being, and how they learned about the Veil or this other universe."

"Doesn't sound like you're sure of much," Jack interjected.

Claire gave the leg of his chair a soft kick. "Hush. Let them finish. None of us came here to learn debate skills, did we?"

Jack rolled his eyes but quieted down.

Remington leaned back in his chair and crossed one leg over the other. "However they're pulling creatures, they're getting better at it. That's why they're able to only pull vampires right now and there's such a glut of them. They're looking for the head one, though. There's going to be trouble if they find him."

"Why?" Claire asked.

It was Marissa who gave the answer. "He's the oldest, meaning more people have believed in him. He'll be the most powerful. That one we saw last night was probably young and not that strong. If they bring Bram Stoker's Dracula over, the real terror will start." She continued staring down at her lap, and she didn't let go of Claire's hand.

"So basically, we don't know how this cult is doing it, or why, but we think we know what they're trying to bring through the Veil?" Claire asked.

"That's right." Remington nodded. "It's up to my organization to figure out the hows and whys. It's up to you and your classmates to stop them from bringing these creatures across."

"Our *classmates*," Jack interjected. "You seem to be forgetting about them in this whole mess. I don't see any of them picking up stakes and going out into the night to fight the undead."

"He got accepted to Yale, but he's not that smart." Remington smirked as looked past the students to Pritcham. He shrugged then found Claire's eyes. "If we send you all out into the field right now, what's the worst that can happen?"

"The entire class gets killed," Claire answered.

"That's right." Remington tapped his knee with his forefinger. "I'm going to be honest with you three, because lying won't get us anywhere. We can't afford to have the entire first class die. We needed to see if you three could perform in the field, and you can. If we'd told you we were there to jump in and help, we wouldn't have found out what you were capable of. We had to be certain. Right now, you're our only weapon against what's coming. The other members of your class are going to continue with the regular curriculum. We're nearly halfway done with the semester. You three are going to be trained more as, well, assassins. At least until we deal with this vampire threat. Then you can join your classmates again."

A wide grin spread across Jack's face. "Maybe I was smart enough to get into Yale and maybe I wasn't, but one thing is for sure. You two couldn't sell a life raft to a drowning man. All you had to tell me was you were training me to kill stuff and we could have avoided the whole kerfuffle."

Marissa's face grew even paler. "I..." She tried to speak, but words failed her.

Claire turned, ignoring the rest of the room. "Hey, you're with us now. You're part of this team, this unit. We're not the same without you, that I know."

Jack leaned forward so that he could see Marissa too. "Don't you worry. I'll protect you." His grin was as wide as ever.

"See?" Claire told her. "If you don't stick around, we're not going to be able to embarrass Jack-ass over here."

Marissa actually smiled.

"Claire, hold on a second, would you?"

Claire had her hand on the door and was about to leave the room. She paused as Jack and Marissa turned around to look at her.

Claire shrugged. *I don't know,* she mouthed.

"I hope they treat you better than me," Jack remarked, raising his wounded arm and pointing to it.

Marissa was clearly ready to be done with the entire conversation. "See you in the dorm."

The two left, and Claire went back inside the office. She looked at Remington, who'd been the one to speak. "Yeah?"

"Close the door." He nodded to it.

She did, shutting it silently but not moving away from it.

"We need you to talk to Frank." Remington leaned back in his chair. "We know he's here in Boston."

Claire raised one eyebrow. She didn't like this. These people were here to kill the Mythers, and she didn't know what they were going to do about Frank over the long haul. "What makes you think he's here?"

"Hey," Lance raised his hands with the palms facing outward. "We've shot straight with you. There's no need to do any less with us."

Maybe that's fair, Claire thought. *But I'm still not giving Frank up.*

"What about him?" she asked.

"You don't have to bring him to us or anything like that," Remington assured her. "We know and respect your feelings toward the little green creature. We do want you to talk to him, though."

Claire crossed her arms over her chest. "I've got some questions first, things you should have answered on day one. How can you see Frank? How can any of you see him?"

Remington nodded at Pritcham. "She can see all Mythers. She's like you and Jack and Marissa."

Claire glanced her way, understanding that much. She turned back to the agents. "And you two? You told me back at the bowling alley you could see him somewhat clearly? How did you know he was even in there?"

"You've had a class on this, correct?" Lance asked.

Claire nodded. "It's still confusing, and I want to know if you two have any more information."

Remington smiled and leaned back. "Always probing for more. That's fine. Lance and I here are changing. It's slow, but it's happening. We first heard about Frank and you chasing him down because another teenager saw him at the park that day. The word traveled upward, and so we came down to see about it. We learned you'd chased him down, and then we began recording you. You know about recordings, right?"

Claire nodded. "Everyone can see Mythers if it's on a video."

"That's right." Remington moved his hand slightly forward in the air. "So, we saw Frank on the recordings. When we walked into the bowling alley that day, we didn't see him like you did, but he looked slightly green to us. Because we'd been seeing him on camera. It takes time for the brain to bend and change, but Lance and I both believe, and so our brains are slowly allowing us to see them. Now, we see Frank just as clearly as you do."

Claire's eyebrows were drawn together, but she didn't

have any argument against what they were saying. "Fine. What else did you want to talk about?"

Remington continued. "Wherever these cults pop up, there's a lot of Veil activity in the area. More creatures coming across, and not all of them are bad or evil. We think there's a chance your green friend might be in contact with some of them, and if so, we want to know what he's hearing. That's all." Remington shrugged as if to say, *no games.*

"I don't really know how to get in touch with Frank," Claire told them, ignoring the fact that they knew the leprechaun was in Boston. "He usually gets in touch with me."

"That's fine." Remington nodded. "But if he does get in touch with you, let him know what we're thinking. If he's your friend, and on your side, he may be able to help. Tell him it's imperative we find these cult members, okay?"

"You guys don't understand leprechauns that well, do you?" Claire's right eyebrow raised, as she realized how foolish they sounded.

"They're not usually at Thanksgiving dinner, no," Lance responded.

"Well, these guys don't do things for free. They're more or less misers." Claire uncrossed her arms. "If he comes around, I'll talk to him, but he's going to want something in return."

"Like what?"

Claire smiled. "Depends on how much information he gives you, but I can almost guarantee it's going to have something to do with beer and bowling."

Lance looked at Remington. "The one insider we may

have is a damn derelict."

Remington shrugged and turned his attention to Claire again. "Just tell him we're the FBI. We can get him whatever he wants, so long as we deem the information relevant, informative, and impactful."

Claire barely held her grin. "Relevant, informative, and impactful, huh? That's what you want me to tell the little green leprechaun who drinks more than any human on Earth?"

Lance raised a finger. "You tell the little green goblin—"

"Leprechaun," Claire corrected, raising her own finger into the air to mock Lance.

Remington stared at her as if he wanted to choke her, which only made Claire's grin grow. "Just tell him what we said and see if you can get us some freakin' help. Between you and Teams, I'm going to have an aneurysm."

Claire opened the door to her right and turned to Dean Pritcham. "Anything else?"

The dean nodded toward the hallway. "No. Dr. Byron knows the changes we're putting into place. You three go see him."

Claire left the group, wondering exactly what Frank would say when he finally showed up and got a load of this.

Claire wandered quietly into the lobby. The room was dark and empty. Her feet padded softly on the hardwood floors. She wasn't completely sure where she was going, only that she couldn't sleep.

She passed by shadow-draped couches, heading to the door on the other side of the room. There was a nice garden outside, and she thought she might go sit in it for a while until she got tired.

"Running away?"

Claire whipped around to the sound of the voice.

"Jack! You almost gave me a heart attack!" she whispered harshly. She could see Jack now, and had only missed him because she'd been so sure this place was empty. He was lying on one of the couches, staring up at the ceiling.

Claire's heart rate started to fall, and she felt herself calming some. "What are you doing down here?"

"Can't sleep," Jack answered without turning over to look at her. "This is some pretty heavy stuff. Heavier than I thought when I signed up."

Claire looked at the door she'd been headed to, then decided against it. She walked over to a leather chair across from Jack's couch and curled up on it instead. "Yeah, I know what you mean. I don't think I actually considered what I was getting myself into before I came. I just wanted to get away from home. I wanted to try something new, I guess. To try for a future."

Jack blinked in the darkness, quiet for a few seconds. "Maybe that's true of all of us here. We're gifted, that's obvious, but there are other people with gifts too. Yet, they're at Harvard, ya know?"

Claire didn't hear his usual bravado in his voice. *Is he actually showing vulnerability?*

"What are you trying to start new with? What kind of future are you looking for?" she asked, unsure exactly where this conversation would go. Most likely nowhere, because he'd shut it down with some kind of joke.

She saw him shrug in the darkness. "I don't know."

Claire was quiet for a few seconds, thinking that maybe it'd be best if she just went out to the garden. He seemed happy enough here by himself anyway. She decided to say one more thing first.

"I was proud of how you handled yourself at the club. You did a really good job."

"I wanted to get away from my father," Jack whispered as if Claire hadn't said anything. "My father and my mother, I suppose, but mainly my father."

"You don't like him?" Claire whispered, not wanting to pry, but not wanting him to think she didn't care either.

Jack shook his head. "It's not that I don't like him. He's my dad. I love him, and I guess I do like him, too. In a way. I don't like the life he had planned out for me, though."

Claire's eyes narrowed. "What life was that?"

"He's a neurosurgeon. He's smart as hell. Smarter than I'll ever be. My whole life, people have compared me to him and...." His voice trailed off, and he shoved his hands in his pockets. "That's why I talk so much trash, I guess. I mean, I think it's funny, don't get me wrong. I like my sense of humor, even if it grates on other people. But I talk a lot of trash because when I was younger, it helped deflect the comparisons. Over time, it just sort of became my personality, I guess."

Again he shrugged, although Claire thought he was attempting to pretend this didn't matter.

It matters a great deal, to him, and to me. "What did your dad want you to be?" she asked.

"A doctor like him. He wanted me to go to med school and probably be a neurosurgeon." Jack pulled his hands out of his pockets to create air quotes for the next sentence. "'To continue the family legacy.'"

"You don't want that, though?"

Jack looked at her, one eyebrow raised. "Hell. No. When I was growing up, I saw my dad on vacations and every couple of Saturdays. He worked constantly. He had no time for family. When I have a family, I want to be there for them. I want them to know who I am beyond the things I can provide for them."

Claire nodded. She understood that well because her own father had been there for her so much.

Jack turned back to stare at the ceiling. "Sorry, I don't know why I'm going into all of this with you. Just a lot of heavy stuff going on, and..."

His voice trailed off again.

"Sometimes it's nice just to be able to talk to someone," Claire finished, looking at her feet in the darkness.

Jack nodded. "Yeah, I guess that's right." He turned his head to once more. "Hey. Don't go tell anyone about this stuff, okay? I had a good childhood. I know that. I never wanted for anything, and the last thing I need people thinking is that I'm some rich kid who thinks his life was so hard because Daddy wasn't around, ya know?"

She met his gaze. "I won't tell anyone, Jack. We're teammates. What you tell me stays with me."

"Thanks, Claire," he responded. He grinned. "Plus, if people know I'm a Jack-ass because of deep-seated parental issues, it'll take away some of my sting."

Claire rolled her eyes. "You're ridiculous."

CHAPTER FOURTEEN

"You didn't say anything about us being hunted." The vampire stood in the same room as before, when he'd first met these three summoners. David hadn't been much impressed with them then and was even less so now. He could, without a doubt, open their insides and spill them across this floor in a matter of seconds.

Yet, he didn't understand the power they wielded. They had brought him forth, gave him life, some might say. Perhaps they could send him back to the other side, and he didn't want that. He was enjoying Earth, despite what had just happened.

"We didn't know," the fat man, Bradley said. He sat in the same place as last time, to the woman's side, with the scared skinny man on the other. "It doesn't change anything."

"It doesn't?" David asked. He turned his back to them and shoved his hands into his pockets. "Seems like creating havoc while a group of people is trying to kill us is a bit tough to do. What if it had been me in that club?"

"We understand your concern," Bradley answered. "But this was something we thought might happen."

David chuckled icily. "You thought that we might get killed?"

The woman spoke next. She was by far the tougher of the three, if not the leader. "We couldn't keep ourselves clandestine forever. Sooner or later, government agencies would catch on to us. That's what is happening. That's who those people were."

"Have you seen the recordings?" the vampire asked. "I have. I went down to the club and managed to convince the owner to let me see the tape from inside the building. The people who did this were little more than kids. Probably still teenagers."

He turned around and folded his hands in front of his belt.

"Teenagers don't sound like government agencies to me."

"You really up to date on Earth's programs?" Hannah asked. "Understand how they all work, huh?"

The vampire only smiled and shrugged.

"Thought not." The woman pulled a cigarette from her pack and lit it. She took a long drag before speaking again. "Not everyone here on Earth can see you. You know that much, right?"

David nodded. "I'm up to date on that part."

"Well, younger people can. They haven't lost their ability to believe. That's why there were teenagers in that club. Most likely, they're government recruits trained to hunt you down, as well as other creatures from across the veil." She looked at the tip of her cigarette, the ember bright red. "They're not a problem. We've nearly found him."

David knew who they meant, although he wasn't sure *they* actually did. Or, that they understood the ramifications of what they were doing. He'd let them find that out on their own, though.

"Of course, the government was going to fight us," Bradley told him. His hands were crossed in front of him as before. "That's never been in question. They don't know what we're doing yet, but when they truly figure it out, they're going to fight us with everything they've got. This right now is just the beginning."

The frightened man on the end, Matthew, spoke next. "We need you to handle them."

David raised an eyebrow. "Handle them? Would you mind explaining that a bit more?" He wondered what the man's blood would taste like. He imagined sour.

Matthew's lips quivered as if he might cry, so the skinny woman picked up the slack. "We'd like you to kill them."

The vampire was quiet for a moment, thinking about how he'd gotten himself into this mess. Certainly through no fault of his own, or at least not much fault. He'd been brought to this world and now was basically working for a triumvirate of cowards.

"If I kill them, do I get my freedom? I'm tired of organizing for you three, and now that vampires know they're being actively hunted, it's going to be harder to get them to listen to me. They'll leave. Go to other parts of this world, parts without so much scrutiny. I'll kill these teenagers, but when I'm done, I want out." He stepped forward, walking closer to the table. "You understand?"

"When he gets here." Hannah eyed the vampire with something akin to distaste. "You will do as he says, and you know it. For now, you and your cohort go kill those kids. If you don't, we'll ship you right back to where you came from. When you get done, we should be ready to bring him over, and then he can decide whether you're free or not. Do *you* understand?"

David leaned forward on the table, closing his eyes. He felt rage growing inside of him at the insolence of these humans. The sheer arrogance.

Yet, he didn't want to go back, and he was kind of looking forward to what would happen when the ultimate vampire finally arrived.

"Okay," he responded, opening his eyes. "I'll take care of them."

Hannah watched the vampire leave the room. Matthew opened his mouth to say something, but she raised a bony finger into the air. "Quiet."

Slowly she let it down, and no one in the room spoke. A minute or so passed, and Hannah lit a cigarette. Finally, after taking a long drag, she spoke.

"Now we can speak without any fear of him hearing it. We probably should do that any time they're around." She looked at Matthew. "Sometimes I wonder if you have enough brains to make it out of this alive, let alone enough courage. You were about to speak, knowing he could probably hear us."

Matthew looked down at the floor. "Sorry."

Hannah ignored his apology, only taking a pull on her smoke and then looked toward Bradley. "We're in a precarious situation."

He unfolded his hands and leaned back in his chair. He let out a heavy sigh. "We've got to find Dracula soon. We can't keep this up."

"Hush." Hannah stood and slowly paced toward the closed door. "We can keep it up because we hold the power to send them back across."

"We *believe* we hold the power!" Matthew shouted, his voice shrill and echoing off the ceiling.

Hannah whipped around, her eyes narrow. "Don't even think such foolishness. Not for a second. You let that creature who just left here believe we might not be able to send his ass back, and it's over for us. Do you understand that? Our mission doesn't end with that two-bit vampire. He's only the beginning. Even Dracula isn't the end, and you know it."

Matthew's left leg began shaking, bouncing up and down on the floor.

"It's fine," Bradley assured them. "We're close to finding him. We're getting better at this, and I'm sure the other sects are too. The vampires will go take care of the kids, and by the time they're done, we'll have him."

He stood up from the table and pushed his chair in. His large gut hung over his pants, covered by a *Death Becomes Her* shirt.

It was Bradley's favorite book, Hannah knew. She

wasn't loving what he was doing to the ass of the character on the t-shirt. No wonder the red-eyed woman looked pissed.

"Even if we kill them." Matthew's voice shook as hard as his leg. "They won't stop. The government will just keep coming."

Hannah flicked her cigarette onto the concrete floor. "I don't know why we ever let you in, Matthew. You're more pathetic than I imagined possible. *Of course,* they'll keep coming until they can't any longer. But we don't serve them, do we?"

Matthew refused to look at her. He kept his eyes on the ground in front of him.

"No. We don't. Their little kids running around playing ninja might scare you, but they don't scare me. I serve things greater than man, and that's what I'm here to do. Serve them." She shook her head, a sneer on her face. "I hope they can't see how you're speaking now for your sake. I don't think they'll be kind in the face of such cowardice."

CHAPTER FIFTEEN

"Faster!"

Claire's heart raged inside her chest, and she felt a cramp clawing at her side.

"Faster!"

She whirled around and met the oncoming attack with her pole. The combatant was faceless to Claire, just another person trying to beat her to a pulp. She swiped forward with her pole, but the attacker danced backward, causing her to slice through the air as if he'd never been there at all.

"Behind you!"

Again Claire turned. A giant figure swiped down at her with massive claws. Claire twirled to her right, but not fast enough, the claws cutting through her shirt and nearly her flesh.

She swiped up with the pole, hoping to land a kill shot.

"I got you."

The voice was little more than a whisper, but Claire didn't need it to be any louder to feel the blade in her side.

She looked down and saw the knife ready to pierce through her flesh and then kidney.

"Damn it!" Claire shouted. She threw her pole to the ground and bent over, placing her hands on her knees. She breathed heavy, looking at Dr. Kilgore. "It's not fair."

"Life not fair, girl," Dr. Kilgore told her in his heavy Russian accent. He was a bald, stout man.

Claire had a feeling that if he stood in the middle of a road and a Mack truck hit him, the truck would end up with the bad end of the deal. Dr. Kilgore was ridiculously strong thanks to his thick shoulders and chest, and legs like tree trunks, but what had surprised her was the sheer speed of the man.

He moved like a ghost, as if physical objects didn't really exist for him. He could just move through them. He was the first person to make her feel slow.

"I've got these weights on my wrists and ankles, and you've got five guys helping you. That's more than unfair. It's ridiculous." She gestured with her left hand to the ankle weight strapped on her leg. It was seven pounds, and it made moving hella hard.

"Jack," Mr. Kilgore called. "What does the girl sound like to you?"

"She sounds like a baby," Jack called from ten feet away. The three of them had been taking turns all afternoon, with the weights on their extremities getting heavier each time they trained.

"That right. A baby." Dr. Kilgore smiled broadly, real glee in his eyes. The other trainers were all nameless to Claire. She heard them talk from time to time, but in Russian, never in English. It was clear Kilgore led them.

"You're not even a real doctor." Claire spat on the ground, feeling stupid for saying such a silly thing.

Dr. Kilgore tucked his blade into the small sheath, not caring at all about her slight. "Me? *Da*, I am a doctor. I have two Ph.Ds if you must know."

"In what?" Marissa asked from the side.

"Suck-up," Claire grumbled.

"First in sports science. I know how your body works and how to get the best from it. Second in psychology. That means I know how your brain works. That is why FBI brought me here." He looked at Jack. "Your turn, Jack-boy. Come fight us."

Jack stepped onto the grass. "It's 'Jacky-boy,' and you guys better be careful with this freakin' arm. Last time, one of you numbskulls hit it."

Dr. Kilgore grinned largely. "Claire, what does he sound like?"

Claire couldn't help but match it. "A baby."

"That right. Jack-boy sounds like a baby."

Claire stepped off the training field. They were using three trainers against her, including Kilgore. He had only sent two against Marissa. Because of Jack's injury, Kilgore faced him alone.

"You tired?" Claire asked as she reached the sideline.

"I'm exhausted," Marissa answered.

They'd been out here for six straight hours. First they'd stretched and listened to Jack mouth off about how he was a fine physical specimen and didn't need to stretch. Then they'd worked on their technique for two hours, which was now solid.

Build a foundation, Dr. Kilgore had told them.

Finally they'd gone into action, live fighting mixed with more technique training.

Claire's legs were shaking. She'd never been put through this much physical exertion.

Jack grunted as he fought Kilgore on the grass.

Claire's eyes darted to the right. "Wonder what he wants?" She pointed at Dr. Byron.

It had been seven days since they met with the FBI agents and Dean Pritcham. They spent the first half of each day with Byron and the second with Kilgore. Claire didn't have a clue what the rest of the class was up to. They hadn't even seen them.

Dr. Byron reached Claire and Marissa. He stopped by Claire's side to watch Jack fight. "I see that Mr. Teams finally has shut his mouth."

"Don't make me come over there," Jack shouted as he blocked a blow from Kilgore.

Dr. Byron pointed to Marissa's wrist. "Ms. Hallor, why are there weights strapped to your legs and arms?"

"Vampires are faster and stronger than us. It's to train our muscles to react quicker and get us ready for when we face them again."

Dr. Byron nodded and turned back to the action on the grass. "Interesting technique."

"Yeah, but not exactly cutting edge," Claire complained. Her lungs were finally starting to relax and her heart felt like it might remain inside her chest. "I was told we'd be fighting with weapons that even the damn military didn't have. Instead I've got stakes, garlic, and holy water."

Marissa grinned, her face beautiful despite the dirt and

sweat across it. "You can't shoot a vampire. It will just heal. We have to fight them with what will work."

"You should listen to Ms. Hallor," Dr. Byron mused. "She might be as quiet as a church mouse, but she's got brains, unlike you and Mr. Teams out there."

Jack made a foolish attempt to bring his stake down on Kilgore's back. The professor dodged it and swept Jack's leg, bringing him down to the ground with a thud.

"Were you bored in class, Dr. Byron?" Claire walked out to the field and picked up the pole she'd thrown in anger. "Or did you just come out here to mock me?"

Dr. Byron grinned as she returned to the group. Jack was getting up, ready to fight again.

"I always get a little kick out of mocking you, as you well know, Ms. Hinterland. However, that's not why I'm here. We don't have class until tomorrow, and I wanted to give you an update on what's happening outside of these grounds."

Marissa turned away from the action on the field and looked at the professor. "What do you mean?"

Claire leaned on the pole, shoving it into the dirt. "Yeah, this is new."

Dr. Byron didn't take his eyes from Jack. He was fighting valiantly, especially for someone with only one good arm. "I know you three are scared, and I know you're not exactly exuberant about getting out in the field. When I went to war, I was the same. I imagine all people are their first time. It's fallen on Dr. Kilgore and me to get you ready for it, though, and that includes letting you know the truth about what we're facing."

Claire sighed. "Quit with the preamble. What is going on?"

Dr. Byron's face didn't change with her pressure. He kept staring stoically at Jack, who was retreating from the physically superior Kilgore. "These cults don't appear to just be in America. I wasn't aware of them until a few days ago. The FBI was playing that very close to its chest. However, there was a serious attack in Europe last night."

"Europe?" Marissa's eyes grew wide. "Vampires?"

Dr. Byron shook his head. "No. The cults don't seem to be seeking the same creatures in each instance. Last night, a group of hellhounds ran through London, savaging anyone they came in contact with. The death toll is still being counted." He grew quiet.

Claire watched his face. "Hellhounds?" she whispered.

Marissa nodded as if to herself. "Dogs that supposedly guard the gates of Hell."

Byron nodded. "For that many to show up in one place, they think it's cult activity. It's not like the one-offs, or those Asclepius staffs that keep falling from the sky." He shoved his hands into his pockets.

He's scared, Claire thought. *He won't ever say it, but that's what the severity written all over his face means. He's scared of what's coming.*

"I just wanted the three of you to recognize how important it is that you get up to speed quickly," the professor told them. "But, if Mr. Teams out there is taking it as seriously as he appears to be, then I imagine you two are as well."

Jack dropped to his knees and swiped forward with his stake, actually hitting Kilgore's leg. The bigger man's hand whipped out and slapped Jack's face with his knuckles, sending him sprawling across the grass.

"Good work, Jack-boy." Kilgore smiled and reached to help lift him off the ground. "You touched me, though. You left yourself open to die."

Jack took his hand away from his reddening face. He was smiling. "I don't give a flying fuck. I got you, ya big bastard." He took Kilgore's hand and pushed off from the ground.

Claire didn't look at Dr. Byron as she spoke but kept her eyes on the smiling teacher and student. "We're taking it seriously. I promise."

Exhaustion didn't begin to describe what Claire felt. Her very bones wept with weariness, but she couldn't rest yet.

Do you know when you'll actually be able to? she asked herself.

Of course, she didn't.

"Lass, you look like a bag of smashed assholes." Frank handed her the basket of fries. "Hopefully, these will help."

"Thanks, Frank. You always know how to make a girl feel better." Claire took the fries and placed them on the small bowling alley table.

They were at the twenty-four-hour place again.

Claire had told Pritcham she needed a ride to the bowling alley after classes were done for the day.

"Why?" Pritcham asked.

"You heard Remington and Lance. They want me to talk to Frank. He's got a predilection for coming and going as he pleases, so I don't know when I'll see him again unless I show up at one of his haunts."

Pritcham hadn't argued, only asked if Claire wanted the dean to drive her or to request an Uber.

Claire took the Uber because she didn't want to have to worry about getting picked back up. She certainly didn't feel comfortable calling the dean at three in the morning and asking for a ride. Claire *might* ask Frank, but after his driving last time, she thought that might end up with her wrapped around a telephone pole.

If he gets pulled over, he better teleport quickly, or he's going into the slammer. No way he's got a driver's license, she thought.

Claire had shown up here, and sure enough, Frank had been bowling alone. He got a strike and turned around, his eyes spying her immediately. A grin broke out across his face, and true happiness that warmed Claire's heart. The two of them talked a lot of shit, but they were close friends, even if they weren't able to see each other much.

Now, Frank ignored the pins waiting for him and sat down across from her. His hand darted forward to grab a fry.

Claire probably could have slapped it away, but she was too tired to even try. "Enjoy it while you can, green man."

Frank chomped loudly on the fry. "Never insult Frank like that. A man? Ha! I'd rather be a *liderc*."

"A *liderc*?" Claire took a fry. Her arm hurt to move, the muscles full of lactic acid and very sore.

"A wannabe leprechaun. Either way, lass, don't call me a man." He winked at her and Claire shot a faint smile back.

"Now, tell Frank why ye came out this late at night if you're clearly feeling so awful?"

Claire looked at the upright pins. "You not going to bowl?"

"Ye let Frank deal with Frank's business," the leprechaun told Claire, pointing at her. "I'll bowl when I'm damn well ready. Now, quit ignoring me questions. What's goin' on with ye, lass?"

Claire chuckled. "I think I'd rather know about where you've been first. You seem to have kept yourself busy over the past week."

"Church," Frank replied quickly.

Claire raised both eyebrows. "Oh, no. You haven't been at any church, Frank. Not unless you've been drinking communion wine?" Her eyes narrowed as she studied her friend. "Oh, I know where you've been."

She smiled at Frank's look of worry. "There are lady leprechauns here, aren't there? You've been getting a workout in at night, but not by bowling?"

Claire couldn't be sure, but she thought a red hue was growing across Frank's face.

The leprechaun stood up without saying a word, grabbed a bowling ball, and then sent it right down the gutter. "*DAMN IT!*" he shouted, stomping his foot. He whipped around. "That's your fault! All these accusations! False, might I add! False and inflammatory!"

He stomped back to the table and sat down.

Claire started laughing because there was definitely red beneath his green skin.

"Enough o' that. Mayhap I do have a lady friend, and

mayhap I don't." Frank tapped his finger hard on the table. "It's none o' yer business."

"Hey, Frank, I'm happy for ya." Claire grabbed a fry and popped it into her mouth to keep from laughing anymore. She could tell Frank was genuinely embarrassed.

Frank frowned. "Now, what brings ye out here this late?"

The sound of pins being set up echoed through the empty alley.

"You trust me, Frank?" Claire asked, meeting her friend's eyes with a solemn look.

"Aye, trust ye as much as I trust anyone, which isn't much. Us leprechauns are not a trusting breed by nature." Frank reached for the beer to his left and took a large sip. "But, aye, I trust ye, Claire."

Claire hesitated. "Good, because I would never do anything that could get you hurt, Frank. You're my friend, and I value that a lot."

Frank sat back in his chair, a skeptical smirk on his face. "Something is most definitely going on. Let Frank hear it."

"The FBI wants your help." Claire tried to keep a straight face as she said it, but a grin broke out. "Seriously. They asked me to ask you."

"This is the group who is training you to kill creatures like me?" Frank folded his hands over his chest. "Ye expect me to believe they're asking for help?"

Claire put her hands out, palms up. "I know. I know. It sounds crazy, but you have to hear me out. I'm telling you the truth."

Frank shot Claire a skeptical look and sunk deeper into his chair. "Go on, lass, but Frank didn't get to be hundreds of years old by believing in fairy this establishment such atales."

"Frank, you *are* a fairy tale," Claire told him with a quizzical look on his face.

Frank's expression grew more exasperated. "Are ye going to tell me what the hell you're talking about, or are we going to argue about who created who?"

Claire sighed and looked at her fries. "Okay, so there's real trouble here in Boston. You know what vampires are, Frank?"

"What, do you think I'm some kind of an idiot?" he asked. "Of course, I do. Where I'm from, everyone stays away from 'em. They're not to be trusted."

Claire glanced up. "That's a tough judgment coming from a leprechaun. Either way, they're here now. In Boston. I don't know if you've seen the news, but they're on a killing spree. The FBI thinks that you might have some avenues into how this is happening, or who's in control, or *something*. They want to know if you can work those avenues."

Frank's eyes lit up, although his face remained in a stern pout and his arms were still crossed. Claire knew what that meant. Frank was playing tough, but his mind was counting riches. If the FBI needed something from him, they'd have to pay for it.

"What kind of avenues do they think someone like me might have? Do they think I can just wiggle my toes and information is handed to me? Do they not *know* the amount of work I'd have to engage in to do what they're asking?" Frank raised a finger into the air self-righteously. "These things they ask of me aren't *easy*."

Claire rolled her eyes. "Frank, they'll pay you, I'm sure of it. They just want stuff they can use. They're looking for the group of people bringing the vampires over, or maybe if you can get them to one of the head vampires? I don't know. Just something they can use." Claire leaned forward. "Plus, it'll help me."

"How so, lass?" Frank said skeptically.

It was Claire's turn to frown. "What do you think I'm doing over there at that university?"

Frank's eyes narrowed, but his lip twitched into a smile. "Most likely drinking booze in ungodly amounts and flirting with the opposite sex, methinks."

"Hush it, greenie," Claire told him, not unkindly. "You going to help me or not?"

"Aye, lass. I'll see what I can do." Frank leaned forward and grabbed his beer. He brought it to his lips and paused. "But you make sure those FBI jokers understand that Frank doesn't work for free. I'm going to help my good friend Claire, but I expect to be well-compensated."

CHAPTER SIXTEEN

F rank turned down the dark alley, making sure to look above him and scan the entire length of the roofs on either side. Humans didn't see a lot of the flying creatures being called over. Mainly because they couldn't see shit, but also because they simply didn't look *up*. Frank wasn't about to be picked up by a harpy, though.

The coast appeared clear, so he lowered his head, shoved his hands into his pockets, and continued down the alley. There was a light at the far end on the right, and that was the place Frank was looking for.

Can humans see it? he wondered. He imagined they could, but it wasn't a friendly-looking joint. Not something they'd want to venture into, and once inside? It would probably look even weirder unless you were someone like Claire, who could see creatures from beyond the Veil.

Frank reached the door, the single light overhead casting a dingy yellow glow on the ground. He knocked three times in rapid succession. No more, no less.

A few seconds passed, and then the door cracked open.

One huge eye stared out through the crack. It was nearly the size of Frank's head.

"You leprechauns must have the strongest livers ever created," the doorman said.

"All of our organs are strong." Frank grinned as he reached down and cupped his crotch.

"Not from what I heard." The creature opened the door, revealing himself as a massive cyclops. He stood up to his full height of eight feet. Frank stepped in, barely coming up to the creature's knees.

"Your hearing is shittier than your depth perception, Timmy," he told the cyclops as he moved past him and went into the bar.

The music was loud, but Frank understood the crones had cast a spell to keep it from reaching the alley outside. They didn't want to make more noise than was necessary to have a good time. Certainly didn't want to alert humans if they could help it.

The place was pretty busy for a Wednesday night. You had the crones—witches—at a table in the back. A few brooms leaned against the wall. A lone centaur Frank knew as Bosephus was throwing darts by himself to the right of the bar. The bar itself had seven or eight customers, a mix of leprechauns, what appeared to be a lone werewolf, and another being Frank couldn't identify.

"Frank!" Norstrom, the bartender, shouted. "Haven't seen you in thirty-six hours. Figured you must have quit drinking!"

"Fat chance," Bosephus called without looking away from his game of darts.

"Don't you ever put on any clothes?" Frank asked the

centaur as he made his way to the bar. He reached the stool and put his hands on the seat, which came up to his shoulders. "What the hell is it with these things? This is speciesism if I have ever seen it. Just because you've got that big animal with one eye at the door, it doesn't mean we can all climb up onto these stools."

"Put a beer in front of that stool, and I'm sure the drunk will climb up just fine," Timmy called from the door. The cyclops had pulled out a paperback book and begun to read as he waited for the next knock.

"I shall ignore these barbs about my height and continue fighting the good fight for equality." Frank looked at Norstrom. He was a winged creature that Frank wasn't exactly sure about. Most people in this place looked frighteningly ugly, but not Norstrom. His wings were currently tucked behind his back, although you could still see them poking above his shoulders. If one were to ignore them, one might think him human, perhaps an up-and-coming movie star. "However, the dumb lug over there is right. I would definitely prefer a cold beer in front of me."

Norstrom had already begun pouring it. He put it down just as Frank finished his sentence. "Good to see ya, Frank. When you planning on paying the tab?"

The leprechaun climbed up the stool and sat down. "Very soon, lad. Very soon now. Frank might have come into some good fortune." He picked up the beer and drank half of it in a single swallow. He put the mug back down and gave a mighty belch.

"I wish they would have left him behind the Veil." Bosephus walked to the dartboard and started plucking off darts.

Frank ignored the barb and continued sipping his beer. He looked up at the television hanging behind the bar and watched, although his mind wasn't on it. He was sensing the mood of the place now, and it felt different. More tense than it had been thirty-six hours ago.

Time passed, and Frank ordered another beer. The other patrons left him alone, and he did the same for them. Most creatures came here to have a few drinks without being harassed. To the outside world, they looked weird, and that often lent itself to confrontations, which usually ended poorly for the humans. Frank understood as well as anyone that no one had volunteered to be pulled across the Veil. It had just happened, sometimes by accident, and other times because of external forces.

All these people had been ripped from their place of birth, and whether they enjoyed Earth or not, there was still something awful about being brought to a land that didn't want you.

Thought you looked weird.

Frank knew that Claire thought he was doing this for booze and money. Hell, he was, partly. That was a leprechaun's nature, and he couldn't change that part of himself. Yet, it wasn't all about that. Frank cared about Claire. In a new world where no one wanted you, she'd accepted him.

If that meant snooping around to figure out what was going on, so be it.

Frank clicked his tongue against the roof of his mouth. "Norstrom, got a second?"

The winged creature turned. "What ya got, Frank?"

Frank gestured with his head toward the television.

"You been watching the news?"

"Hard not to. All anyone in here wants to watch anymore is the news. These vampires have everyone freaking out." Norstrom stepped closer to the bar and placed his hands on it. "It's going to bring more heat down on all of us."

"It's curious," Frank continued as he looked up at the television. "Why there are so many vamps coming across all of a sudden? I mean, I was pulled across the Veil in one of the Southern states, but even so, we didn't have any vampires down there. At least, none that I knew of." He looked at Norstrom again. "You got any ideas about it?"

Norstrom's eyes narrowed, and he continued leaning on the bar. He stared at Frank hard for a few moments, then said, "What are you getting at?"

"You heard anything about it is all I'm asking." Frank reached into his pocket and pulled out a wad of money. It hurt his leprechaun heart to do it, but he wasn't here for himself. This was for Claire, and hopefully those cheap FBI bastards would reimburse him when this was all said and done.

Frank unfolded the wad and stripped off three hundred-dollar bills from it. He glanced to his left and right to see if anyone was looking, but the other patrons appeared to be minding their own business. "I'm willing to contribute a bit to yer personal fund, if not the bar's, if ye have heard anything."

Norstrom glanced at the money and then flashed his eyes back up, quickly glancing across the bar. He stuck his hand out and motioned for Frank to put the wad of cash away. "Meet me upstairs in ten minutes."

"Upstairs?" Frank's raised both eyebrows. He hadn't known there *was* an upstairs to this place. *Then again, I don't really go anywhere but to this exact spot.*

Norstrom stepped back from the bar. "Yeah. Over where the bathrooms are, there's a closed door across from them. Go upstairs. I'll meet you there in ten."

Frank glanced down at his glass. He grabbed it quickly and downed the remaining alcohol. He looked up to Norstrom. "One for the road?"

Frank sat in Norstrom's living room. The place was pretty large for a studio apartment and resided right over the Veil Room. Only creatures from beyond the Veil called it that; Frank wasn't sure humans had a name for the shitty little bar at all.

Ten minutes turned to twenty, but then Frank heard heavy footsteps coming up the stairs.

Damn, Norstrom does not look big enough to sound like that, he thought. He didn't move from the chair, his legs splayed out on a footrest. His beer sat on the table next to him.

The apartment's door opened, but it wasn't Norstrom who walked through. Instead, the half-man, half-horse stepped through the doorway.

Bosephus was built like a tank, the man half of him as muscular as a Greek god and the horse half looking like a thoroughbred.

Frank sat up, alarmed to see the horse instead of the bird. *If he gives me trouble, I can always teleport.*

Bosephus closed the door and then turned around to

study the much smaller leprechaun. He eyed him suspiciously. "Norstrom said you were asking questions downstairs. He said you were waving around more cash around than he'd ever seen you carrying."

"Just because Norstrom can't see very well, it doesn't mean I'm broke." He took the beer from the table and put it in his lap. "Why did he send you up here?"

"Because he's working, and I needed to get a look at you." The four hooves clapped as they walked across the wooden floor.

"You sure you're not going to fall through this damn floor?" Frank stared down at the massive hooves. "Frank can teleport, but methinks you'll have a tougher time."

The centaur stopped about three feet from Frank's chair. "Why are you asking about vampires? Why did you pull out money to learn about them?"

Frank looked at his pants, seeing a speck. He wiped it away nonchalantly. "Bosephus, let's get a few things straight. You may be huge and strong, but I'm a leprechaun. You might not know a lot about us, but trust me, my Veilian brother, I'm not someone ye want to mess around with." He rubbed his nose. "Why I'm asking about the vamps is me own business. If ye want to answer about them, that's yer business."

The centaur gave a horse-like sneeze, sounding annoyed. He turned his body so he was staring out the window to the right of Frank. "A lot of creatures are asking about the vampires, and whether I give you any information depends on why you're asking. I don't need your money, and neither does Norstrom. But, if you're asking for the wrong reasons, I'll politely have to decline your request."

What's his angle? Frank wondered. He studied the large horse creature. He saw no deceit in him, but he didn't get this old by trusting beings he hardly knew.

Frank looked down into his beer. He finally shrugged. *To hell with it. Tell 'em the truth.* "I'm asking because I want to stop them or help stop them if I can."

Bosephus turned his head to look at Frank. "How are you going to do that, little man?"

Frank sighed. "Speciesist. Look, it doesn't matter exactly how. I'm just curious what's bringing us over here. Whether these vampires are coming on their own and congregating, or whether it's something more sinister."

The centaur's large legs backed him up so that he was square with Frank. "Listen, little green man. I sense you're on the right side of things, but no one can be certain. Either you level with me and perhaps we can talk, or you take your tiny legs down those stairs and don't come back to this place. Either is fine with me."

Frank looked down at his beer. Almost out. What's it gonna be, Frank? Get more involved with this business, or finish your beer and get on out of here like a good leprechaun?

The decision wasn't hard. He remembered back to when those FBI agents had showed up at the bowling alley and Claire stood up, telling him to cut loose. He'd listened to her, letting Claire handle the agents. Now she needed him, just like he thought he'd needed her back then.

"You're not going to like the answer I've got for you, horse-man." Frank stared into his quickly disappearing beer, the amber liquid looking sadder the closer to the bottom it got. "But I'll tell ye all the same."

Frank went through the spiel. He explained about Claire, although he didn't mention the lass's name. He told Bosephus about the FBI coming for her, and the university, and all the way up until last night.

"So that's why I'm here." He drained the last of his glass and set it down hard on the table next to him. "Because they're asking for help against the vamps, and I thought I might be able to give it to them. I don't have any business with the FBI, and I don't want any besides whatever I might gain from this little endeavor. Now, do you know anything about this?"

Bosephus had turned during Frank's talk and was staring out the window again, his broad, hairless shoulder facing Frank. "The university. I've heard rumors about it, and then there were whispers that one of the vampires was killed. The humans are fighting back, it would seem?"

Frank said nothing. He was honestly tired of all this talking, and consequently, the lack of drinking.

"Okay, green man," the centaur conceded. One of his hoofs rubbed idly on the wooden floor, causing a light scraping sound. "You go home now and come back tomorrow first thing in the morning. I'll have you some answers, or as many as I can get."

"First thing in the morning?" Frank raised an eyebrow. "What time is that for centaurs?"

Bosephus grinned. "Six. Don't be late."

Frank groaned as he stood up from the chair. "That means I'll have to stop drinking in a few hours. The lass gonna pay for this."

CHAPTER SEVENTEEN

It was mid-afternoon when Frank appeared on Claire's computer chair. "I got bad news, and I got worse news."

"What the heck?!" Marissa shrieked from her side of the room. She scurried off the bed and stared at the leprechaun.

Frank turned and grinned. "Oh, my, my, Claire. She's a cute one." He stood and offered a hand. "My name's Frank. Nice to meet ye."

Claire sighed. "Marissa, this is Frank. Frank, Marissa."

Marissa turned her face to look at Claire, eyes wide and mouth ajar. "You *know* it?"

"It?" Frank was aghast. "I'll have ye know, Frank is no *it*. Got a big stick and beach balls within me pants, I do!"

Claire shook her head and turned her body so she faced Marissa, who was still standing on the bed. "He's not the most couth creature to cross the Veil."

Marissa swallowed and slowly turned to the leprechaun again. Her mouth remained open, but she wasn't trying to dart away any longer.

Frank had turned his offended shock back to humor and was smiling. "Claire, you didn't tell me your roommate was so beautiful."

"Because it's none of your business, Frank. Plus, she doesn't practice interspecies dating with jerks. Which you most definitely are." Claire stepped forward and slapped Frank on the arm, getting him to look away from Marissa. "Now, why are you here?"

"Hold on, hold on," Marissa interrupted. "How do you know him? Won't we get in trouble for him being here? I mean, he's clearly not human."

Frank sighed. "Our love is over before it even started, me dear. You're clearly a speciesist." He waddled into the room and bent over to look under Claire's bed. Then he pulled a trunk out from beneath it. "Hmmm... This is new."

"Hey." Claire marched back across the room and slapped his hands. The leprechaun stood up, and she kicked the trunk back under the bed. "Enough, Frank. What the hell are you doing here?"

Frank put a hand over his heart. "I'm wounded, me lady, at your harsh words. Especially in front of such a lovely being as this." He gestured with his free hand at Marissa. "I am here, of course, because I've been out doing your bidding and finding out what you need to know. What your *FBI* asked me for, if I have to remind ye?"

Claire stepped back and sat on Marissa's bed. She patted the mattress next to her, indicating that Marissa should sit down, too. "I know this little green monster. His name's Frank. He's okay most of the time. Just likes shocking people is all. Trust me, he knows I can kick his ass if it comes down to it."

Frank raised one finger into the air. "Once. She bested me once in a race, but I was drunk. It doesn't count."

Marissa slowly sat down next to Claire, understanding for the most part that the creature wasn't going to hurt her.

Claire put her hand on Marissa's knee, trying to calm her. "You remember when they asked me to stay behind after that meeting?"

Marissa nodded.

Claire pointed at Frank. "This was why. They know about Frank. In fact, when they came to pick me up, Frank was with me, and I thought they were after him. When I stayed back the other day, they wanted me to ask Frank if he could help, so I did."

"Lass, Frank is not here to hurt ye." The leprechaun leaned forward, putting his elbows on his knees and looking earnest. "I'm here to help me friend Claire. If ye're with her, then I'm here to help ye as well."

Claire tapped Marissa's knee gently, then focused on Frank. "Okay. Before you disrupted everything with your antics, you said you had news. What is it?"

"Aye, it's bad and it's worse, me dear." Frank stood and walked over to one of the bookshelves. He started pulling books off it one by one as if checking their titles.

The little bastard is rummaging for things to steal, Claire thought. *No doubt about it. I'll have to make sure he doesn't get anything from Marissa, who isn't wise to his ways yet.* "Careful, Frank. I know what you're doing."

"I'm sure ye do. Just looking to see what ye're educating yourself with," Frank commented as he thumbed through a book. "Now, can I tell ye what I came here to relate so I can be on me way?"

Claire leaned back on the bed, placing her hands behind her to hold her up. "You want to tell me, or you want to do it in front of the bigwigs?"

Frank looked skeptically over his shoulder. "I'd rather not go in front of the group wanting to kill me if ye don't mind, me dear. Right here is fine. I expect ye to let them know they owe me a drum of ale for this. Not beer, but actual ale." He stared at Claire.

"Fine!" Claire agreed in exasperation. "Now get on with it!"

Frank moved over to a few knickknacks on the small shelf. "You're right about the cult, although they don't think of themselves in those terms. It's *people* who are pulling the vampires across, and best Frank can surmise, they aren't too keen on helping the human race."

Claire couldn't believe what she was hearing. "What do they want?"

"That, I'm not sure about," Frank answered as he picked up one of the small items on the shelf. He held it up to the light and studied it. "But it doesn't really matter for your purposes. So, right now, these guys are calling creatures over, and they're focusing on vampires—"

"*Frank,*" Claire interrupted. "We know all this. Do you have anything else for me? You're a long way from your barrel of booze right now."

"Well, did you know there is a hit out on you and the rest of your cohort?" Frank put the knickknack down and turned around. He smirked. "That worth any booze to you?"

Claire was stunned. *A hit? What the hell is a hit?* She turned to Marissa but her eyes didn't leave Frank.

"You mean, an assassination?" Marissa asked. "That's what you're talking about?"

"Well," Frank mused, "assassinations are usually reserved for important people. You two don't reach that milestone. However, ye might if ye married me. With your beauty and my brains, we could really be something."

Claire slapped his hand. "Quit it!"

"Aye, okay." Frank nodded with a smile. "Yes, an assassination. A hit. The group apparently didn't take kindly to what you did to that vamp, murdering the poor fellow and all. So now, they're going to try to take you all out before you can do any more damage."

"How do you know, Frank?" Claire was leaning forward now, worrying for the first time. It was one thing to go hunting these creatures. It was something altogether different if they were hunting you.

Frank stood and raised his hands into the air in mock exasperation. "I bring news, and you want to know my sources! This is absurd!"

"Come on. Be serious." Claire was staring at her shoes, ignoring Frank's antics. "How did you find out?"

Frank let his hands drop back to his sides. "There's a group of creatures from the Veil, and they're not taking kindly at being removed from their homes. Apparently, not everyone enjoys Earth as much as I do. They aren't looking at targeting all humans, just the ones responsible. They've got some kind of insight into the group and what they're planning to do."

Claire looked up. "Do they know who's behind the cult?"

The leprechaun sat back down on the bed. "No, or if they do, they didn't tell Frank."

"Do you know anything else?" Claire pressed. "When the hit is coming? Where?"

Frank shook his head. "No one is sure yet. They just know this cult wants you guys out of the way."

Claire nodded and looked at Marissa. "There might be something good that comes out of this."

"What's that?" Marissa whispered, staring at the floor.

"We end up getting rid of Jack?" Claire said, hiding her grin.

"We're not that lucky," Marissa whispered back, unable to hide her smile.

Frank sat in the corner of the room, stiller than Claire had ever seen him. It'd taken her a freakin' *hour* to wrangle him into coming to this meeting. He'd fought her tooth and nail, refusing over and over. He'd almost teleported out of the university before she guaranteed him she'd pay the next ten times they went bowling.

Claire didn't have a damn clue where she was going to get the money for that, but she needed him here when they talked to Remington, Lance, and Pritcham if for nothing else than to back up what she was saying.

Claire, Marissa, and Jack sat in the same three chairs as last time. The FBI attendants occupied the same couch, and Dean Pritcham was behind her desk. Frank had stationed himself in the far corner. He looked much smaller in the overlarge chair.

Claire had given everyone the rundown, and now the two FBI agents were staring at Frank.

"That's the truth?" Remington asked. "Because we haven't heard anything about retribution."

Frank raised an eyebrow and looked at Claire. "You made me come for this? If ye don't believe me, don't believe me. I don't care."

Claire paid the sullen leprechaun no mind. "Remington, he's telling the truth. He didn't come here to lie to us. Anyway, it makes sense. If this cult thinks we're a danger, why wouldn't they try to wipe us out?"

Remington stared for a few more seconds, considering whether to trust Frank.

"Hey," Claire snapped. "You asked him to help us, and he did. That's my friend, and he's telling the truth as best he knows. I trust him, and you better start, too, or there's no reason for any of us to be in this room. The three of us can just go back to training and then see what happens."

Jack turned his head to her with an odd smirk on his face. He started slow clapping, then mimicked Professor Byron as he spoke. "Well done, Ms. Hinterland. Well done, indeed."

Claire didn't even show the hint of a smile. *I'll be damned if they call Frank in here to accuse him of lying,* she thought. She kept her eyes on Remington, and the FBI agent finally turned and met her gaze.

"Fair enough." He glanced Lance. "You good?"

"Yeah, I'm good."

Remington focused on Pritcham. "This changes things again."

The dean laughed. "Of course it does. The only constant around here is change."

"This isn't necessarily a bad thing." Marissa stared down at the open notebook on her lap as she spoke.

She'd written some notes, although Claire didn't know when it had happened. She'd been so focused on making sure the FBI treated Frank correctly that she hadn't seen what her friends were doing.

"It's not bad?" Jack asked, leaning forward. "Seems like having a vampire hit on our lives could very well be interpreted as a bad thing. At least in my book."

Marissa's voice rose in strength. "It allows us to control the situation a bit better."

She's getting good at this, Claire thought. *She's starting to recognize her value to the team. Maybe her whole life, she's only been thought of as gorgeous, but now she's understanding she sees things differently than other people, and in a good way.*

"Go on," Remington instructed.

"Well, if we know they're going to attack us, we can prepare for it." Marissa smiled slyly. "Like in that *Home Alone* movie—"

"Hold on," Lance spoke up. "You've seen *Home Alone*? You weren't even alive when that movie came out."

"Ageist," Frank grumbled from his seat in the corner. "Speciesists and ageists, the lot of ye."

Claire stifled a grin. "We've all seen *Home Alone* because old folks like you make us watch it. Now, quit interrupting."

Marissa continued. "We can prepare for when they come. There are a lot of ways to fight vampires. They're the most dangerous when you don't know they're a vampire, or when your faith is weak, or when you don't have any weapons. The faith stuff only comes into play if you try to use crosses and such, but there are a lot of weapons we can use. We can also remain *here*, which means they'll be on our territory." She looked at Remington. "Have you ever tried to kidnap a vampire?"

Remington smiled. "Can't say I have."

"Well," Marissa met his smile with her own, "this could be your chance. And a captured vampire might just lead us to this cult you're chasing."

CHAPTER EIGHTEEN

"You know you're pretty smart, right?" Claire asked as she and Marissa pushed a large spotlight through the hall.

Marissa didn't look at her, just kept her head down and pushed. "I'm okay."

Everyone had been busying themselves with preparations all day. Claire was covered in sweat and grime. The three of them had been working for hours, with Remington, Lance, and a host of other FBI guys throwing their muscles in too.

"No, I'm serious," Claire continued. "You're smarter than Jack and me combined. Legit."

Marissa shook her head, red appearing in her cheeks. "Nah, no way. You guys are plenty smart."

"Please." Claire course-corrected the spotlight. The thing was heavy despite its wheels, so it took a good bit of strength to make sure it didn't bang into the wall and break.

Probably cost ten grand, she thought.

"Back in that meeting, neither Jack nor I had thought that far ahead. We were still busy trying to wrap our heads around what was happening, but you came up with this entire plan. Now here we are, enacting it." Claire looked at Marissa, hoping her friend was taking in the words she said. It was important that Marissa understood. Claire thought she saw the girl's confidence growing, but she wanted it to blossom fully.

The three of us will never be as good together if it doesn't.

Marissa swallowed, then nodded. "Thanks, Claire."

"We're going to need you to keep stepping up like that. Jack sure as hell doesn't have the brainpower, and neither do I. We'd be outta luck if it wasn't for you."

Marissa grinned a bit, her face turning bright red now. "I know what you're doing."

Claire smiled. "What's that?"

"Trying to build me up and give me some confidence."

Claire nodded and looked down at her feet. "Yeah, maybe a little bit, but what's wrong with that? I'm not building you up falsely. There aren't any lies to it. I'm telling you this to get your confidence up, but that's because we need it up."

The two reached the end of the hallway and rolled the spotlight to a stop.

The door to the right was open, with stairs leading down. Jack stood at the bottom. "Took you long enough!"

He and a group of men climbed them, ready to lug the spotlight down. The mansion hadn't been built with this kind of furniture in mind, so no elevator was available.

Claire ignored them but looked at Marissa. "Just keep remembering that, okay? We're a unit, the three of us.

That's not because of any school designation. It's because we three have to keep each other alive, and right now, your brain is doing more to assist that than anything Jack and I have. So keep it up."

Marissa was still staring at the floor as Jack came up the stairs, but Claire thought she saw some pride in her. Red cheeks, still beautiful and shy, but Marissa was hearing Claire.

Good, she thought. *Because even with all these preparations, when it finally happens, we're gonna need her brainpower.*

The preparations went on for days. At night, Claire lay in her bed, wide awake. She didn't know what to expect; no one did. Truthfully, no one even knew if these vampires knew the university existed.

The bet was that they did, though, and as long as the group didn't leave, the vampires would come here soon enough.

How many? How dangerous would they be?

Frank didn't have any answers, which meant the group of Mythers he'd found didn't have any, either.

They were in a prepare and wait situation, in which something might come, or it might not. Frank dropped by on the second night, but he didn't have any more real information.

Claire thought he'd come for two reasons. He was scared for her, and he wanted to get a look at Marissa. She thought Frank had a crush on her friend.

Marissa had gone to sleep, Frank had disappeared, and Claire was alone again.

Three nights went by like that. Preparations during the day, mostly sleepless nights for Claire. On the fourth night, Frank returned...with actual information.

Claire was lying on her back, staring up at the ceiling. She heard him near the window and looked up. "You were just here two nights ago, Frank. Why are you back?"

"Tonight's the night, lass. He or *they* are coming." His eyes twinkled in the moonlight.

Claire sat up on her elbows. "You're sure?"

Frank nodded. "Aye, as sure as I can be. I'm here to help."

Claire raised an eyebrow, not quite sure what he meant. "Here to help?"

"Aye, I didn't like vampires when I lived across the Veil." Frank stepped away from the window light, his green skin growing much darker. "Maybe I'm speciesist, too. Or maybe I just don't want to see them make mincemeat out of ye, but either way, ye should put me to good use."

"Frank, you're three feet tall and slower than me," Claire told him with a sly smile on her face. She knew how to bug him.

"Aye, slower, but not weaker. Those silly vamps won't know what hit them when Frank takes over. It will be like a whirlwind for them. You'll see." Frank reached the bed and put his hand on the comforter. "We need to get ready. You need to wake everyone up, lass. This is no joke. My group got word that they're coming tonight."

Claire flipped out of bed but kept the lights off. She

didn't want to wake Marissa just yet. "Did they say how many?"

"No!" Frank hissed, showing real anger for the first time. "But it's time to get a move on. It's nearing the witching hour, and I imagine that's when they're going to strike!"

"Hush!" Claire scolded. "What's the witching hour?"

"Three in the morning," Marissa mumbled as she rolled over in her bed. She looked down at her watch. "It's two-thirty."

"You see, Frank? You woke her up." Claire turned to Marissa. "I wasn't going to wake you until I knew for sure. Now, what is the witching hour?"

"It's for sure, lass." Frank turned to Marissa. "Ye've heard of it? The hour?"

Marissa sat up, sounding groggy as she spoke. "Yes, of course. In mythology, it's when evil acts occur. Witches fly, demonic possessions, things of that nature. It makes sense that the vampires would attack then." She blinked a few times and wiped at her eyes, then gazed at Claire. "We should ready the others."

Claire looked down at her feet. *Okay, it's happening. You need to get focused and decide what comes next.*

"We've got to get the other students into the basement. That's the first part." She glanced at Marissa. "How long until three?"

"Exactly twenty-two minutes."

Claire stood up. "Get dressed. Frank, turn around."

"Damn it," Frank complained with a sly grin, although he stood and immediately walked to the window. Claire wasn't worried about him trying to catch a peek. He was all bluster.

The two ladies dressed as quickly as possible and then opened the door. Claire looked at Marissa. "You go get Jack. I'll get Dean Pritcham."

Marissa nodded and headed off to the right.

Claire looked back at Frank. "Come on, let's do this."

Twenty-two minutes was barely enough time, but they managed to round everyone up. The other students were brought down into the basement. Thankfully, they'd all been briefed about what was happening before.

Another great idea by Marissa, Claire thought.

Remington and Lance looked more awake than the rest. Jack appeared to be half asleep, rubbing his eyes as he walked in.

The group of seven reached the University's lobby, where they'd spent the previous day fortifying. The room was large and the ceilings high, and the three large UV spotlights had been placed in different corners. Black sheets were draped over each of them, hiding their true natures. Each were remotely operated, so once the drapes came off, anyone in the room could turn them on. "You're helping?" Remington asked as Frank waddled into the room.

"Trust me, human, I'll be of more help than ye," Frank retorted. He glanced around the room. "I don't suppose anyone has any beer I can drink before this shindig gets started?"

"No, sir," Dean Pritcham replied.

"Everyone has their tools?" Lance asked.

"Not yet, bucko," Jack replied. "I don't know if you've noticed, but we were all woken up barely twenty minutes ago."

"Over here." Remington walked toward the large table in the middle, where a vast array of weapons effective against the undead waited. "Jack, please tell me you have the items we asked you to keep on hand in your room?"

There was a two-pronged approach to the attack plan. The major preparation in the lobby, and then sleeping with weapons near in case the vamps infiltrated the university undetected.

The rest of the group followed Remington over, with Jack responding, "Yeah, it's all up there. The wooden stake. The garlic. The cross that won't work since I can't even remember the Hail Mary from when I was a kid."

Marissa smirked and shook her head. "It's like four sentences."

Jack wiped his eyes as the group looked at the weapons. "I wasn't the best student." He pointed to the crossbow on the table. "That's what I want."

"Probably the best bet," Claire agreed. "Given your arm."

Jack smiled.

Someone cleared their throat from across the room. Everyone at the table jumped, and Claire whipped a wooden stake off the table, ready to stab whoever the hell just entered the lobby.

"Damn it, Byron." Pritcham's hand was over her heart.

"If I'm going to die tonight, I'd prefer it not be from a heart attack."

"Sorry," Dr. Byron murmured sheepishly. He stood just inside the door, having snuck in too quietly for anyone to hear him. When he'd heard about the vampire threat to the city, he'd requested that he move in here. He said it would allow him to study more and travel less, so he had a room here now, like the students.

"My apologies." Byron remained at the door. "I was wondering if I might have a moment with the three students?"

"You're supposed to be downstairs," Remington scolded as he stepped away from the table. "With the students."

Dr. Byron held up his hand as if to acquiesce. "I know. I know. I just wanted to take a few moments to speak to them, and then I'll hustle back down. Scout's honor."

"Let's make this quick," Lance instructed. "We're already past three, and who knows when they're going to attack?"

Claire glanced at Jack and Marissa. They both shrugged, so she started across the room, and they fell in behind her. They reached Dr. Byron in a few seconds and formed a semi-circle around him.

He looked at all three, and when he spoke, his voice was soft. "When I went to war the first time, I was your age. Eighteen. I was scared as hell, as I imagine you might be right now. They put us in a jungle, fighting people we didn't know for a cause I didn't fully understand. But I went, despite being scared."

He shoved his hands into his pockets and paused for a moment.

"If you're scared, that's okay. I don't know if these other

people have been in a war, so this might be their first time as well. What I came here to say is, trust each other. Do your best. Protect the people you care about." He grinned, meeting their eyes with his sweeping gaze. "Oh, and do your best not to die."

Claire grinned back.

"Aye, aye, Captain!" Jack replied with a smile. "Don't die. Check and check."

"All right, go on back, and be ready to kill those blood-suckers." Dr. Byron looked beyond them at the others in the hall. "Thank you. I'll be on my way now."

"Hurry up!" Pritcham shouted back.

Byron said nothing else, only slipped out the door as quietly as he'd entered.

"Don't you think you should be down there as well, Dr. Pritcham?" Remington asked as the students reached the table.

"No, I'll be right here defending the institution I helped build. Now, give me what I need."

The group focused on the table, and Marissa helped hand out the necessary items. A bag of garlic. Everyone got a cross that hung around their necks. Two stakes apiece strapped into leather holsters at their sides. The FBI agents passed out vials of holy water, and everyone stored them in their belt loops. It was an easy pull—you simply ripped the bottle off and the top would pop off.

Jack turned away from the table and looked out the large bay windows. "You see that?"

Claire did the same. "Yes, I do," she whispered.

The room had grown darker, although the lights still burned above them.

"It's a powerful one." Marissa moved closer to Claire, her hand reaching down to grip the stake on her right. "He's pulling clouds across the moon."

"I hope it's Dracula." Jack's hand held onto the garlic pouch. "Because if that asshole woke me up this early, he's definitely going to die tonight."

"Not Dracula," a voice boomed from all around. It seemed to exude from even the *walls*. "You can call me David, and I definitely think you should try to kill me for waking you from your slumber. I look forward to it."

Frank grabbed a stake from the table; he was the only one that they hadn't made holsters for. "Come on in, creature. I'm tired of waiting. There's beer to be had when we're finished."

Something dark dropped outside the window. It landed softly, and Claire saw it was a person, or at least shaped like one. No human could survive such a quick drop, at least not without breaking bones.

The figure landed on a knee and then stood. The bay windows held a single door, and it swung open of its own volition.

"Nice cape," Jack remarked as the creature stepped through the doorway. "You guys must be big on theatrics."

"I didn't know there would be such a large welcoming party." The vampire smiled, surveying the group in front of him, his eyes landing on each individual. "I'd hoped I could slip in and out without causing much of a fuss." He didn't appear worried in the slightest, but rather seemed amused by everything. As if this was all a joke.

"You probably should have brought backup," Jack said.

The group grew tighter together, forming a straight line where they stood shoulder to shoulder.

"Who says I didn't?"

Four more dark figures dropped from the darkness, all landing as softly as the first vampire. They stood as one, then walked through the doorway to form a large half-circle behind their leader.

"How should we do this?" the first vampire asked, turning a palm up into the air. "Would you like to just present us with your necks?" He lifted his other palm. "Or do we want to tussle first?"

Claire watched Frank slip behind her quietly. He gave her left calf a light pinch and she knew what to do, stepping closer to Marissa on her right and filling in the space. She didn't know exactly what he was up to, but she trusted him.

Claire unsheathed one of her stakes and gripped the garlic in her left hand. "Why don't you see if you can get to my neck first?"

"So be it," he answered with a smile. The vampires spread out and moved across the large expanse of floor, the leader in front.

Okay, Claire thought. *Time to organize ourselves quickly.*

"Jack, get in the back and fire that damned crossbow," she demanded. "Dr. Pritcham, you're on water duty. Spray it around this place like you work for the fire department."

Pritcham dashed back to the table, where more vials of holy water sat.

Claire headed straight for the main vampire. *You're mine.*

He smiled as she approached, spreading his arms out to throw his cape behind his back.

Claire couldn't worry about what anyone else was doing. They were all as trained as they were going to be. Time to get to business.

She brought the garlic up and the vampire hissed, revealing his fangs as his face stretched in a grimace.

"Come on. You're not scared of a little seasoning, are you?" Claire swept the stake forward with her right hand, knowing it wouldn't mortally wound the creature. She only wanted to keep him at a distance.

The vampire easily dodged the blow by moving his head back slightly. His hand darted forward, his nails daggers beneath the bright lights. They cut into Claire's hand, the one holding the garlic. Blood spurted onto the floor.

"Oh, you sonofabitch!" Claire snapped, her eyes alight and her hand burning with pain. She still held onto the garlic.

"Back up, bitch!" the vampire hissed, looking to his right. Dean Pritcham had approached softly, but she didn't waste time with words. She flung the holy water at the undead monster.

It hit his face and the flesh started sizzling, just as Claire had seen in the club. Bright red gashes appeared where the water seared him, and his hands jerked up to his face. The water coated them as well, his palms burning.

"Keep going!" Claire shouted.

Dean Pritcham didn't hesitate. She flung more water from the vials, dousing the vampire with it.

His screams filled the hall, drowning out the sounds of

scuffles elsewhere. Claire dashed forward, moving faster than anyone else in the room besides these vampires. She dropped the bag of garlic, wrapped both hands around the stake, and lifted it above her head. She brought it down hard, plunging it into the creature's heart.

The vampire didn't even see it coming because his hands still covered his face. His arms fell to his side, and his eyes grew wide as his mouth fell open.

Claire stepped back and watched the creature twitch for a second, unable to pull away from it.

My first one. My first kill of these evil things.

The lead vampire fell, landing with a thud on the floor, the stake wobbling in his chest.

"Come on, there are more." Dean Pritcham grabbed Claire's shoulder, breaking the dead vampire's spell over her.

Claire whirled in time to see Jack's crossbow bolt miss his target by mere inches. Claire immediately saw the problem—her group was fighting with their backs to Jack, meaning he had to miss *them* before hitting the vampires.

Claire found Marissa next.

The girl was retreating fast, the vampire slashing and hissing at her. Marissa tried to parry a blow with her stake, but the vampire slapped it to the ground and sent it skidding across the floor. Marissa was fast, if not as fast as Claire, and she reached for her second stake, but the vampire grabbed her wrist.

"Time's up," he hissed.

No, it's not! Claire's mind screamed. Her feet carried her across the floor as if she were floating.

The vampire leaned forward to bite. Marissa was paralyzed with fear, her eyes large as she watched the fangs come for her neck.

Claire leapt onto the creature's back, not knowing what else to do. She hadn't even considered her stake. She'd only been concerned with stopping the vampire. She wrapped her arm around his neck, trying to choke him.

The vampire reached up and grasped her forearm in his iron grip.

He yanked Claire forward, pulling her over his head. Claire groaned as her body slammed to the floor. Stars danced over her vision as pain bloomed across her body.

Marissa suddenly appeared above her. The vampire had her by the hair and stared down with a sick grin.

"You killed one of us," he said. "Now you'll watch me kill one of you."

He wrenched Marissa's head back, revealing her neck. Claire stared, the wind knocked from her lungs, barely able to make noise. She couldn't do anything. She couldn't t help her friend.

"Lass, hit it!" Frank's voice boomed across the lobby.

Claire's eyes narrowed. She knew what he meant. She now knew why he'd slipped out behind her.

God bless that little green bastard, she thought, hoping she wasn't too late.

Her hand shot into her pocket, and she pressed the remote's button.

Light flashed out from three different corners of the room. It was so bright, it felt like actual stars were burning inside the hall. Claire had to squint to see, but her ears worked just fine.

She didn't hear the *light*, but rather its effects.

The vampires' screams echoed off the high ceiling. The one holding Marissa dropped her immediately and wrapped his arms around his face as his skin burned worse than it would have with holy water.

Claire rolled over and tried to climb to her feet. The four remaining vampires were retreating, trying to find the door or a window they could shatter to escape through.

"I don't think so." Jack stepped up next to Claire and aimed the crossbow. He let a wooden stake fly, and it landed in its target.

The vampire stopped retreating and fell to the floor. The bolt's impact caused him to slide three feet before he finally came to a stop.

Jack reloaded quickly and pulled the trigger again. Another vampire dropped to the ground. "You idiots should have just let me shoot them all. I'm twice as good as any of you."

Claire was on one knee now and looking at the two remaining vampires. One was a male, one a female. Neither had any idea what was happening around them. They couldn't handle the light now shining—ultra-powerful UV radiation lamps.

"We need to capture one," Claire croaked.

Jack looked at her with a raised eyebrow. "Huh?"

"Can't kill them all. We need to get information." She nodded at Remington and Lance, who were slowly circling the two remaining creatures.

They appeared to have had the same idea as Claire. They were trying to figure out some way to capture one of the burning vampires.

"I got 'em." Jack looked down the crossbow's scope and

pulled the trigger. The female vampire hit the ground. He glanced at Claire and winked. "Watch this freakin' skill." He loaded the crossbow with another stake from his belt and let it fly, and it hit the last vampire's leg, dropping him to the floor. He loaded again and hit the other leg.

Damn, he's good with that thing, Claire thought.

The vampire was on the ground, burning alive with smoke fluttering into the air around him.

"Got 'em." Jack lowered the crossbow and reached down to offer Claire a hand. He pulled her to her feet as Remington and Lance fell on the injured vampire.

Frank waddled over to the group of three, Dean Pritcham joining them as they watched the two FBI agents subdue the screaming creature.

"I kind of feel bad for him," Marissa admitted.

Frank looked up at her. "Pretty, but not many brains." He shook his head. "One of them almost drank from yer neck, lass. No pity for the wicked."

"Come on, you lazy bastards. Let's go help them." Jack walked forward, neither injured nor out of breath.

Claire looked at Marissa, blood dripping from her hand. "Must have been nice to sit back there and watch us do all the freakin' work."

CHAPTER NINETEEN

The room in front of Hannah appeared to be full of electricity. Or rather, a wall of electricity stood in front of her and her two compatriots.

A single light bulb glowed overhead, although it was unnecessary now. The electrical wall in front of her shone brighter than the bulb could. Hannah's eyes glowed with the wall's reflection, and she paid no attention to the other two in the room. She was only concerned with the wall.

With the Veil.

A black globe sat on a small table to her left. It hummed with energy, but Hannah hardly heard it. As long as it kept working, everything she wanted would be right in front of her. There were other ways to summon creatures from across the Veil, but none were as sophisticated as the globe.

The electricity crackled, which it made the fine hairs on her arms rise.

Come, she thought. *Come through and help us end this.*

Matthew dropped to his knees, folding his hands as if in prayer.

Bradley remained standing on the other side of Matthew, his fat body sweating as if he were on a treadmill. His pits were stained dark, and he had a wet ring around the collar of his black shirt.

The electrical wall picked up in intensity, and the black globe's hum grew louder. It was searching for the being they'd programmed into it. Looking for Dracula, a creature who should only exist in myth, but who was alive in the world beyond the Veil.

The light grew brighter. Hannah squinted but didn't dare cover her eyes with her hand. She didn't want to miss this. They'd worked so hard.

The wall of electricity was no more than a foot thick. It sliced through the middle of the room. It flashed, turning completely to gray static. No one could see through it for a moment, and then it was gone.

Vanished.

In its place stood a creature of singular magnificence. He didn't look like the vampire who had come before him, the one called David. This creature was older, both in looks and in aura. His hair was black and sleek against his skull. He wore a cape, as he did in the myths. His clothes were black, resembling the same suit he would have worn in his castle before Van Helsing rained hell on him.

"Where...is this?" the creature asked in a heavy European accent. He sounded nearly like the Count from *Sesame Street*. "Who are you?"

Hannah dropped to her knees as Matthew had already done. It took Bradley a bit longer, his gut getting in the way of him reaching the floor.

"This is Earth, and we're here to serve you, master," Hannah intoned with her head bowed. "We called you here to serve you."

"It's you the rumors speak of? The reason my vassals are disappearing?" Dracula didn't move but stood staring at his three minions with an eyebrow raised. "It's not only my kind who have been called, but others as well. Many, many others."

Hannah raised her head slightly but didn't meet the vampire's eyes. "There are a lot of things happening between our world and yours, but we, us three, called you specifically. We've been looking for you for years."

"For years?"

Hannah nodded. "Yes. This effort has been long in the making, and we are your loyal servants. We will do as you bid, and all we ask is that when the world is remade in your image, you hold us next to you."

"Hmmm...." The vampire walked to the table on his right and looked down at the now-silent globe. "And the others not like me that were brought here? Do they serve the same purpose?"

"Yes, but not with us. We are here to serve you," Bradley blubbered, sounding like he couldn't get the words out fast enough.

Dracula turned his head slowly and looked at Hannah's partner. "You're a plump one, aren't you?"

A small laugh burst from Hannah's lips, and she was unable to stop it. Bradley was a disgusting blob who she tolerated because he believed the same as her. Matthew? Even worse, but in personality and not looks.

"Why should I not drink all of your blood and simply go on my way?" the vampire asked.

"You need us." Hannah nodded quickly, hoping to assure this creature of the truth before he ended their lives. "You need humans to help you move around in the world, at least in the beginning."

Dracula turned completely toward them. "True, I don't understand this place. Perhaps you can live until I do. You've brought others over here, others like me. Some were even my children. Where are they?"

"Some are still here, master." Hannah lowered her head further. "Some were killed last night."

"Killed?" the vampire hissed. "Did you fools somehow bring that dastardly Van Helsing over? Is he chasing me again?"

"No-no-no," Matthew stammered. "He's still on your side as far as we know. These are humans that killed them. Humans from Earth. We were-were-were—"

"*Hush!*" Dracula commanded. He slowly walked to the three, stopping just in front of them. "Van Helsing isn't here?"

Hannah stared at his black shoes, shiny beneath the yellow light above. She wanted to bash Matthew's head through the floor. He always sounded so *weak*.

"No," she answered before the stammering idiot Matthew had a chance. "These are humans who have learned about our presence. We tried to preemptively kill them, but we learned early this morning that they killed some of your kind."

The vampire was quiet for a second, and Hannah didn't

dare look up to see his face. She didn't want those eyes to fall on her, freezing her. This was who they'd been searching for, and now that he was in front of them, she felt his power in full.

"They're just kids, master," Bradley babbled from the other side of Matthew.

"Kids?" Dracula asked.

Bradley nodded. "Teenagers. Nothing more."

The vampire started laughing. It was a deep yet raspy thing. It went on for a few moments and then finally died away. "Children... Children are killing my kind?"

Hannah didn't know what to say. She didn't want to affirm the answer and end up with two holes in her neck.

Dracula stepped away, his heels clicking softly on the concrete floor as he did.

He walked around behind the three kneeling worshippers, which made Hannah even more nervous. She couldn't see him. She didn't know what he was doing.

"Where are we?" Dracula asked.

"A city called Boston, in the United States. We're underground," Hannah answered. "In abandoned subways."

"That's smart. Perhaps you are all not complete idiots after all." The vampire chuckled. "No matter about these children. I will vanquish them. Rise, and go bring me my kind. We will prepare for this battle, and then I'll do what I should have done with Van Helsing."

Hannah closed her eyes and sighed softly. This creature wasn't anything to mess with. She heard Matthew whimper quietly.

Is he going to piss himself? she wondered and smiled

inwardly. *Maybe Dracula will get tired of his weakness, and then I won't have to deal with it anymore.*

Claire, Melissa, and Jack were still in the lobby they'd used for the fight. Twelve hours had passed, and the three of them were still exhausted. It had taken a few hours for their nerves to allow them to sleep, but eventually they had.

Frank waddled into the room, his voice slashing through the silence. "Time to wake up, lazies."

Claire groaned, rolling over on the couch she was using. "Go away, Frank."

"What's the saying you have here? No rest for the weary? Well, that's the truth, lass," Frank grabbed Claire's feet and yanked them off the couch, causing her to either sit up or fall off.

"Damn it, Frank." She flipped up on the couch, drowsily rubbing her eyes. Her arm was bandaged from where the vampire had cut her. "What are you doing? We're trying to sleep."

The leprechaun stood in front of her, an amber beer in his right hand.

"Where did you get that?" Jack asked from across the room. He slowly sat up, leaning forward and putting his elbows on his knees.

Frank turned partly around and raised the glass to him. "If you look hard enough, lad, you can find anything. Just need a little faith, persistence, and luck." He took a sip, then turned back to Claire. "They've gotten some information out of the vamp. That's why you gotta wake up. There's more work to do."

Jack groaned loudly, his voice echoing across the room. "These people are slave drivers. They don't stop. Just go, go, go." He rubbed his eyes with his palms but didn't stand up.

Claire looked at the third couch, where Marissa was waking up. "How are you feeling?"

Marissa sat up, looking the most disheveled Claire had ever seen her. "My scalp hurts like hell, and so does my arm. But I'm all right."

"She complains about *her* arm," Jack grumbled. "I'm the one with stitches." He stood up and stretched, giving another groan as he did. "Just kidding, Sissy. You did a good job. You both did. I did the best job, but that's to be expected. I'm a guy."

Marissa raised an eyebrow. "Sissy?"

Jack shrugged. "Seems to fit on multiple levels. You're as scared as anyone I've ever met, and you're becoming like a sister to me. Plus, 'Marissa' has too many syllables."

"You're a Jack-ass." Claire stood up too. "I'm not even going to dignify the chauvinistic comment with a response. Just know if it wasn't for us, you'd be a corpse right now."

"Or walking around looking for something to suck," Frank added with a mischievous grin. "Not that there's anything wrong with that."

Jack and Marissa walked toward Claire to form a half-circle in front of Frank. "Where are Remington and Lance?"

Frank took a step back. "They just finished with the vamp. They're coming upstairs now."

"Did they kill it?" Marissa asked.

"Frank didn't ask, and they didn't tell. I asked where beer was, then did my part to relieve this establishment of such a valuable substance. If people were to know about the stores of alcohol in this place, it could quickly become a target for scoundrels and thieves." Frank winked at Claire. "That we don't want." He drained the remainder of the beer and belched. "All right, lad and lasses, Frank needs more beer."

"Your liver is going to give out on you," Marissa told him. She looked at Claire. "You let him drink like this, and he's your best friend?"

Frank raised a finger. "First, I don't like this lass. She's rude, crude, and socially unacceptable. I deal with only the highest class of people. Second, how do you know leprechauns even have livers?"

Marissa opened her mouth to say something but paused. She grinned. "Do you?"

"We could always dissect him to find out." Claire jarred Frank lightly with her elbow. "Okay, where are the alphabet boys?"

"Alphabet boys?" Frank asked with a confused look.

Claire rolled her eyes. "You don't know everything, little green man. FBI, FBI, NSA. The alphabet boys. Where are they?"

"This way, lass." Frank started walking and called back over his shoulder. "You see why I don't like her? She's always got something smart to say."

"Only because she's smart!" Marissa called.

"She wishes," Frank retorted with a chuckle.

Claire smiled, and the group of three followed Frank

out of the lobby. The vampire bodies had all been removed. Besides the weapons and huge lights, the place looked as if nothing had happened at all.

"You both feel okay?" Marissa whispered, slowing down to let Frank get farther ahead.

"What do you mean?" Jack asked.

Marissa frowned. "I mean, with what we did. We killed those things last night, and now one of them might be being *tortured*."

"It's most definitely being tortured!" Frank clarified cheerfully.

"You heard me?" Marissa asked.

Frank nodded without turning around. "Of course. Leprechauns are better at everything than humans."

"It doesn't matter," Claire patted Marissa's hand. "He's good people. No, I don't feel bad about it. Do you?"

"I don't know what to feel," Marissa answered.

Jack took hold of Marissa's hand and pulled her to a stop. He looked Marissa right in her eyes. "No. I don't feel sorry for those creatures at all. First, I'm not even sure how real they are. It's a mind-fuck to think about, considering whether they exist, what they know, where they came from if not from our freakin' heads. So I don't know if they're real like you and I are, or if they're just smoke and mirrors. Second, what I do know is my arm has a scar on it, and while I think it's going to be a good story to pick up chicks in the future, I know that thing was trying to kill me. Those things last night? They would have laid waste to every one of us if they'd been able to without a second thought. They're evil, and they're invading my fucking *world*."

This was the first time Claire had seen Jack so serious. She was sort of taken back, but also proud of him.

"So no, Sissy. Don't you start feeling bad for those evil bloodsuckers. If one of them shows their head, put a stake through it."

Marissa gave a sly smile. "It wouldn't kill them, you dolt."

Jack smiled back, his seriousness breaking. "Maybe you couldn't kill 'em like that, but I could."

"He's right," Claire agreed. "I don't feel bad, and you can't either, not if we're going to make it out of this alive. They're the enemy. Frank up there, yeah, I wouldn't harm a hair on his green head, whether or not he's from this world or not. Them? I'm going to hunt every last one of them down until I find the people bringing them over."

Marissa looked at her feet and nodded. "You're right. They would have killed all three of us last night. There's nothing to feel bad about."

"You're damn right, there isn't," Frank called from far ahead. He'd stopped and turned around, one hand on his hip, the other holding his empty glass. "No one better touch my hair. It looks too good. Now hurry up. We've got work to do. Or ye do. I've got beer to drink."

The three followed Frank around a corner and then down another hallway. Claire didn't know exactly where they were since she hadn't been in this part of the building much.

They turned another corner and saw their trainer, Dr. Kilgore, standing outside of a room.

"You aren't to go into this room. Nothing good to see,"

the trainer told them as they approached. "Go to the end of hallway. Door on the right."

Frank kept leading, and Claire looked at the closed door. *So that's where they have the vampire. It's still in there.*

A chill rolled across her as they passed it, knowing how dangerous the creatures were. *We stopped them, though,* she thought. *With a little forethought and courage, we stopped them all.*

They reached the door Kilgore directed them to and Frank opened it wide. "Ah, Remington, you're a good lad." The room was almost completely empty. A beer keg sat in the corner and there were five chairs against the wall, but other than that, nothing. Just white walls, Remington, and Lance.

Frank grinned and walked over to the corner of the room where the keg was. He pumped it hard a few times and filled his glass.

"I figured all that walking to get them would make ya thirsty, Frank," Remington joked. "So we wanted to make sure you had reserves ready."

"You know me as well as I know myself." Frank pointed to Claire. "Go on. I woke the lazies up. Tell 'em what they need to know."

"Where's Dean Pritcham?" Claire asked.

"She's still got the school to run. We had some new recruits coming in today to replace you three."

Jack raised both eyebrows. "Replace? That means we're leaving, and if you think I won't sue the federal government for every penny it earns each year in taxes, you've got the wrong person."

Lance smiled; it was the first time Claire had seen him

do it. Remington showed a lot more personality than Lance, but Claire liked the smile. It lit his face and made him appear younger.

"Anyone ever tell you that you're a jackass?" Lance asked.

Jack cracked his own grin. "Just these two every hour or so."

"No," Remington said. "We've got no plans for you leaving. There are talks at higher levels than you three can imagine about what to do with you. The way you performed last night was amazing, and with the green munchkin back there throwing in his weight—"

"Leprechaun," Frank corrected casually before taking a sip of his beer.

"Well, with him helping, you four were lethal. Lance and I didn't do much except keep from dying. You three... Well, we knew what we were doing when we picked you and put you together. So just know that you're important to the operation. No suing necessary."

Remington nodded toward Jack, and Claire understood he was giving them respect. Everyone in the room was tried and tested now according to the FBI agents.

"Okay, let's get on with it," Remington said. He walked over to the keg and picked up an empty glass from the floor.

Claire noticed his dress for the first time, seeing that he was in a t-shirt and basketball shorts. Tennis shoes too. She'd never seen him look so casual, not even last night at the fight.

You don't torture a vampire into giving you what you want wearing a suit and tie, she thought.

Remington filled the glass and handed it to Lance. He grabbed a third one, filled it, and took a sip. "Sorry, kids. You may serve your country, but the drinking age is twenty-one. I don't make the rules, I just follow 'em."

Jack rolled his eyes.

Remington continued, "We know where the cult is. We know a lot more now than we did before, thanks to our friend in the other room."

"How did you get it out of him?" Jack asked.

Remington took a small sip of the beer. "Well, we tried a lot of ways, but in the end, we used light. Those damned things *hate* light worse than Frank hates being sober."

"Doubtful," Frank disagreed, leaning against the keg.

"With enough light, they'll tell us whatever we want to know," Remington continued. "The cult is three people, or this sect, at least. Two men and a woman. The leading vampire was the one you killed, Claire, although the cult treated him as someone beneath them, more or less."

"How did they get the vampires to do what they wanted?" Claire asked.

"Sounds like they threatened to send them back across the Veil."

Frank's eyebrows raised. "That's possible?"

Marissa shook her head. "The vampire wouldn't know. It's only going to know what it's been threatened with. Maybe it's possible, maybe it's not."

"Told you," Lance remarked to Remington, clearly talking about how smart she was.

"Yeah, she's right," Remington commented. "It doesn't matter right now. We'll figure that all out later. In Boston, there are miles and miles of unused tunnels. Goes back to the fifties and sixties when politicians started all kinds of projects to get elected, but they never finished them because they ran out of budget. The cult somehow infiltrated them, and that's where they are. We got the vampire to map it out, though we obviously can't trust it completely."

He paused and took a deeper sip.

Looks like what he's going to tell us next is harder than what he just told us, Claire thought.

"You three, and Frank here if he wants, have to go into those tunnels. We're not sure if they pulled over Dracula, but the vampire thinks it's possible. Something was supposed to happen today. You've got to go in there, kill Dracula, and apprehend the cult members. You can kill them if you have to, but it's much better if you bring them out alive."

Remington looked at the three, his eyes deadly serious.

Frank took a sip of his beer. "Sounds easy. Just one problem, Frank won't be able to make it. Got a date and other stuff I need to do."

Claire ignored him, her eyes narrowing. "Us three? That's all you're sending in there? We've got a school with nine other kids, plus three new recruits, and whatever other power the FBI has. But it's us three you're sending?"

Remington shrugged, no kindness in his eyes. "Plus Frank."

"That's *bullshit.*" The steel in Claire's spine was firming up again. She wasn't scared. She just wouldn't let her crew get slaughtered. "We're walking into forgotten tunnels in pitch black with the undead roaming around. There's no way we make it out. Why aren't *you* all coming?"

"Told you," Lance said. "Stubborn as a mule. We can't go, Claire, because we don't know what else is there. What if we can't see them at all? You three didn't see what we did back in that lobby, but I didn't see fangs until the thing was attacking me. It looked *normal* to me. There are myths about creatures that literally *trick* people into seeing something that isn't there, like a beggar, or a little child. That, combined with our inability to already identify the creatures, would surely result in our deaths. That's why you're here. All of you. Because you *can* see them."

Remington swirled the beer in his cup, looking down at it. "The sad fact is, we're not like you three. We saw the vampires when our lives depended on it, but now?" He looked up. "We're not there yet. Our brains simply can't see them like you can. Not yet. Maybe not ever. Both of us." He moved the cup back and forth between Lance and himself. "We both want to see. We both want to be down there with you. But all it takes, Claire, is one of us to mess up once. We see someone we think is a Myther, and we kill them? Then what? Then we've killed an innocent, and that can't happen."

Lance took a step forward. "We want to go. Neither of us wants to let you all go down there alone. That's not the way this works, though. It's why the government has spent millions on this school and training you three. You're our weapon against this invasion. You're our first and last line of defense. Right now, Remington and I can't fight this war. Maybe not ever."

Jack reached up and touched Claire's shoulder.

Her anger was hot, but it cooled some at her teammate's touch. "This feels like a suicide mission."

"Lass." Frank had turned back to the keg and was refilling his beer. He spoke as if he hadn't a care in the world. "This isn't impossible, and if you're nice to old Frank, I'll cancel my other plans and go down there with the three of ye. We can beat Dracula." He turned around and leaned against the keg. "I saw him once."

"Bullshit," Jack said.

"I tell ye true." Frank took a short sip. "The old-timers like him all live in one area, and I saw him at the market. He doesn't look like any of those cute vampires from downstairs or the ones in that book *Twilight*. This man is a scary one, at least looks-wise." He pointed a finger at Claire. "Now ye may be scared, lass, that you'll die if ye go down there. I'm not. I took one look at that old man and knew I could square up with him anywhere. Vampires have nothing on us leprechauns. He doesn't want any piece of Frank, that I tell ye true."

"You scared, Claire?" Jack asked with a hint of humor. "Going to let the creature who can't see over the counter at the bank be braver than you?"

"Fear's got nothing to do with it, and you all know it. I don't want to send you two down in there if there's no way we're coming out." Claire kept her eyes on Remington. "I want to hear you say it since this is your operation. You tell us you really believe we're getting out."

"I believe it." Remington's eyes kept a level look at Claire. "I've got faith in the three of you, and even the green thing behind me. No doubt about it. I'm not sending anyone to die."

"Green thing. You're a bunch of colorless wannabe

giants." Frank lifted his arm into the air, showing off his skin. "I've got the greatest pigment out of all of us."

Claire took a step back and her two partners turned to her, forming a circle. "You two are in? You're both willing to go down there and fight this thing?"

"If we don't," Marissa countered. "Who will?"

That's the truth, Claire thought. *Because the fate of this city is coming down to us three. No one else is showing up. No one else is going down into those tunnels.*

She looked down at her shoes and nodded, mainly to herself. "You're right." She raised her head and looked past Marissa and Jack to Remington. "Okay. We'll do it. But I want more than stakes and garlic."

Remington winked at her. "I thought you'd say that."

"What's this?" Claire asked.

"This is a part of the university we don't show to very many people," Dr. Pritcham answered. "In fact, you're the first people besides the FBI and me to see it. Not even the professors have been here, save one."

"Okay?" Claire's eyebrows were raised as she looked at the doors in front of her. "What is it?"

The doors weren't like any other doors inside the university. While the rest opened and closed on hinges as you would expect house doors to do, these were sliding glass doors like you'd see at shopping centers. The glass was an opaque gray, and Claire couldn't see anything on the other side.

"This is where we work on more advanced items.

Things that we haven't had to use yet, but we think we might." Dr. Pritcham held a small remote in her hand. The doors still hadn't opened. "What you'll see in here are a lot of prototypes. Regardless, you're not to tell anyone of this. No one else in your class is to know about it."

She turned around and looked at the three students standing behind her. Frank and the FBI agents made up the rear.

"You understand?" she asked. "The secrecy of these weapons is paramount."

"If you trust us to go kill Dracula," Jack said, "then you'll have to trust that we won't tweet about your gadgets."

A faint smile pricked at Dr. Pritcham's lips. "True enough." She turned back around and faced the door.

"Frank!" Claire called over her shoulder. "Keep your hands in your pockets. Don't even think about grabbing anything that's not yours."

"I'll stun him if he tries," Lance told them.

Not sure if he's kidding, Claire thought. *But it would serve Frank right.*

"Ye all have the wrong idea of me." Frank waved his hand. "I'm an upstanding citizen."

Dr. Pritcham pressed the button on the remote, and the opaqueness of the doors fell away as they slid open to reveal a man standing directly on the other side.

"Hello, Dr. Pritcham." The man's accent was crisp and English. "I am glad you have brought me some students."

"This is Dr. Mitchen." Dr. Pritcham stepped to the side, letting the three students get a look at him. "He is in charge of research and development. This is his laboratory. The people you see behind him are his engineers and technicians."

Claire's eyes grew wide as she looked past Mitchen into the room. *This isn't a room,* she thought. *It's a freakin' factory.*

Rows and rows of long tables lined the floor. Some had computers on them, others workstations, and still others what Claire could only think of as "robotic engineering." People were constantly moving through the place. Claire couldn't count how many people were in it. Some were hunched over desks working. No one was paying attention to the group at the door.

"Ho-lee-shit!" Jack's eyes were as wide as Claire's. "Why haven't we gotten any equipment from here before now?" His voice sounded far away as if he couldn't fully focus on what he was saying.

Remington had the answer. "The moment we understood we were facing vampires, we got to work on weapons that could stop them. However, it took us some time to get it right."

"A few weeks isn't too long if I do say so myself." Dr. Mitchen's voice sounded cheery. "I'm very glad to meet you three. Dr. Pritcham has told me a lot about you. I certainly hope our additions to your arsenal will help bring you home safely. I believe they will."

"Pleased to meet you *four.*" Frank stepped up beside Claire.

Dr. Mitchen's face grew confused, and he looked at Pritcham. "You didn't say four, and he's certainly an odd-looking chap, yes?"

Dr. Pritcham smiled and glanced at Claire.

Frank stepped forward, his fists balled. "'An odd-looking chap?' Is that what this Brit just said?"

Claire reached forward and lightly touched his shoulder. She met Mitchen's eyes. "He's a leprechaun."

Mitchen stared for a moment, his eyes narrowing. Finally, he shook his head. "You're pulling my leg, aren't you?"

Claire looked at Frank. "It's up to you if you want him to see you."

"I could attack him, I suppose," Frank mused, staring up at the man.

"Attack me?" Mitchen asked.

"Then you could see him," Claire said. "He *is* a leprechaun, though."

Mitchen kept looking at Frank. "It's amazing. I believe you, but I can't see him. No green skin. Just an odd-looking man with a large nose."

"Call me odd again and I *will* attack ye," Frank grumbled.

Mitchen nodded, although Claire didn't think he was listening to Frank much. *He's realizing he's actually in front of a Myther,* she thought. *For maybe the first time.*

"Dr. Mitchen?" Remington asked. "Do you think we can get started? Sort of have a city to save."

"Ah, right," Dr. Mitchen responded. He pulled his eyes away from Frank, breaking the spell that had taken hold of him. "Just so remarkable," he commented again. He looked at the three students and clasped his hands together in front of his chest. "Right, right. Vampire hunting. Let's go. I think you're all going to like what I have here for you."

"This is like some James Bond shit," Jack enthused as

the group walked through the doorway. "What's the guy's name from James Bond? The one with all the gadgets?"

"Q, I think," Marissa answered.

"You think he'll get mad if I start calling him that?" Jack asked with a grin.

"Oh, just try to pay attention," Claire grumbled, though she thought the place around her too wondrous to feel any actual animosity.

They made their way past multiple rows of tables, and Mitchen pointed toward the back wall. "There's a door to the right over there that will take you to our server room."

"Server room?" Jack asked.

Mitchen kept leading the way. "Precisely. We need a lot of compute power to do the things we're doing here. We didn't feel safe using a private company, so we built our own."

Claire had no idea where they were going.

Another minute or so passed with the group winding by various tables and people. Claire stared at the things they were working on. Some looked like odd-shaped guns, others little more than circuit boards. She had a million questions but knew to ask any right now would only slow the whole procession down.

"Here we are." Dr. Mitchen came to a stop.

Claire looked over her shoulder at how far they'd come. The sliding doors were closed and once again opaque to the outside world. This room truly was cut off from the entire university. It was a world unto itself.

Claire glanced at the table in front of them.

Dr. Mitchen "The problem with vampires, besides that

they want to drain your blood, is their supernatural abilities."

"You're a smart one, Doc," Jack shot back.

Claire put a not-so-gentle elbow into his ribs.

Mitchen ignored Jack's barb and continued on in his cheery tone, "So when we began creating weapons to fight them, that was what we primarily focused on. How can we give *you* supernatural abilities? It was a very interesting question to ask, and a challenging one to answer. I think we did it, though. Answered the question, I mean."

Frank stepped up to the table, pushing past Claire. His head was about a foot above it. "Enough with all the talk. Tell me what we're looking at."

"Right. Right." Mitchen pointed at a small circular object on the table. It looked like a thick compass, except where the face should be, it was just black glass. "We call this a Nova, although that's just because I like fancy names." He picked it up in his hand and turned to the group. "This is a smaller-sized version of the lights you used upstairs when the creatures came. It fits in the palm of your hand, but the blast it sends out is extremely concentrated, meaning as the light spreads out away from your hand, it's not going to dissipate. These will light a very large area of space, and any vampire in its radius is going to wish they'd worn sunscreen."

Jack smirked and glanced at Claire. She knew he wanted to say something about the lame joke. He kept quiet, though.

Mitchen replaced the Nova on the table. "That's going to create space between you and the creatures. However, you might be tempted to simply turn it on and walk, keeping them at bay at all times. I would caution you against it since that's only going to make it harder to find them." Mitchen leaned forward and picked up what appeared to be a black metal rod. "I heard that one of you actually managed to shove a stake through a vampire's chest plate last night. Is that true?"

Marissa nodded. "Yup. That was Claire."

Jack spoke up. "Well, I did it, too."

Marissa rolled her eyes. "Yeah, with a freakin' crossbow. She did it with her hands."

"That's more impressive than you probably realize." Mitchen turned, creating space for himself and the black rod. "The chest plate is bone, and we wanted to give you an advantage when you get close enough to attack. We also wanted to allow you to not have to be right next to the creature."

Mitchen moved his hand so that the tip of the rod faced the wall. His thumb pressed the opposite end. A black object shot from the opening, flew through the air, and slammed into the wall twenty feet away. It sank so deep into the concrete that only a small piece was still visible.

Claire's mouth opened slightly. "It's like a blowpipe activated by your hand."

"Precisely," Mitchen agreed. "The main thing you need to do with this weapon is aim."

"Yeah, but once you shoot it, you're out of stakes," Jack observed. "So you have to make sure you hit on the first try."

"Erroneous, my dear chap." Mitchen reached into his pocket and pulled out a black stake that was about six inches long. He popped into the rod, an audible click letting everyone know it had hit home. "What you have to do is reload, but with a bit of practice, you can get it down to about one second. The good thing is, with this, you won't have to be directly on the vampire, so reloading is possible. I call it the Impaler."

"Any other problems you see?" Claire asked Jack sarcastically.

He shrugged. "Just making sure they've thought through everything."

Mitchen placed the Impaler back on the table. "Everyone here knows what mace is, I assume?"

Frank looked up at the doctor. "We're not all from here, Mitchen. So no, I don't."

Mitchen looked curiously at the odd man. "Very true. My apologies."

"Apologies! That's the first time one of you humans has done that." He turned to Claire. "You could learn a thing or two from this man."

Mitchen seemed to not notice Frank's show. "Mace is something law enforcement uses to subdue people. It's an irritant that we put into aerosol form. Holy water is something like mace gas for vampires, although it's more damaging. That's what we have here." He picked up a small cartridge sitting next to the Impaler. "Want to be my test dummy?"

Before Jack could answer, Mitchen pressed down on the cartridge and a concentrated spray shot out. Jack raised his hands to try to block it but couldn't do anything quickly enough. The spray hit him in the face just as his features turned to complete fear.

He was prepared for pain.

He blinked as the liquid dripped down on his face, his mouth open, ready to scream.

"Looks like you're not a vampire." Mitchen grinned.

"What the hell?" Jack asked as he wiped the water from his face.

Mitchen again ignored him, looking at the rest of the group. "Now, had he been a vampire, his face would be burning. We've acquired a large quantity of blessed water and turned it into an aerosol spray. You don't have to throw anything at the creatures, hoping the water hits them. Just point and spray."

Jack finished wiping off his face.

Claire grinned at him. "Did you get a bit scared, Jack-ass?"

"Thought the guy just maced me," he grumbled.

"Moving right along." Mitchen put the aerosol can back on the table. "The last thing we wanted to combat was their speed and strength. This was a much more complicated endeavor since we can't build you exoskeleton suits that might give you superhuman abilities. So the next obvious question was, how do we slow them down? How do we make them weaker?"

"Not a problem for me," Frank said. "I took it easy on them upstairs, wanting to give these young whippersnappers some confidence." He pointed a thumb at his chest. "I won't need any assistance in slowing them down. When I get up and running, they're going to wish they'd slowed *me* down."

"Is that why I caught you the first time we met, Frank?" Claire asked.

The leprechaun paid her no mind. "You'll see, Chatty Cathy."

Mitchen looked at Frank as if he were viewing an alien. Something technically possible, but not something he ever thought he'd see. "Very well, then." He smiled and looked back at the table. He grabbed a blue ball about the size of a tennis ball. "I call this the Immolator. The name is sort of apt for what it does." He turned to Jack. "Want to be my guinea pig for this?"

"If you do it, we're fighting," Jack warned.

"Oh, come on, Jack," Claire teased. "You can give it, but you can't take it?"

"*You* be his guinea pig," Jack returned.

"Hard pass." She smiled and found Mitchen's eyes. "Sorry, please continue."

"Anyone know what the one thing is you haven't used against vampires, but that they are susceptible too?" Mitchen asked as he looked over the three.

"Fire," Marissa answered. "There are some myths that say fire can actually kill them. At the very least, it hurts."

"Bingo." Mitchen lifted the ball in front of his face. "We're not sure if it will kill them or not, but we do believe it's going to incapacitate them. The problem with this, however, is that fire will also incapacitate you as well. Or, obviously, worse." He offered the ball to Claire.

"Is it going to set me on fire?" she asked skeptically as she eyed the blue orb.

"I'd like you to demonstrate how to work it." Mitchen pushed the ball forward again.

Claire took it very gently.

"You need to think of it like a grenade, only without the

explosion," Mitchen told her. "If you operate it under that line of thought, you're going to be safe. Now, Claire, squeeze the ball hard. After you do it, throw it at the wall over there. You'll have four seconds from the time you squeeze until it detonates."

Claire stared at the thing. *What the hell is about to happen to me?*

"Who's scared now?" Jack teased.

Claire shrugged, squeezed the ball hard, and threw it overhand at the wall.

Four, three, two—

It hit the wall, and fire blazed across the concrete surface. The ball dropped to the floor, a burning orb now. It rolled away, although the ground didn't catch on fire.

The wall continued to burn.

Claire stared at the flames, which were spreading in a circle with a diameter of about five feet. "I can feel the heat."

"That's actually an engineering masterpiece." Another blue ball rested on the table and Mitchen picked it up. "The ball is capable of telling which way it's being thrown, and after four seconds, it sprays an accelerant *in front* of it. Then its internal reactions cause it to burst into flames. Thus, any vampires you throw it toward are going to be doused with gasoline and immediately hit with a fireball." Mitchen grinned as two workers went to the wall and started spraying it down with fire extinguishers. "It should slow the bloodsuckers down a bit."

"I like that," Jack told him. "I like that a lot."

Remington spoke from behind the group, a smile on his

face. "I told you guys. You're not going into those tunnels with just your hands."

Frank pointed at the table. "I want one of those light things and the Impaler. Give the kiddos the rest."

"Frank, hold up a second." Claire stepped out of her room and closed the door behind her. The sun was down, and Marissa had already climbed into bed. Everyone was exhausted. She could tell how tired Frank was because he hadn't teleported from the building but was actually walking out. Teleporting took more energy.

Frank turned around. "What is it, lass? I need a beer and some shuteye."

Claire nodded and hustled down the hall to him. "Sorry. I just... Why are you coming down there with us? I know you're not doing it all for ale. So why risk it? You don't have to. I won't think any less of you."

Frank looked up at Claire, his shaggy black eyebrows contrasting with his green skin. "I thought you were brighter than this."

Claire shrugged. "I'm too tired to verbally jab with you right now. I just wanted to say I never expected you to come with us. You've already helped a tremendous amount."

Frank sighed and looked at his feet. "I'm not doing this for beer, lass. I didn't come to Boston for better beer or bowling alleys. Will I take that?" He shrugged. "Sure." His eyes found Claire's again. "I came up here and I'm going down *there* because of you. Because you were my friend when no one else would be. Because when the world wanted me to die, you ate french fries and watched me bowl. Now things want *you* to die, and I'm not going to let that happen. You're my friend, maybe my only friend, so we're going down there together, lass."

Claire felt hot tears in her eyes. Before they could fall, she took Frank in her arms and hugged him tightly.

"Thanks, Frank. You're my best friend too."

"Calm yerself, lass," Frank said, although he put his arms around her. "And don't tell a soul about this. I've got a reputation to uphold."

CHAPTER TWENTY

"What have we gotten ourselves into?" Matthew's hands were shaking, and he was rocking back and forth in his chair.

Like some kind of invalid, Hannah thought. "Shut up, Matthew. I don't want to hear it."

She pulled a cigarette from her pack and lit it. She inhaled the smoke, feeling the familiar burn. *I wonder if vampires can do anything about cancer. Or, if I have to become one to rid myself of it.* Hannah didn't have cancer, though she thought she certainly would at some point.

Still, she wasn't going to quit smoking.

"This isn't what we planned," Matthew complained, ignoring her instructions. "We thought we'd be, I don't know... Appreciated."

The wuss did have a point, and Hannah wasn't exactly sure how to get out of this situation.

She, Bradley, and Matthew were still underground in the tunnels, but they'd been relegated to a single room. They hadn't seen Dracula once since he'd shoved them in here. No, now lackeys came to deliver their food or allow them to use the restroom. Dracula had nothing to do with them.

Matthew stared despondently at the floor. "They're going to kill us."

"Give it a rest," Bradley grumbled.

At least he hasn't cracked yet, Hannah thought.

"They're not going to kill us," Hannah told them pensively. She took a drag on the cigarette. "Did you see that, though? How quickly they all came to him? David was barely able to hold them together, and as soon as word spread Dracula was here, they flocked down to these tunnels."

"What does that matter?!" Matthew shrieked.

"Oh, I wish they would come kill you," Hannah mumbled. She started to pace the room. Her watch told her they'd been down here almost twenty-four hours. There were three cots against the walls.

Hannah hadn't slept much. "What we need to be focusing on is how we get back in his good graces. Does either of you have any idea why Dracula lost in the myths? Or why vampires rarely won?"

Matthew looked up at her, appearing lost.

Bradley's stomach grumbled. "No, and right now, I don't care. They've got to bring us more food than they have been. That's all I know."

Hannah rolled her eyes, took another drag, and breathed out the smoke. "Because Dracula was *alone.* They're always alone, vampires, so when humans come for them, they don't have enough concentrated power to win. One vampire against a horde of humans will lose, and I think Dracula understands that. That was why he called them, and that was why they came. They don't *want* to lose."

She nodded, not caring if the other two were listening.

"He's smart, and he's planning this out. They're going to win. They'll take over all of Boston, maybe New England. The government will have to bring in the National Guard or the entire military. This is going to be a fucking war zone by the time he's finished."

Yes, she thought. *We're on the right side of this. We just have to find a way to ingratiate ourselves with him.*

She turned around and looked at her two partners, people she wished she'd never teamed up with.

Bradley's stomach rumbled again, but at least he was matching her gaze. "We've got to get in touch with the other cells. We've got to try to get up the ladder to people with more authority. They have no idea what's happening here."

Hannah shook her head. "Come on, Bradley. They aren't idiots. Everyone in our organization is seeing what's on television, the Vampiric invasion. They know about the work we're doing."

"What about now?" Matthew chimed in. "That we're locked up and completely out of power? You think they're sending someone to save us?"

"No," Hannah mused. She flicked the ash from her cigarette on the floor. "Nor should they. That's not how this works, and you know it. We were chosen very specifically to join, and the reason was that we can work independently. If we're overrun by the creatures we call over, then that's on us. Not anyone else inside this organization."

Her eyes narrowed as she stared at Matthew. "How did you get in here? That's the real question I want answered. You're far too weak to be involved in something like this. Just because you believe in them and can see them, it doesn't mean you should be given a place such as you currently have."

"What place is that?" Matthew asked. "Sitting in this room, locked away as potential food sources for the creatures we brought over?"

Bradley turned with a raised eyebrow. "Do you realize what you're saying?"

Matthew looked at the floor again. He gripped his pants, although that didn't stop his hands from shaking. He didn't respond to the question.

"He knows." Hannah sneered. "He's just too scared to admit it. He's forsaking his entire reason for joining this organization. He's turning against those who can rule humanity because he's too scared to stand next to them." She took a few steps closer to Matthew so that she was about a foot away from him. "When this is over, I'm going to make sure you pay for what you just said. We're here to serve, and to serve at our master's feet. The master is Dracula, and if he wants us to sit in this room, then that's what we'll fucking do."

Her voice was ice, and had it not been against the organization's rules, she would have murdered him right then.

The door opened.

Hannah turned and glared at the intruder, her eyes still narrow, her anger still hot. "What?"

A young vampire stood in the doorway, a female. She had dark brown hair and looked to be maybe seventeen years old. Her skin was the color of chalk. "He wants you."

The vampire looked at Hannah like she was a bug, one the vampire wanted to squash.

Hannah's eyes opened slightly. "'He?'"

"Dracula, you fool," the vampire snapped. "Who else?"

She looked at Matthew and smiled. "What was it you were saying a bit ago?"

Matthew was almost as white as the vampire at the door.

"Cat got your tongue?" Hannah asked. She turned to the vampire. The three had decided long ago that the only vampire they would allow to rule them would be Dracula. If they let any vampire besides the Supreme One gain control, they would quickly be relegated to little more than slaves. "Well, errand girl, bring us to him. The next time you snap at me, don't forget that I control how you got here. I control how you are sent back as well."

Hannah looked down at her dwindling cigarette pack and pulled out a second one, trying to portray that she didn't care one way or another what the vampire thought. *I hope she buys it, and I hope Dracula lets me get a new pack of smokes,* Hannah mused. *Or else this room is going to get a whole lot more annoying.*

The two men in the room stood and moved toward the door. Hannah looked up after she'd lit her cigarette. The vampire was staring at her, but she hadn't bared her fangs, so that was probably a good sign. Either the girl believed Hannah or Dracula didn't want them touched. Either way, it was working out.

Hannah followed the group into the main lobby of the

dead subway station. They hopped into the empty tunnel and traveled a ways in the dark, then pulled themselves up to another drop-off station. Dracula had placed them farther away because he needed the space for the vampires he'd brought to him, and now, as Hannah stood in the lobby, she saw how many there were.

"We were so foolish," Matthew murmured as he stared at the ground. "To think we could control this."

It wasn't control we wanted, dumbass, Hannah thought. She didn't say anything, though. She felt confident Matthew would get what was coming to him for his treacherous ways.

They walked through the crowd of vampires.

They're all looking at us, Hannah thought. *They know we're the ones who brought them here. I wonder if they want to thank us or kill us?*

The group finally reached a room off one of the back halls of the subway station. The vampire opened the door but didn't step inside. She simply moved out of the way and glared as Hannah passed her.

"See ya around, darling," Hannah said as she entered.

Dracula was alone in the room.

I feel it, Hannah thought. *I feel his power. It's different than anyone else's. I chose wisely, and Matthew will see that soon.*

"Your thoughts betray you, frightened man." Dracula sat in a chair with one leg crossed over the other. He didn't look up but studied his nails instead. "I heard them as soon as you stepped off the railroad tracks. You think you should not have called me over, yes?"

Hannah forced a smile from her face.

Dracula's eyes darted to her. "Your friend here, she

wants me to hurt you, frightened man. She thinks you have betrayed your oath."

Hannah held the vampire's eyes, although it was tough as hell to do so.

Finally, he looked back at his nails. "I will deal with all this when we are done with these pesky children. I would like to know more about your group since I am coming to believe there are more like you, yes?" He turned his attention to his other hand without looking up.

"Yes, that's true," Hannah answered.

Dracula nodded. "There will be time, then. For now, the children have arrived."

"*Arrived?*" Hannah could hardly believe it. "That's imposs—"

She caught herself before correcting the creature she'd called here to worship.

Dracula shrugged. "Yes. It would seem they somehow got information about your lair, and now they are traversing these tunnels in hopes of finding me. A silly notion at best. I'd planned on going to their homes and killing them with the overwhelming force you see outside this room, but to think they can find me in a lair such as this? I could hide forever, and they would never know it." He looked up and smiled. "I do not wish to hide, though. I wish to end this foolishness so I can get on with my plans of ruling."

Hannah nodded. "That's what we want as well."

Dracula lazily flicked his hand in the air as if swatting at a fly—or Hannah's thoughts. "I called you three here because I want you to join me as we destroy them. I haven't quite figured out what to do with you yet, at least two of you. Frightened man here will meet the demise he deserves for having little faith in my gratitude for bringing me here. In my world, there are checks and balances on what I may do. The different species who live there are powerful enough to hold me back. But here?" Again he waved his hand. "There is nothing that can't be done. They should have firebombed this city, but instead they send children? Humanity is full of idiots, and soon you will be nothing more than a food supply for my offspring and me."

Matthew dropped to his knees, unable to help himself any longer. "Please! Please don't hurt me!"

Dracula glanced at him, his eyes narrowed. "Do not do that. Do not beg. It's unbecoming."

Matthew looked at the floor and sobbed. Dracula turned to Hannah and Bradley. "Okay, fat man and old lady, now we find the children, yes?"

Old lady? Hannah thought. Quickly realizing her thoughts were as apparent to this man as her words, she followed it up with, *I've been called worse. Plus, Bradley is fat as hell.*

Dracula stood from his chair and went to the door. He placed his hand on the doorknob and glanced over his shoulder. "I do not wish to live in these tunnels anymore, so it is good they come. We end this now."

Claire stared down through the manhole.

"You sure this won't drop us into a sewer?" Jack asked from his place next to her. "Because if I go down there and the first thing I smell is shit, I'm coming right back up and beating someone's ass."

The group of four—Claire, Jack, Marissa, and Frank—formed a circle around the open manhole. Remington and Lance stood behind them. Everyone else was back at the university.

"It's not a sewer line, you dope," Remington told him.

He's really getting familiar with us, Claire thought. *Oddly, I like it. He may not be a part of the core group, but he's still one of us.*

"The amount of money and time we've invested in you all?" Lance asked. "And then we mess everything up by dropping you in a sewer? The two of us wouldn't be able to get a job as greeters at Wal-Mart."

"Hey," Claire snapped without looking away from the manhole. "My mom was a greeter at Wal-Mart."

"Nothing wrong with that," Lance responded. "But it would be a cut in pay, and I know Remington here likes strip clubs too much to risk it."

Everyone but Frank chuckled.

"What's a strip club?" the leprechaun asked.

Jack raised an eyebrow and looked at him. "You're kidding?"

Frank shook his head, frowning. "Never heard of it."

Jack closed his eyes, and a smile appeared on his face. He looked into the sky as if God was blessing him at that very moment. "When we get out of here, Frank, I'm going to change your world."

Claire rolled her eyes. "Enough. It's time to get down there. Everyone ready?"

The group was loaded down with the weapons Mitchen

had shown them earlier. Claire felt like she was GI Joe—*or Jane*, Marissa had corrected. She had two wooden stakes attached to her belt and twelve metal stakes that would be used in the Impaler. Each of them had six Immolators attached to the vests on their chests, three on either side. Four cans of Holy Mace (as Jack was now calling it) were attached to their arms. Each had a Nova in their pants pocket as well.

"Yeah, ready," Jack confirmed.

"Your arm going to let you actually fight this time?" Marissa asked with a grin.

Jack smiled. "It's nearly healed, so don't you worry about that. The main problem you're going to have is how you're going to write epic poems about my triumphs down there when we get back. It's going to take you the rest of your life to give me my due."

Good, Claire thought. *Joking is good. Better than being scared.*

"Okay." Remington stepped through the four and got down on his knees. He slowly dropped the rope ladder until he felt it touch the ground. He stepped by and tied it off on two small bolts they'd drilled into the cement. "Enough chatter from the peanut gallery. Time to do what we get paid for."

"Only person paid here is Frank, and that's in beer." Jack stepped up to the ladder and carefully put his foot on the first step. "Which is another thing I want to talk about when we get back. Jack here is going to need some paychecks."

Claire stepped forward and lightly placed her foot on his head, pushing him down.

"Keep him under control down there," Remington said.

Jack started down. Frank went next, then Marissa, and finally Claire.

She looked at Remington and Lance as she stepped onto the rope ladder. "See you when we get out."

"Bet on it," Remington assured her. "Go give 'em Hell."

"That's the plan." Claire started down the ladder, the silence of the tunnel quickly assaulting her senses. No wind. No voices. No noises at all except the rope ladder slowly creaking as the four climbed down.

Claire reached the ground. The other three had already turned their headlamps on, casting light out across the darkness.

"Tight space," Jack commented. This was definitely a subway tunnel. The walls on either side stretched maybe ten feet, but Claire thought that was a good thing. There weren't a whole lot of places to hide, which meant they'd see their attackers quickly.

"Marissa, you got the maps memorized, lass?" Frank asked.

Marissa giggled. "Nope, forgot 'em on the way down."

"Funny," Jack whispered.

He doesn't like the way our voices echo, Claire thought, *and neither do I.*

Marissa had memorized the maps the captured vampire had drawn out over the past few nights. No one wanted to waste time consulting them or not focusing on what was in front of their faces, so she'd volunteered to memorize exactly what the vampire said. He'd known it all because he said this is where they broke the Veil—down here in these tunnels—and so to get out, you had to have an intimate idea of where you were going.

"Onward then, ye lazy bastards," Frank called. "There's not a bar in sight, and Frank wants to start drinking as soon as possible."

Marissa moved forward with Claire right behind her. The headlamps did a decent job of lighting up the darkness, and they traveled like that for about ten minutes before reaching a crossway.

"Left," Marissa guessed. She turned without slowing at first and then stopped, causing Claire to almost run into the back of her.

"Hello, children." The vampire stood ten feet from them, her skin pale in the light from their four headlamps. She had blonde hair and was distinctly beautiful, like a goddess dropped from Mt. Olympus.

"Well, I don't think that's Dracula. Unless he had some kind of sex-change operation," Jack joked.

"What do we do?" Marissa whispered. The four stood shoulder to shoulder, blocking the entire tunnel.

"Start taking notes, Sissy," Jack told her. "Because these poems about me will be remembered like *The Iliad*." Jack's hands moved like vipers, although his feet remained in place to avoid giving away what he was doing. He pulled the bar from his waist, pointed it toward the vampire, and pressed on the end. The stake flew through the air like a missile.

The vampire barely had time to blink.

The stake struck it in the chest, pulverizing bone and the undead heart behind it.

Jack didn't even pause, simply unhooked another stake and loaded it into his weapon.

The vampire fell to the ground.

"You all saw that, right?" Jack looked at the other three. "I want to make sure that's on record. While you three were twiddling your thumbs, I stepped up and saved everyone's asses."

Claire gave him another of her elbows. "Good job, but save it. There's going to be a lot of them up ahead. At least we know we're on the right path. Let's keep going."

The four walked on, passing by the dead vampire without looking down at it.

A thought came to Claire as they continued forward. "Frank, why can't you just teleport around this place and kill them?"

"Because I don't know where I'll end up, lass," Frank replied. "Could end up inside a wall, or maybe in a room full of the bloodsuckers."

"Couldn't you just teleport out if that was the case?" Jack asked.

"I'm going to put a serious request in that the university start teaching you about leprechaun culture. It's ridiculous how little ye all know." Frank shook his head, his light shining back and forth across the tunnel. "We're taught since wee ones that we never teleport unless we know where we're going. Doing that is a good way to end up in front of a bus."

"You have buses beyond the Veil?" Marissa asked. "Who drives them?"

Jack rolled his eyes. "We're not having an economics class right now, Sissy. Ask him later."

They reached another crossing. "Right."

The group turned as one this time, wanting to take on whatever waited beyond the corner.

"Sonofabitch," Jack mumbled. "You three going to help? Because I don't have enough hands for all of them."

Four vampires stood twenty feet off, a bit farther away than the last vampire. Three males, one female.

I wonder if they know about the mechanical stakes already, and that the distance is to make us more effective with them? Claire thought, keeping her cool. A month ago she would have been terrified and the other night extremely nervous, but now she felt pretty confident they could take out the four of them, especially with these new weapons.

She stepped forward, but Frank put his hand lightly on her leg. She looked down at him. He was staring at her with a wild grin. "When I get done with these four, I want you to admit I could have gotten away from you at the amusement park if I'd wanted to."

Claire's eyes narrowed but Frank didn't give her a chance to say anything. He stepped away from the group. "I don't recognize any of ye bloodsuckers, but then again, I try to stay away from your type. Always trying to take from others what isn't owed ye, mainly our blood."

The vampires all smiled at the same time, looking creepily like robots.

"Come, little man. Let us end your torment," one of them offered.

"I'm not a man," Frank ground out through gritted teeth, reaching for one of the wooden stakes on his belt. He yanked it off. "I'm a fucking *leprechaun.*"

Claire's eyes widened at what happened next.

Frank moved faster than anyone she had ever seen. He darted to his right, and rather than stay on the ground, he launched himself onto the wall. He landed on one foot, then shoved himself off it, flying through the air like a suicidal acrobat.

The vampire closest to him turned but appeared to be moving in slow motion compared to Frank. The small green creature thrust his stake into the vampire's heart and removed it just as quickly. He kicked off the dying vampire, but instead of heading toward the ground, he launched himself back into the air.

The other three vampires were still in the process of turning, trying to gather themselves to attack this mythological ninja.

Frank began his descent, stake tip pointed down. A vampire reached up to grab him, but only touched a flash of light.

Frank teleported to the ground. He sliced upward with the stake, dropping the vampire who had tried to lay hands on him.

Two left, Claire thought, bewildered at how fast all of this was happening.

Another flash of light, and Frank was on the other side of the vampire. The stake darted once, twice.

All the vampires lay on the ground, and Frank turned to the group. He smiled, blood dripping from his weapon. He tucked the stake under his arm, then took a bow. "Thank you, thank you! Thank you! Seriously, the applause is too much! Thank you!" He bowed over and over as he spoke.

Claire started laughing, her voice echoing off the walls.

"Frank..." Jack shook his head, mouth slightly open. "You move like someone from *The Matrix*."

Frank stood up, stopping his ridiculous bows. "The what?"

Jack nodded, still in awe. "I'll show it to you after the strip clubs."

"Five dead?" Dracula's voice cut through the stillness like a blade through water. "Five of *us* dead?"

The vampire in front of him looked down at the floor, refusing to meet his gaze. She'd brought the news, though how she knew it, Hannah had no idea. She, Bradley, and Matthew were seated in three chairs against a wall. The vampires had congregated around the departure station, all of them apparently waiting for news that the kids had been killed.

But that was not what appears to have happened, Hannah thought.

Matthew sat two seats over from her. He was doing his rocking thing again, and Hannah wanted to smack him. She kept her hands to herself, though, knowing that Dracula's punishment would be far worse.

The vampire turned around, his eyes falling on Hannah. Vampires surrounded him, probably close to seventy, representing all the work Hannah and the other two had done in searching for *this* one. Building him a following.

"You said they were mere children. Teenagers." His voice carried ice in it that chilled all the way to Hannah's bones.

"They are." Hannah nodded. "You don't understand yet. Very few people can even see that you exist, but kids can more than most. The government found the oldest who could see you. Otherwise, they wouldn't be able to fight you."

"*STOP!*" Dracula screamed, his voice carrying farther than it had any right to. "Nothing you say makes sense. These aren't *children*. Van Helsing himself couldn't have wiped out five vampires in such a short time. What is it that you bring this way, woman? What is coming to attack us?"

Hannah's eyes were wide. She was stupefied. Dracula thought *she* was conspiring against him? She, the one who had engineered his arrival in this world?

"Master," she whispered, "they are teenagers, not even old enough to drink alcohol in this world."

Dracula turned his gaze on the rest of his brood. "They know where we are, and they're coming this way. So be it. We will meet them in force if we cannot defeat them with stealth."

He looked over his shoulder at the three.

"If you are right, you will serve at my right hand. All except frightened man. If you are wrong and I take heavy losses, you will die right after these *teenagers*."

***

Thirty minutes had passed since they saw their last group of vampires, and Frank wouldn't shut up.

"You tell me now, lass, that I could have gotten away from you. Tell me, or Frank is done helping. I'll watch Jack here try to take your glory, and keep watching while you all fall."

Claire shook her head, her light moving back and forth across the dark tunnel. "Frank. One, you're not ever going to do that. Two, a footrace is different than fighting. Sure, if you'd teleported when I was after you, you probably could have gotten away. There's a difference between quickness and speed. You've got me on quickness, I'll give you that, but in a footrace?" She huffed. "Hardly. I'll beat you any day of the week and twice on Sunday."

"All these ridiculous sayings ye humans have," Frank mumbled. "Twice on Sunday. Like Sunday makes any difference. When we get out of here, ye and I are racing, lass. I've had enough of yer mouth."

Jack interrupted their arguing. "How long have we been down here?"

"About an hour," Marissa answered.

"Why haven't we seen any more vampires, then?" Jack asked. His right hand gripped his Impaler, ready for action.

"Jesus, Frank," Claire snapped, looking over her shoulder at the leprechaun. "Stop all your yip-yap. I haven't even thought about why there haven't been any others, and it's because I'm focusing on your nonsense."

She turned her head to Marissa. "Any thoughts?"

Marissa was quiet for a second, her feet leading them all over the forgotten tracks. "Hmmm...The only thing that comes to mind is not something you're going to want to hear."

"Well, let's hear it anyway," Claire instructed.

Marissa shrugged. "Probably an ambush."

"You're fucking kidding." Jack kicked a rock in front of

him, sending it scattering up the tracks. "They couldn't kill us with a few so now—"

"They're going to do it with a group," Marissa finished.

Does that change things? Claire wondered. Everyone in the group was important, but she knew her role was to make the major decisions. She was the leader, and if she made a wrong choice, everyone would suffer from it. *No, it doesn't change anything. We can't go back to the surface without killing these things. That's our mission, and that's what we're going to accomplish.*

"How far are we from where the vampire said their home base was?" Claire asked.

"A half-mile. Another ten or fifteen minutes, I'd guess."

"We should have brought a map," Jack complained.

"We don't need a map," Marissa responded over her shoulder. "I've gotten us this far, and I'll get us the rest of the way."

"Okay, enough," Claire demanded. "We can't be arguing right now over a stupid map, and Jack knows it. His fear is getting to him, and he's taking it out on you." Claire turned around so she was walking backward and looked at Jack. She knew she had to be careful here. Insulting him wouldn't work. It would only drive him further away from the group. Make him focus. "What do you think, Jack? She can remember things better, or you can hit things from a distance better?"

"Is that a serious question?" His face was stern.

"Well, you doubt her mapping abilities. Maybe I'm doubting your shooting abilities."

A small grin appeared on the left side of his mouth.

"How many have you killed? One? My count has me at three."

"Okay, so if we're about to be ambushed, how many do you think you can get?" Claire looked down at his belt. "Looks like you have about ten stakes left."

"Plus one in the chamber." He lifted the Impaler. "That's eleven. Given my usual accuracy, I'd say I'll get eleven."

Claire spoke over her shoulder to Marissa. "How many minutes until we're there?"

"Ten," she responded.

"Got a watch?" Claire called.

Marissa waved a hand. "On my wrist."

"Time it." Claire resumed looking at Jack. "Okay. We'll see how accurate she is, and we'll see how accurate you are. You owe me eleven."

Jack chuckled. "Owe you, huh?"

Claire nodded. "Yup. She owes me ten minutes, and you owe me eleven kills."

Jack looked down at his Impaler for a moment, then met her eyes. "I'll get you eleven."

"Damn right, you will." Claire turned back around and started walking normally again.

A minute passed in silence, and then she felt Jack's hand on her shoulder. "Thanks."

It was a small whisper, but she heard it. Claire didn't need to respond since they both knew what had happened.

The minutes seemed to take forever to tick by as if they'd entered a time warp. *That's only because you're ready to fight.*

"There," Marissa told them, coming to a stop.

Claire had been deep in her own thoughts, but she

quickly pulled out of them. The light was faint but visible. Four hundred yards off, perhaps, but she could see the ancient subway stop.

"Where are they?" Jack whispered as he pulled up next to Claire.

Frank finished the line of four. "What do they teach you in that school? Don't you know anything about vampires? They don't exactly wear neon lights and dance around. Those blood-sucking bastards are down there, but they're hiding."

"What do we do?" Marissa asked.

Claire squeezed her Impaler, then brought her hand down to feel the pointed stake sticking out of the tip. It was hard and deadly, like her. "They know we're here. No sense in trying to hide. Let's go down there and make ourselves known."

Jack grinned. "Sounds good to me. I owe ya eleven."

"Damn right." Claire stepped forward, taking the lead for the first time since they'd entered the tunnels. As she walked, the station's light grew brighter, but she still didn't see any movement. They went a hundred yards, then another, and after the third, Claire understood.

"They're on the ceiling," she whispered.

She tilted her head upward, her light illuminating the ancient ceiling. There were no vampires there, but there would be if they kept walking.

"Jack, I want you to walk with your head tilted back," Claire instructed. "Keep the light focused on the ceiling, about twenty yards ahead of us. Just be careful not to trip."

She watched as Jack's light followed hers, showing the ceiling in front of them. They could all do it, but Claire understood they needed a designated person. "They're going to drop on us like bats. Frank, you have apparently been around them. You got any advice?"

"Turn into a leprechaun, and then you can fight like me." Frank grinned, his own light shining on the ceiling with Jack's. "No, lass. No advice. Don't let them bite ye."

"Great, Frank." Claire sighed. "Thanks for all your help. Let's go."

Again she started forward, knowing they were nearly at the end of their travels. The subway stop grew closer by the step.

Jack grabbed Claire's shoulder. "We've got company," he whispered.

Her head flashed to the ceiling, and she saw the first row. Vampires lined shoulder to shoulder, their skin pale and their eyes reflecting the headlamps.

One hissed, and the others followed.

They dropped from the ceiling like falling night. Claire couldn't possibly count them all. Row after row fell, one after the other.

"Excuse me." Frank stepped forward. "I've got a date with destiny."

He rushed forward, and the first row of vampires fell on him. Six at least, blocking out any sign of the little green leprechaun.

He's dead, Claire's mind though in cold fear. *Just like that.*

She was stunned, unable to move. They thought they'd had a chance, and now it was over.

"You three going to frickin' help?" Frank's voice rose above the commotion of the oncoming undead. Claire still couldn't see him.

Frank burst up through the crowd of six who had all bent over to drain his blood without a scratch on him.

There's not a scratch on him!

Frank touched down on one vampire's head, his Impaler plunging through its back and into its heart. He didn't even shoot the thing, just used it like a regular stake. It was like he was walking on air, bouncing from head to head and ruthlessly cutting them down.

The vampires fell around him, and Frank finally landed on the ground, one foot resting on the chest of the now-dead creature. He looked at the three. "Seriously, any of ye going to help me?"

He turned to the vampires. They'd all paused, watching the small creature decimate the first six. "Who wants some more?"

Claire didn't look at her friends. Frank was an amazing warrior, but if they didn't jump in now, it wouldn't matter. There were simply too many vampires. "Time to soldier up."

"My pleasure." Jack raised his Impaler and fired. The stake soared past Frank and nailed a vampire in her chest. She stared as if unable to believe what was happening, then fell forward.

That broke the hold on the horde. A few hissed, fangs bared.

They surged forward.

Frank darted to the left, bounding onto the wall. Vampires flung themselves at him and Claire lost sight of him. She had to focus on making sure *she* didn't fucking die.

Four vampires came for her. A stake whooshed by her side and impaled one a bit farther away.

Thank God for Jack, she thought as the first vampire swiped at her face. She dodged back, her moves almost as quick as theirs. She grabbed the Holy Mace from her belt and started spraying. The aerosol liquid shot out, misting the creatures, and they screamed into the dark tunnel.

Claire wasted no time. Her hand darted forward with the Impaler, using it like a regular stake so as to not waste ammunition.

Wham. Wham. Wham. Wham. The four dropped around her.

"How's everyone doing?" Claire yelled.

"Could use some help!" Marissa called.

"Focus forward, Claire!" Jack yelled. "I've got her!"

Claire glanced to her left. Three vampires were nearly on top of Marissa. She simply wasn't as fast as Claire. Jack's Impaler slung stakes at them. Two vampires went down in seconds, leaving Marissa to face one alone.

"This way, bitch."

Claire turned her head toward the voice. She'd just put down four, but now she looked at nine.

A dark-haired female stared back at her. "Go ahead and spray that shit. There's too many of us." She raised a hand and pointed behind Claire.

Claire turned around, not understanding—until she saw. Vampires flocked to the ground, falling from the ceiling as they had moments before.

I didn't realize it soon enough, she thought. *We'd already passed them by the time I understood what they were doing. Now we're trapped.*

"Jack! Behind you!" Claire shouted, pointing. "Hold them off as long as you can!"

Jack slowly turned around. "Christ on a cracker."

"There are too many of us, human," the female vampire sneered. "Even with your little tricks, you'll never kill us all."

Claire whirled back around. "Maybe not, sweetie, but I can kill you." She pushed on the back of the Impaler and the stake ripped through the air, landing in the creature's chest.

Claire heard hisses and saw the crowd rush forward.

Reload. Fire. Reload. Fire.

Vampires dropped in front of her but more came, replacing the ones she killed as if there was an unlimited supply.

"Frank!" she called. "Can you help?"

"Sorry, lass!" he yelled from somewhere else. "Got about twelve of these bastards trying to give me a hickey!"

The horde came on, reducing Claire to hand-to-hand combat. She batted left and right, spraying her mace and stabbing as many as she could.

It's too close for the Immolator, she thought. *I'll burst into flames, too.*

She grunted, feeling a slash on her shoulder and knowing she was bleeding. Nails scraped across her face. Still she fought, the Impaler cutting through chest plate after chest plate.

There are just too many!

She shoved the Impaler into her holster, knowing that it didn't matter anymore. If she relied only on that, she would be dead. She pulled the Nova out of her pocket and pressed its button. Bright light rushed out all sides, a star in the palm of her hands.

One last hand slashed across her other cheek, then screams replaced the attacks.

"Novas!" Claire screamed as she thrust her light forward, forcing the horde back. She saw the rest of the tunnel lighting up; her team knew what to do.

The screams were awful, like dying animals being thrown from cliffs.

Claire kept marching forward. They covered their faces, howling as smoke rose into the rafters. Some broke away from the pack, fleeing into the darkness. One dropped in front of her, rolling on the ground as if that would somehow put out the flames.

"Run!" Claire hissed back at them.

More did take off, trying to reach the darkness. Anywhere to make the pain go away.

"Badda-*bing*!" Frank shouted, and Claire heard a body drop. She glanced to her left and saw him still using his Impaler. He hadn't pulled his Nova out and was offing the ones around him who were trying to hide their faces from the burning rays of light.

He moved fast, and vampires fell wherever he went.

Claire turned all the way around, her Nova high in the air to keep the killers at bay. Marissa had moved closer to Jack and was standing across from him on the other side of the tunnel. Both held their Novas out from their chests, shoving them toward the vampiric masses.

Many had broken and run on the other side, while the rest were simply trying to shield themselves from the pain.

"Watch this!" Jack shouted. He grabbed his Impaler off

his belt with his right hand. Using only his right hand, he placed it below a stake hanging from his belt, and jammed the Impaler upward, loading the weapon. It took only a second.

He's definitely better with it than I am, Claire thought.

Jack raised it and fired, and a vampire covering her face dropped to the ground.

Claire looked over her shoulder to see if anyone was coming, but between the Novas and Frank's killing spree, her side was empty. "Come on, Frank. Let's take care of these."

"Hold yer little glass orb there, lass. I'll do the real work." Frank didn't look at her as he spoke, just grinned maniacally.

He's enjoying this, Claire thought and smiled. *He* hates *vampires.*

Claire followed Frank, reaching the line Jack and Marissa had already set up. Frank walked past them, and Jack raised his Impaler to shoot again. Claire touched his hand before he could. "No, don't waste them. Let Frank do his magic. Dracula wasn't here. We've still got another vampire to find."

Jack nodded and grinned. "His magic." He shook his head in awe as Frank got started. "That's what it is. Magic."

Frank moved through the remaining vampires like a phantom, something they couldn't see or touch.

"I think he likes it," Marissa said with more than a bit of awe.

"Yeah. We might wanna be careful around Frank from now on." Jack grinned. "The little guy has a taste for killing, I think."

The last vampire fell to the ground and Frank stood above him, breathing heavily and holding his Impaler.

"Did you shoot even one of those?" Claire called.

Frank shook his head. "No. You can't see 'em as good when they die if you're far away, lass."

"One of those vampires must have done something to you, huh?" Jack asked.

Frank looked up. "Fuck vamps, every single one of them. I hope that once we kill Dracula, I never have to see one again. I just pray they don't appear back in my world." He walked over to the group and stood in front of Claire.

"What makes you hate them so much?" she asked.

"Besides the fact all they want to do is drain your blood? Oh, I've got a few reasons." Frank shook his head and looked at his feet. "They're awful, awful creatures. They bring no one joy. Their only purpose is to take from others." He tilted his head and grinned, light in his eyes. "Not like Frank. Not like leprechauns. Sure, we'll chase gold or beer, as the case may be, but we can bring joy. Those creatures don't."

"I've had boyfriends like that," Marissa volunteered.

"Eh?" Frank raised his Impaler. "I'll go take care of them when we're done here."

Jack laughed. "Sissy's never had any boyfriends." He surveyed the scene in front of him, then turned around. He didn't see any more vampires. He looked at Claire and raised the Nova. "Think it's okay to turn these things off now?"

"Yeah. I think so." Claire pressed her button but didn't shove the thing back in her pocket. She wanted to be ready in case they were surprised again. She looked at the subway station. "How do they have lights on down here?"

"Probably running a generator," Marissa answered as she turned off her Nova. "Or they've got some other kind of technology that we don't understand. I imagine it's that."

"Why?" Jack asked. He hooked his Impaler back on his belt.

Marissa glanced quickly at Claire and winked. "Oh, I don't know. Maybe because they're somehow breaking down a thousand-year-old barrier to a universe we didn't even know existed? I doubt they're doing it with rain dances."

"Hardy, har, har," Jack mocked. "Well, however they're doing it, I'm glad they are. Makes it easier to see once we get up there."

At that, the lights in the station shut down. Their head-lamps were still on so they could see around them, but the subway station was shrouded in darkness.

"Nice going, Jack-ass," Claire told him.

Jack shrugged. "Don't blame that on me! They would have done it anyway!"

Claire smiled. "Don't get your panties in a wad. We just killed I don't know how many vampires. We've only got one left."

Frank moved in front of the three, his headlamp shining on a bench in front of the station. "This one's different, lass. Make no mistake. Dracula is not like the rest of them. He's the most dangerous. I don't know how all this works—if it's true you all dream us up over there, or if maybe we're over there already so we come through your dreams, but I know this vampire has been around a long,

long time. I know the power he holds makes these things we just killed look like mere children."

"Why didn't he come get us himself, then?" Jack thumbed one of the stakes on his belt. "If he's that strong."

Frank didn't turn around, but for the first time, he seemed scared. "You don't know Dracula, lad. He doesn't do anything unless he has to. He always has some lackey sticking around to do it for him because he's lazy and only moves when it's necessary. It's become necessary now, though, because his little army just got killed."

"Well, let's not keep him waiting." Claire walked past Frank and over to the platform. She grabbed the top, then used her legs to push herself up. She turned around as the rest of the crew came. "Frank, how are you going to get up here? You're too short." She grinned as she spoke.

"I won't even honor that with a response." Frank crouched, then jumped. He landed next to Claire. "Ye humans are a rude bunch, I swear."

Next came Marissa. Claire grabbed her hand and helped pull her up. Finally, they got Jack onto the platform, and the group stared into the shadows.

"Left or right?" Jack asked, turning his head in both directions.

The voice came down the hall to the right, deep and loud. "This way, children. This way..."

Claire shivered. Without some kind of bullhorn, no one should sound like that.

"I guess that answers that question." Jack shrugged and glanced at Claire. "Go on, fearless leader. You first." He nodded toward the dark hall.

"Yes, fearless leader. Come. Bring your friends.

Everyone come in. No one will be leaving." The voice mocked them as it spoke, half-laughing, half-daring them.

Frank looked over his shoulder at Claire. "He's a cocky bastard. Let's go take care of this nasty business so I can get meself to a bar."

Claire was quiet. She unclipped her Impaler and grabbed her Nova, then walked past Frank and led the way down the hall, seeing her group's headlamps light up the way as they fell in line.

"Yes, yes," the voice mocked. "This way. That's right. Keep coming."

Claire stopped. She'd learned her lesson about not having a plan back at the club. She wouldn't do it again.

"It's the room on the right down there. That's where he is." She pointed. "I'll open it and turn on the Nova. I'm going to duck and hide behind the door. Frank, you go in first. You're the fastest. Jack, cover him with your Impaler. I want you to take a few of my stakes since you're almost out. Marissa, once Frank is in, you and I will slip past Jack. You're on water duty. I'll set the Nova on the floor so it'll still shine and go after him with my stakes. Everyone got it?"

"Got it," Jack answered, his voice firm.

"Got it," Marissa whispered.

Frank unclipped his Impaler. "Aye, I'll go in first, but this is going to cost ye some serious beer when we get back." He reached into his back pocket and took out a small flask. He unscrewed it with one hand and tilted the thing up, draining it in one chug.

"What the hell, Frank?" Claire asked as she looked over her shoulder.

Frank put the flask back in his pocket, then wiped his mouth with his arm. "Thirsty, lass." He nodded, psyching himself up. "Okay, let's go."

Claire went forward, unsure of what to expect. All she knew was that this was the end of the line. Everything would be over very shortly.

She reached the door and looked back at Frank. He nodded in return. *Ready.* She nodded back, then grabbed the doorknob. Silence reigned in the hallway, the deep voice no longer speaking.

Claire pulled out the Nova with her free hand and raised it. She put three fingers up while holding it, and slowly folded each one down.

Three.

Two.

One.

She twisted the knob and shoved the door open while lighting up the Nova. It burned brightly as she knelt and threw it into the room.

Frank darted past with his Impaler raised.

Claire caught a quick glimpse of the creature inside. Old. Black hair. A face that looked worn but regal.

The face of a king, she thought before she realized what was happening. *He's not hiding from the light!*

Dracula smiled at her and flicked his fingers toward the wall. Her Nova was yanked from her hand by an invisible force much stronger than she ever dreamed of. It flew across the room and slammed into the concrete wall, shattering. The light died, and the dead technology fell to the ground.

"*GO!*" she shouted, understanding Frank was in real

trouble. She shoved past the door with her Impaler in the air, ready to fire. Marissa and Jack came next. Jack moved toward the wall, his back to it so that he could fire without getting ambushed.

Claire took in the room with one glance. A single light burned overhead, and three people who *looked* human sat in the far corner. The room was otherwise small and empty.

Frank flew toward the vampire, his leprechaun speed in full display. He leapt off the floor, stake bared.

He's got this, Claire thought, even as she rushed to his defense. *No way can anyone stop him.*

Inches away, Frank froze in the air. He was almost nose to nose with Dracula, the stake aiming right at his heart.

What the fuck? Claire wasn't able to move either, not even her eyes. She was frozen stiff. Everything inside her kept trying to push forward, to reach the vampire and kill him, but she couldn't move an inch.

"This is who you send?" Dracula asked, his European accent thick. "This is the best you have to offer? A tiny green midget and three children?"

Frank's mouth didn't move but his words were clear enough. "Stop with the magic and let me cut you down to size."

Dracula rolled his eyes, an insanely creepy thing coming from such an ancient creature. "Begone." He flicked his hand again, and Frank flew through the air like the Nova had. He smacked into the wall *hard* and slid down to the ground, falling sideways as he landed.

Dracula turned his attention to the others in the room. "The kiddies. Ah, yes. How cute." He stepped into the middle of the room. "You are having trouble moving, yes? Did you think you could come here and simply attack me with your gadgets, and I would fall down like those weaklings you got through?"

He shook his head and looked at the floor, smiling.

"I have lived for centuries, children. *Centuries.* Here, there, wherever you want to put me, I cannot die. I am the undead. Gadgets and weapons will not stop me. You are no Van Helsing. You are no savior. You..." He paused, looking at all three now. "You are simply food."

He raised his palms up into the air as if to say, "What can I do?" After a moment, he lowered them and turned to the humans in the chair. "You three. You see now why you cannot be equals? Why you will at best be lowly servants in a world I dictate? You are as they are. Nothing but food."

Dracula smiled and turned his attention once more to Claire.

"I hear your thoughts, girl. I hear them loud. I let your green friend talk because I wanted to hear his boast. I will not let you talk, though. Your thoughts...they are enough. You want to kill me, yes? You think you can if I simply let you go. Your confidence, it would seem, knows no limits."

Claire forced her mind to go silent. No thoughts. She just stared at the undead creature.

"Would you like a go, little girl?" the vampire asked. He raised his hand and gestured between the two of them. "Would you like to try to kill me? I'll let your friends here watch, and then they can decide whether to join me or die. How does that sound?"

YES! Claire shouted in her mind before silencing herself again.

The vampire nodded. "Very well, then." He raised his hands and touched his fingertips together, then dropped them quickly.

Claire's control of her muscles come back to her. She nearly fell over but caught herself, straightened, and went still.

"What would you like to use?" the vampire asked with a smile. "Would you like to spray me with holy water?"

"How about this for starters?" Claire whipped the Impaler up and pressed the back; the stake flew from her hands like a missile, aimed right at the creature's chest. She reloaded again immediately.

When it was twelve inches from him, Dracula raised his right hand and slapped it away as he might a gnat. Claire didn't pause. She fired another, reloading at the exact moment it was free of her chamber.

Another slap. The stake clattered to the floor.

The vampire shrugged. "These are nothing, poor girl. Nothing."

Fine, then, she thought. *Hand to hand it is.*

Claire went forward, her feet as light as feathers, her stake raised. She took out the Holy Mace and started spraying, slashing forward with her stake as she did. The aerosol spray hit the vampire's face as her stake came down on him. He smiled and raised one hand to wipe it off and another to fend off her attacks, hardly paying attention to her.

"*AGH!*" she screamed as she brought the stake up again and again, only to have it batted away each time like it was nothing. As if it didn't exist.

Dracula slammed his palm out into Claire's chest. She

was flung backward, arcing into the air before hitting the ground. Her head slammed into the floor and stars appeared in her vision. She blinked hard, immediately climbing to one knee before faintness nearly made her fall again.

She looked up, breathing hard.

Dracula smiled at her. "It's all about belief, poor girl. That holy water? You don't believe. It was blessed by a priest who believed, but you? You have as much faith in holy water as you do in Mt. Olympus. Yes, it worked on those weaker vampires since they didn't understand how weak your faith is. They do not understand anything, but I do. And now you do as well, don't you?"

Claire's mind was still despite the pain tearing through her body.

Dracula cocked his to the side, considering her with narrowed eyes. "Would you like to join me, Claire? Would you like to walk this world forever?"

"Fuck you," Claire grated.

"No, I didn't think you would." Dracula straightened his head. "You are much too stubborn to join, so now you'll die."

He started forward, and Claire knew with cold certainty that she couldn't stop this creature in hand-to-hand combat. She couldn't use blessed water or machines that slung stakes. He was too powerful. He was too old. He was too *strong*.

She either acted now, or she died.

Her mind finally spoke once again, unable to hide its true intentions. Dracula was seven feet from her, but he paused.

He finally saw the thought she'd managed to keep hidden.

Claire's hand whipped to the cargo pocket in her pants and she yanked the Immolator out. "Let's see you dodge fire."

She squeezed the ball as Mitchen had told her and threw it at him. Everything seemed to move in slow motion.

Dracula's mouth dropped open. He was able to read her thoughts now and understood fully what she'd been hiding. The ball flew through the air, its mist spraying outward, and flames quickly followed.

Dracula's hand moved, trying to telekinetically swat the ball out of his path, but it was too late. The flames had emerged, and he couldn't move *those*.

The accelerant covered him first and the fire next. It washed over him like a purifying light, orange and yellow flowing across his entire body.

Whoosh.

Claire felt the heat rush out from Dracula as the flames stretched up and down, turning him into a human...*no*, her mind corrected, *a vampiric torch*.

His screams filled the room, echoing off the walls in a cacophony of pain.

Jack and Marissa stepped up next to Claire. The heat was growing strong on her skin. They would need to leave. The creature stumbled back into the wall and turned to the other three humans.

"Ah, hell," Claire grumbled. "I forgot about them. You got them, Marissa? Jack, you're going to need to grab Frank."

Both nodded, hardly able to stop staring at the stumbling vampire, who was now banging into walls.

One of the men stood and tried to bolt. Jack's hand snapped out and caught him in the temple as he passed. The man fell in a heap.

"One of you is carrying him," Marissa yelled over the vampire's slowing screams. She glanced at the people against the wall. "Because we're not."

"Come on," Claire told them. "Let's get out of here. The FBI can come get whatever's left."

CHAPTER TWENTY-ONE

They made it out of the tunnel without seeing another vampire. Perhaps the fact that they were leaving showed the others they'd killed Dracula. Or maybe the vampires simply didn't want to mess around with the Nova anymore since the pain was far too great.

Either way, with Jack carrying Frank over his shoulder, the group walked their prisoners all the way back to the manhole.

It was nighttime, and a street light cast a glow above them.

"You jokers still up there?" Jack called.

Remington stuck his head into the manhole, cutting off some of the light. "We're here. What about you? Are you all okay? We've got medics up here waiting."

That was smart, Claire thought, and she was also grateful for it. They couldn't come down in these tunnels with her, but they'd been prepared for when they got out. "Frank's unconscious, but other than that, I think we're okay."

"Who are they?" Remington asked, nodding at the three

newcomers. The one Jack had knocked out had regained consciousness, although from his moans, he had a splitting headache.

Claire grinned as she looked through the manhole. "That's your glorious cult. The ones causing all the problems."

Remington's face looked surprised. "You got them?"

"No!" Jack shouted. "We found some homeless people and are bringing them up to you. Jesus, just help us get out of here! Frank is heavy!"

Remington stepped back from the manhole, and after a few seconds, the rope ladder dropped.

The EMTs came down and took Frank up first. They took the cult members next, and finally the three schoolmates made their way back to the surface.

Cuffs were slammed on the three strangers, and agents Claire had never seen before read them their Miranda rights.

"You three okay?" Remington asked, stepping away from the commotion of the ambulance and the arrests.

"I'm exhausted," Claire answered. "How are we getting home?"

Remington glanced at Lance as he walked up. "They need to rest. We can start the debrief tomorrow."

Lance nodded as he scanned the three. "That's fine with me. The EMTs are going to want to check you out in that ambulance over there. When they're done, they'll take you back to the university."

Claire looked over her shoulder, having not even seen the second ambulance. She didn't want to be checked out by anyone, but she imagined it was standard procedure. Plus, she was too tired to argue about it.

Finally, when all their vitals had been checked and their necks looked over for bite marks, the three classmates were loaded into the ambulance and driven home with the lights on but the sirens off.

Claire slept for hours and hours. She dreamed some of the time, and other times it was peaceful. She woke up a couple of times during the dreams, unable to remember what they'd been about. She'd look around the room but decide she wasn't nearly ready to be awake yet and fall back asleep.

No one came for her, not for a while, at least.

Finally, she heard an Irish voice.

"Lass, that's enough. You've been sleeping longer than Rip Van Winkle, and I know the joker. Snores like a freight train. I guess it's a small blessing that you're not a snorer."

Claire slowly opened her eyes, an annoyed frown forming on her face. "Go away, Frank. I'm tired."

"That may be, me dear, but Frank does not care. Ye have slept for two days straight, and I can no longer let this continue. You're ruining your education and making me look bad." He shoved a thumb into his chest.

"Look bad?" Claire groaned and rolled over on her other side so she couldn't see him.

Frank nodded. "Yes. Those FBI agents keep referring to you as *my* friend and asking when you're going to get up? I won't have it, I tell ye. My reputation will not be sullied by the likes of ye and ye lazy ways. Up!" He grabbed the corner of the blanket and yanked it off her.

Claire sat up, her eyes wild. "Frank! What if I'd had no clothes on?" Luckily, she was wearing pajamas, but *still*.

Frank rolled his eyes. "You're not on my level as far as dating, lass. I go for higher-caliber ladies." He moved his eyebrows up and down. "Like Marissa."

Claire leaned over and looked at her roommate's bed. "Where is she?"

Frank glanced at it for a second, then turned back to Claire. "*She* is up like a normal, productive person in society. *You* are the only one still sleeping. I got knocked out—while acting valiantly, might I add—and I am up before you."

Claire rolled her eyes. She stood slowly and stretched her arms high above her head, pushing up onto her tiptoes while she yawned. "What's the rush? We saved Boston. The school is still intact, and Remington has the cult members. What else is there to do except sleep?"

Frank's face grew quizzical. "Did Dracula bump yer head when we were down there? What else is there to do except *sleep*?"

"No, Frank. He bumped yours when he tossed you across the room like a ragdoll." Claire mimicked Dracula's hand gesture. "I killed him. But for real, why are you barging in here like this? Why are you here at all? Don't you need to be drinking in a bowling alley somewhere?"

Frank turned around and threw his hands in the air in mock exasperation. "First the lass *begs* me to help her. Pleads. Promises me her firstborn children, if Frank will help them stop the vampires who were threatening Earth.

Now, when Frank has vanquished these creatures, beat the hordes back with his bare hands, she asks why I'm here? Why I'm not drinking like some common miscreant? Gods! Help your poor servant!"

He remained standing with his hands in the air, his head tilted upward as if pleading.

"You done?" Claire asked, nonplussed.

Frank turned around. He was smirking. "That was pretty good. I think I might have a chance at this Broadway thing I keep reading about. You ever heard of Danny DeVito? I think somehow there was a mix-up, and he's a leprechaun. Either way, he's a famous actor. No reason I shouldn't be too."

Claire rolled her eyes and went to her dresser. "Just go tell them I'm up, and I'll be out in a minute."

"Atta girl," Frank encouraged. He walked over to the door and opened it, ready to leave.

"Hey." Claire turned around from the dresser. "You okay? Concussion or anything?"

Frank waved his hand in the air dismissively. "Dracula got in a lucky blow. I'm more than fine. Better than ever. I'm just mad ye put him down before I had a second go at him."

Claire smiled. "I'm glad you're okay, Frank."

"Thanks, lass," he told her. "Now hurry up." He stepped out of the room and closed the door behind him.

"Well, you did even better than we expected." Remington nodded appreciatively. "I don't think Lance, Dr. Pritcham, or I thought we'd get all four of you back, *plus* the cult." A grin appeared on his face. "We were just hoping we'd get the four of you back."

"Watch it, Remington," Claire told him icily. "You told me you were planning on us coming back the whole time."

"I'm kidding." Remington turned his palms toward the group in a gesture of peace.

The three students were in Dr. Pritcham's office again, the FBI agents on the couch as usual. Frank was sitting in the corner near the window, although he didn't look nearly as dejected and untrusting as he had before.

He's part of the group now, Claire thought.

"In all seriousness," Dr. Pritcham volunteered, "what you four did was beyond amazing. To say I'm proud would be an understatement."

"We didn't get all the vampires," Marissa protested. "A lot of them fled."

"We know," Remington replied. "There have been a few more attacks over the past few days, but that's okay. We'll be able to round them up. They're scared now, after what they saw happen to Dracula. They aren't nearly as brazen as before, and their connection to the cult is gone. They're on their own."

Claire turned around in her chair. "What happened to the cult? Where are they?"

Lance smiled. "We have them. It's taking time to get what we need out of them, but they're giving it up. The skinny one is the easiest to break. We're already getting a lot of information."

"You going to share?" Jack said, turning around in his chair too.

"Well, for starters, the layout of the organization," Remington informed her. "It's decentralized like Marissa thought, but there is a hierarchy. It goes up pretty high, and the woman in this group was one of its oldest members. That's why she was given Boston. We also know they're *choosing* who they bring over. We haven't figured out why the cult lets them do that yet if it fits into some kind of overarching plan."

Claire's eyes narrowed as a question came to her. "But what do they want? Why are they doing this?"

Remington glanced at the window in thought. "Another question we don't know yet, but we'll get it out of them. This group wanted to be Dracula's right hands, more or less. They would worship him like a god, and in turn, when he conquered Boston and Earth, or whatever they thought he'd do, they would share the spoils." After a moment, he continued. "We're not sure if it's the same for every cell. That's going to be important for us to find out."

More questions were coming to Claire now, her brain waking up from its long slumber. "How are they breaking the Veil?"

Remington smiled at that, his eyes flashing back to Claire. "Oh, that's the good news. We got one of the machines they're using. It's some kind of orb, and we've got engineers looking at it now. We'll figure it out eventually, but it's the first time we've gotten a look at one of those things."

Marissa raised her hand.

Remington smiled. "Just be rude like Claire. No need to raise your hand."

Marissa put her hand back down, smiling. "How did

they see the vampires? They're adults, but they're the ones who called them over. The vast majority of adults can't see anything, so how did they?"

Remington nodded at the question. "We're not completely sure about that either, but we have some theories. It seems the fat one played online video games like ten hours a day before he got involved with the cult. We can't be sure, but we think his mind was so accustomed to seeing fantastical things in the videogames that it wasn't a stretch for him when the Mythers showed up. The woman, Hannah? She was part of a coven before she joined this thing. She believed in witchcraft, so it would only make sense that she could see vampires. The other guy, the scared, skinny one? We think his fear and paranoia allowed him to see. He's constantly looking out for bad things that are going to happen, so it makes sense that his brain would allow him to see Mythers. He believes there are threats around every corner. Once we get done with the debrief, we're going to have scientists run brain scans. Hopefully that will give us more information.

Claire looked down at her lap. "There are still so many questions."

"That's true." Dr. Pritcham nodded. "But, it's not your job to figure out answers. We've got people working on that, and they're the best in the world at it. It's your job to be ready for the next attack."

Claire looked up. "Next attack?"

"Yeah," Jack said. "'Next attack' seems awfully soon. I was hoping for a little rest and relaxation. Take Frank to a strip club. Maybe get a little Spring Break."

Dr. Pritcham deadpanned him. "It's nowhere near spring."

Jack grinned. "You know what I'm saying."

"Sorry, but no can do." Dr. Pritcham shrugged. "You three are going back to class until these nice gentlemen tell us what the next creature to look for is. Then, we'll train on that."

Jack groaned. "Class?"

"Thank God," Marissa whispered.

Claire looked at the FBI agents. "You got any idea what that's going to be? The next creature?"

Remington shook his head. "Not yet, but we've got some leads. You might have to travel."

Jack raised his eyebrows. "Somewhere exotic? With tanned women?"

"You'll be lucky if we don't send the three of you to the Arctic Circle," Lance replied. "We're working on figuring that out. That's another question you needn't concern yourself with. Just be prepared, because what we're hearing is that it's something big. Something even more powerful than Dracula."

Frank rolled his eyes. "Dracula wasn't so fierce. Just an old man with too much confidence."

Remington leaned forward, ignoring Frank. "We're not saying it to scare you, just to prepare you. What's coming next has the potential to be really dangerous, so we need the three of you learning everything you can in all of your classes." He looked at Jack. "Including you."

Claire smiled. "Don't worry about that. He's going to pass everything, or he's off my team."

Jack turned, eyebrows raised. "It's like that, huh?"

Claire nodded. "For sure. Only the best hang with Marissa and me."

"Nope," Frank corrected with a grin. "Only the best hang with Frank."

The End

Book two in the series, Paranormal University: Second Semester is now available as a pre-order at Amazon.com.

The Veil is still tearing.

Which means for Claire and her friends, class is still in session.

Spring has arrived and everything appears calm. Claire and Marissa are studying. Jack is flirting with the new female students. It's beginning to feel a bit like...well, college.

The cult isn't finished. They're just getting started.

On the coast of Florida, evil is brewing. Something far worse than vampires, and something much harder to fight.

Claire is in the calm before the storm, because she will be tested like never before. A choice is coming...

Complete the mission...

Or save her friends.

Pre-order Now at Amazon

AUTHOR NOTES - JACE MITCHELL

OCTOBER 24, 2019

Thanks for taking the time to read this, and if you haven't gone and grabbed Amy's book which is in the same universe yet, you definitely should – it's great. It's tougher than I ever imagined to create a shared universe, and I'd like to thank Michael for his support with it. He's sorta like the Yoda of Universe Creation. You have a problem, you bring it to him – and BAM – it's fixed. However, while Yoda uses riddles and odd sentence structure, Michael uses curse words.

Without spoiling too much, there's a lot going on behind the Veil that we haven't been privy to yet – but don't worry, the answers are coming. Who started tearing the Veil? What's their purpose? And perhaps most importantly, can they be stopped? See you in Book Two.

Thank you for not only reading this book but these *Author Notes* as well!

A very short bit about me. I'm just under four years old as a releasing author. My first book (*Death Becomes Her – The Kurtherian Gambit* 01) was released on November 2, 2015. Since then, I've written dozens of books, and been a collaborator on dozens of series. Along the way, I built a fairly large Indie publishing company.

Jace Mitchell has written pre-LMBPN books under another name. I won't out the name, but it's there somewhere!

He is one of the nicest guys I know. When he believes he isn't meeting expectations, he is the first to offer an apology, and I have to ask...

"For what?"

Half the time, I've no idea what mark he thinks he missed. Other times, I have to put up the results and explain that he needs to realize this wasn't him. He's a remarkable fellow, and so easy to get along with.

But, if he wants to think of me as Yoda and credit me with fixing issues in the time it takes, I'm ok if you are. It is flattering, and I appreciate the sentiment, Jace!

Right now, I have to stop typing. It's 11:24PM, and I'm suffering from jetlag. I am snoring (and waking myself up) as I type these notes. I wish Jace and Amy the absolute best with these stories, and I welcome you guys and gals to our new universe, which is all about the Veil!

Regards,
Michael Anderle

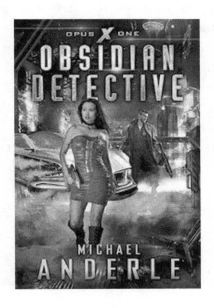

Pre-order now to have the book arrive on your Kindle November 1st.

Two Rebels whose Worlds Collide on a Planetary Level.
On the fringes of human space, a murder will light a fuse and send two different people colliding together.

She lives on Earth, where peace among the population is a given. He is on the fringe of society where authority is how much firepower you wield.

She is from the powerful, the elite. He is with the military.

Both want the truth – but is revealing the truth good for society?

Two years ago, a small moon in a far off system was set to be the location of the first intergalactic war between humans and an alien race.

It never happened. However, something was found many are willing to kill to keep a secret.

Now, they have killed the wrong people.

How many will need to die to keep the truth hidden?

As many as is needed.

He will have vengeance no matter the cost. *She will dig for the truth. No matter how risky the truth is to reveal.*

Coming November 1st from Amazon and other Digital Book Stores

CONNECT WITH THE AUTHORS

Jace Mitchell

Jace Mitchell is an Amazon best-selling author of fantasy novels. He lives in Key West with his dog, and when he's not writing, he's enjoying a cigar and scotch.

John his Mailing List by clicking below

https://www.subscribepage.com/jacemitchell

Michael Anderle Social
Website:
http://www.lmbpn.com

Email List:
http://lmbpn.com/email/

Facebook Here:
www.facebook.com/TheKurtherianGambitBooks/

CPSIA information can be obtained
at www.ICGtesting.com
Printed in the USA
LVHW031501120421
684234LV00029B/1142